P9-DBP-676

Play the Monster Blind

STORIES

Lynn Coady

VINTAGE CANADA

A Division of Random House of Canada Limited

VINTAGE CANADA EDITION, 2001

Copyright © Lynn Coady 2000

All rights reserved under International and Pan-American Copyright Conventions. No part of this book may be reproduced in any form or by any electronic or mechanical means, including information storage and retrieval systems, without permission in writing from the publisher, except by a reviewer, who may quote brief passages in a review.

Published in Canada by Vintage Canada,
a division of Random House of Canada Limited, in 2001.
First published in hardcover in Canada by Doubleday Canada, in 2000.

Vintage Canada and colophon are registered trademarks of
Random House of Canada Limited.

Canadian Cataloguing in Publication Data

Coady, Lynn, 1970–
Play the monster blind : stories

ISBN 0-385-25958-1

I. Title
PS8555.O23P42 2001   C813'.54   C99-932840-8
PR9199.3.C62P42 2001

The quotation on page v is from "Rougeur des Matinaux, XXIV" by René Char, translated by John Thompson. Reprinted from *John Thompson: Collected Poems and Translations*, Peter Sanger (ed.), with the permission of Goose Lane Editions.

Material in this collection has been previously published as follows:
"Play the Monster Blind," *Turn of the Story* (anthology), Anansi, 1999;
"Ice-Cream Man," *This Magazine*, 1998; "Batter My Heart," *Fiddlehead*, 1994 and
Fiddlehead Gold (anthology), Goose Lane Editions, 1995;
"A Great Man's Passing," *The Antigonish Review*, 1994

Cover photograph reprinted with permission from *The Globe and Mail*
Text design by Susan Thomas/Digital Zone
Printed and bound in Canada

Visit Random House of Canada Limited's website:
www.randomhouse.ca

TRANS   10   9   8   7   6   5   4   3   2   1

For Mom, Dad and the boys

"When the ship sinks, its sails survive, within us. They are hoisted on the mast of our blood. Their fresh impatience draws itself up for other obstinate voyages. It's you, isn't it, who is blind on the sea?"

— René Char

Contents

◇

Play the Monster Blind

◇

DRINKING

THE FATHER WAS DRINKING AGAIN, in celebration. John said it bothered him. He remembered being three, tooling around town in the green station wagon with fake wood on the sides, watching his father drink. He would drink and visit his friends, at their homes or at the boxing club. He would pull into the driveway, pause to smile at John, take a quick couple of swallows before reaching over to unbuckle the boy. And he would hoist his young son inside to show him off, both of them pink-cheeked. He showed her a picture of himself then, his little hands tied inside of a pair of enormous boxing gloves, his father perched behind him, holding them up to take aim at a smiling, sweaty man in trunks.

John was strapping then, and he was strapping now. One of the first things the father told her was that they used to have to pin John into three layers of diapers, he was such a big eater. It was obvious the old man and he were close. The second evening after she and John arrived, she stayed inside doing dishes with the mother, and saw the two of them sitting out in plastic chairs on the lawn, facing the shed with rums in hand. The mother said, "That should keep him happy for a while," and the plastic chairs sagged and quivered from the weight of men. The father was built all of hard, stubborn fat, but John was just big. They sat quietly torturing their lawn chairs together.

He told her he used to be fat. He was very sensitive about it. He told her he had never told that to anyone. In high school he stopped eating and started taking handfuls of vitamins, which made him thin and absent-minded, but his mother stopped buying them and he had no choice but to go back to eating. In university he just gave in to everything and ate and drank until he ballooned. Now he was approximately in the middle, a big man with a thick beard. When he was fourteen, his father had him collecting UI for all the dishwashing he had done at the family restaurant, because the workers didn't know any better from the size of him. She had thought, when she met John, that he looked like a lumberjack. He wore plaid shirts and work boots whenever she saw him in class, not because it was fashionable, and not fashionably, but because it was what he wore. She learned where he was from and imagined they all must dress like that, that it must be a very welcoming place, rustic and simple and safe, like John himself.

When his sister showed up, pasty and in leather pants despite the August swelter, the first thing she said to him was, "Hey, you fat shit." Bethany knew that they had not seen each other in a couple of years. He reached over and grabbed one of the sister's wrists. Her knees buckled at once and effortlessly he turned her around, already sinking. Then he grabbed the other wrist and held them together in one large paw while guiding her face-first to the kitchen floor, using her wrists as a sort of steering apparatus. Then he sat on her.

"Pardon?" he kept saying.

"You fat bastard."

The father sat nearby, laughing. The mother saying, "Johnny, Johnny, Johnny," now, as she tried to move around them to the stove. Bethany and the sister were exactly the same age. She felt she should have something to say to her.

When the brother arrived, he at once began to beat and contort the sister in the same way, as if this were some sort of family ritual. She railed at him as he pulled her feet up behind her to meet her shoulders. Whereas John just used the sheer force of his bulk and his size, Hugh, smaller and wiry, was a dabbler in the martial arts. He said he used to box, like his father, but got bored with all the rules. Now he was interested in something called "shoot fighting," which scarcely had any rules at all. He knew all sorts of different holds and manoeuvres, some of which he demonstrated on the sister for them. When he was finished — Ann yanking herself away, red-faced and hair awry and staggering towards the kitchen for a beer — he darted at John, head down and fists up. John responded in the way she had seen him do at bars whenever drunken men, maddened by his size, ran at him. The strategy was to reach out his big hands and simply hold the opponents at bay until they got tired and embarrassed.

Bethany thought of herself as an easygoing person and tried not to be nervous, but she and John were going to get married, and she knew that the family was striving to be civil in a way they were not used to. John kept cuffing his sister in the head whenever she said "goddamn "or "cocksucker," and quietly stating, "Dad," when the father did the same. Bethany and the sister tried and tried to talk to each other, bringing up woman-things like belts and shampoo. She knew that the sister worked in theatre in Halifax and lived with a man who was thirty-five, and everyone was disappointed in her, but hoped she would soon turn her life around. It was touching the way the family spoke of Ann when she was out of the room. The father, overwhelming his armchair, ponderously clinking his ice cubes and turning to John.

"What do you think, me boy?"

"Well, who knows, boy."

"She's getting by," the mother would say.

"But for how long?"

"We'll talk to her at some point," John promised, this being what the father was waiting to hear. The father was always turning to John and waiting to hear the right thing, and John always seemed to know what it was.

The father didn't ask the other son to talk to the sister, and Hugh didn't seem interested in doing it anyway. Hugh and Ann presented themselves as allies, of sorts, against John's authority, even though they fought with one another more furiously than they did with him. They rolled around the living room, knocking over lamps and bothering the mother's nerves, as she complained from the kitchen, and John would come in and bark at them to smarten up. They would call him a big fat fruit and he would sit on them both, the sister on the very bottom of the pile. At one point she looked up at Bethany, blood vessels throbbing to burst in her face, and squeaked, "Can't you control him?" Which Bethany lightly laughed at.

When the parents went to bed, the four of them sat around the table drinking rum. She had never had so much rum in her life. She normally liked spritzers, which John said were for pussies. John tried to talk to his brother and sister seriously about the father. How the drinking bothered him.

"It keeps him in good cheer," said Ann.

"You two don't remember how he used to get. I remember how he used to get."

"Maybe he's too old to get that way now."

"It bothers Mum's nerves."

"I think he's been dandy," said Ann.

"Just because he's not yelling at you all the time doesn't necessarily make it fine and dandy."

"I disagree," said Ann.

Hugh said nothing, waiting for the conversation to turn to sports or parties. Bethany noticed how jolly Ann looked when she said she disagreed with John. She thought, once or twice, that John might grab his sister's head and slam it into the table a couple of times. Ann looked capable of disagreeing with John in her sleep.

Hugh never seemed to bother getting into a conversation with his brother. He merely lurked in corners, behind chairs, waiting for an opportunity to get him in a paralyser hold, but John would always shrug him off like a summer jacket. Hugh showed some of his holds to Ann, who in turn tried them out on her mother, but the mother complained loudly about her arthritis whenever this occurred.

"Hugh said they're not supposed to hurt — they just immobilize," the sister protested, chin digging into the mother's head.

"Well, they do. Get away before I clout you."

Ann released her mother with much reluctance, sorry to loose the fleeting power. The mother had just stood there politely the whole time. She probably could have broken out of it if she wanted to. Like everyone else in the family, the mother was bigger than Ann.

Ann wore combat boots with her sundress. The father made fun of them, and the mother wanted to know if her feet didn't get overheated. Bethany felt sorry for Ann, because when they all were sitting around the picnic table eating lobster, Ann couldn't open hers but she wouldn't ask any of them for help. Bethany finally passed her a cracking utensil under the table.

"I never used to eat lobster until last year," Ann explained. "It grossed me out. Then I decided I want to be the kind of person who'll eat anything she's given."

"She won't eat the pickled alewives," said the father through a mouthful of roe.

"Don't count as food," said Ann, sullen. Hugh was sneaking up behind her with a lobster that had not yet been boiled alive.

BOXING

THEY WOULD PICK UP THE UNCLE and the bunch of them, some in the father's car and some in John's, were going to tour around the trail, staying in cabins and eating in restaurants and swimming at beaches. This was the father's gift. John told her that doing it was important to him and she would have to have fun. She was surprised he would put it this way, because she was looking forward to seeing the island. She was worried about being in the car with the father, however. At the airport after they arrived, he made them stop at the duty-free liquor store and purchased an armload of tiny bottles of Crown Royal. Once they were in the car, he handed one to each of them and said, "Slug 'er back, you two. The vacation has officially begun." Bethany had never drunk straight whisky in her life and had no idea how to properly respond. She looked at John for help and he took it from her and dropped it into her purse.

"Can't be into this on the road, boy," he said, smiling and blinking ahead of him.

"Ach, I'd need fifty or so of these before anything good started happenin."

"Let me drive, boy."

"No, we can't have you drinkin and drivin."

"I don't need to drink."

After scant argument, the father declared, "Betty, it's just you and me!" turning around in his seat to beam at her. "My God," he added, "did you down yours already? Well, good boy, yourself."

So the father sat in the back seat with her the whole way, making jokes that John was their chauffeur and kicking his seat and telling him to step on it while Bethany watched the innumerable veins road-mapping his nose and cheeks begin to glow as if filling up with lava. She was terrified of everything. They were on a stretch of road where one sign after another read things like: JESUS IS COMING! PREPARE THYSELF! REPENT! SAITH THE LORD.

All the way to the house, he told her about boxing. He rhymed off one boxer after another, not famous boxers like Muhammad Ali but ones from, as he said, "nearby." Men with names like Sailor Dave and Fisher MacPhee and Ronnie the Dago. He said he had met more than a few of these fellows in the ring, and could tell her something about the style of each if she was interested. The Dago, for example, was a smart fighter, a thinking fighter. Always went in with some kind of strategy. Archie the Rigger, however, had nothing going for him but a hard head and had the record to prove it. Fisher was the prettiest of fighters, floated on air. Sailor Dave was like a goddamned bull, just an ox. The father went on and on in this vein. He handed one little bottle after another to her so that when they finally got out of the car her purse clinked and sloshed.

"Johnny," the old man pronounced, holding the kitchen door open for her, "this is a goddamned good girl right here." He went to bed almost at once, and so they sat up and had cornflakes with the mother.

The sister very much admired Bethany's luggage as they loaded up the car. She marvelled at it, it was so nice, so much that Bethany was embarrassed. John intuited this and kept making jokes that some people had moved beyond Glad bags and cardboard.

"It would never even *occur* to me to have bags like that," the sister persisted, and finally John told her to shut the hell up and she told him to kiss her rosy red arse and he strode over to her and picked her up and placed her, barely able to squirm, in the trunk of the car and then held the hood down, not completely closed, until Bethany told him, for Pete's sake, to let her out of there, and Ann, who throughout the performance had not made a sound, flung one bare leg out and then the other and hopped away like a crow. Hugh stood by looking pensive, as if he wished he had thought of it first.

Hugh himself was a strange one, because, although he had gone to university, he spoke with an insanely nuanced accent that was nothing like the rest of the family's, and every second thing he said had something or another to do with his hole, and he wore an Expos cap just perched on the top of his head, but when she asked him what he did for a living, he replied that when he was not "partying his hole out," he worked with computers. Bethany asked John about it later on and he said, "Oh, yah. He's the brain. Straight A's. Could have done anything he wanted." What he chose to do was teach courses at the vocational school and help people around town with their systems. He didn't go anywhere after university because, he said, all his friends were here. "Friends're pack a retards," John once remarked. And after a few days Bethany began to realize that Hugh didn't own any shirts except T-shirts with sayings on them. He sat around in T-shirts that said things like: I'D RATHER PUSH A FORD THAN DRIVE A CHEVY and IT'S NOT HOW DEEP YOU FISH, IT'S HOW YOU WIGGLE YOUR WORM!

After the mother, the uncle was the one she felt most comfortable with. They picked him up at a group home where he stayed in Port Hastings the night before the trip. Bethany knew in advance that he was Mentally Handicapped, and having this foreknowledge made her calm about meeting him, far less nervous than she had been about the rest. It was good to have a label, something her mind could scrutinize. It was good to have an idea what to expect.

Lachie was his name, and she found him delightful. He reached out one hand and wished her Merry Christmas as she shook it, and then he extended the other to wish her Happy Easter. He puttered away, then, announcing, "There now! He knows Betty!" to all present. For the rest of the evening he sat in a chair in the corner of the living room and raised his eyes every once in a while to ask if it was time for corn-flakes. Bethany felt at home in the chair beside him. Now and again he would show her the fingers of his right hand to let her know that he'd been nibbling at the nails. Apparently this was a great pastime of his, much frowned upon by the rest of the family, and he seemed to enjoy the disapproval it provoked.

"Breaks his nails," he remarked more than once.

"Tch. Isn't that terrible," Bethany answered.

Lachie would smile back and reach over quickly to poke her in the cheek with a ragged fingertip before reclining again.

"You kick his arse if you catch him at that!" the sister yelled from across the room, the uncle plunging both hands into the tucks of his armchair and closing his eyes.

The uncle was the fattest. John said that his grandmother had spoiled him from birth, heaping his plate and feeding him entire pies, and Lachie had never done anything but follow a few cows around on the farm for exercise. Now he had arthritis in his knees, and he could hardly walk around any more. The fat hung off Lachie in an unpleasant sort of way, like it wasn't quite a part of him, something that had to be strapped on in the morning. John said that was how *he* would be if he let himself go, how would she like that? He said it was in the genes. He constantly had to be working against it.

"Your sister's a bone rack," Bethany pointed out, "and she looks more like your uncle than you do."

"She had the anorexia all through high school," John explained, dismissive and also somewhat grudging. "Sees the nutritionist once a week."

"All she talks about is eating," Bethany said.

"I know."

"What about Hugh?"

"Works out every day," John said with a bit of contempt, because anyone could see this with one look at the chest beneath the T-shirt slogans.

At the dinner table the father congratulated Bethany for her fine appetite, unaware that she was only eating so much because he kept insisting more be offered to her and she was afraid of offending him.

"Get Betty some more potatoes, Annie. Jesus Christ, she's wasting before our eyes."

"Do you want more potatoes, Betsy?"

"Ummm ... sure."

"She doesn't want any more, Dad."

"She just said she did, for the love of God!"

"Quit forcing food down the woman's throat."

"Well, Jesus Christ, I'll get her the potatoes if you're not up to the challenge," said the father, practically spreading himself across the table.

"No, no, no! I can get them for myself!" Bethany exclaimed, horror-struck.

"There now," the father said, emptying a greyish, steaming mound out of a Corningware dish and onto her plate. "Some of us know how to be civil to a guest."

"You're making her sick," said Ann.

Bethany was a big eater most of the time, however, and only went to bed in slight discomfort, having eschewed the evening's cornflake ritual. She asked John if he thought she needed to lose weight and he said who gave a shit one way or another. He would not have asked her to marry him if he thought she was a tub of lard. It was being around Ann and the mother that made her feel that way. The mother said having her "nerves on the go" all the time was what kept her skinny, and Ann, meal-obsessed, hopped about the kitchen a pale crow, swallowing the occasional fastidiously selected morsel. John had said that he and Hugh had teased her about being fat all throughout their childhood but had to stop once she decided to forgo eating altogether, and felt guilty for the rest of their lives. Now John would wrap a hand around one of her thighs whenever she passed by and squeeze, feeling for meat. "Get in the kitchen and eat a tub of ice cream or something, ya stick," he'd say, thinking he was being kind. And the sister Ann would smile at her brother as if she were thinking it too.

Swimming

LACHIE COULDN'T GET HIS CLOTHES OFF fast enough. Scarcely had she put the picnic cooler down than his shirt was in a heap on the sand and rolls of white flesh sprouting the coarsest of black hairs gave salute to the sun and the ocean. The effect of the sight of so much exposed skin caused her to reach instinctively for a bottle of sunscreen. She tried to hand it to him, but the uncle was busy unbuckling his pants and muttered, "No, you put it on me. He can't get his pants, can't get them." She waited a moment to see if any of the family would come down the path before finally squirting a little onto her fingertips and trying to apply some to Uncle Lachie's shoulders, but he had the pants around his ankles and staggered out of her reach a second later. Then he regained himself, muttering about the ocean, and, in his haste, yanked off his swimming trunks on top of everything else. Bethany was not so embarrassed as to be unable to imagine her embarrassment if someone other than John came down the path at that moment, so she said calmly to the uncle, "Put on your trunks, Uncle Lachie. You need to put your trunks back on."

Lachie was irritated at anything keeping him from the sea at that point and protested vigorously for a good minute or so as Bethany stood there beside him, trying to come up with a persuasive argument. She thought it strange that he would argue so much and yet not actually defy her outright, trundling away, a white blur against the blue sky like a walking snowman. Finally she just said, "You can't go *swimming* without your *swim* trunks, Uncle Lachie," like it was the most logical thing in the world, and he gazed meditatively down at the shorts for a bit before hauling them back up about his hips and plunging towards the Atlantic. Bethany thought this a profound triumph and almost wished there had been someone around to witness the crisis, and her unexpected competence. At that moment, Ann appeared. Struggling with a cooler and in a polka-dot bathing suit with moulded bra-cups that must have belonged to the mother in 1968. She lingered beside Bethany for the briefest of moments before taking in the sight of Lachie. White like a plump cloud had fallen directly out of the sky and now bobbing free and independent with the waves.

"Lord lifting Antichrist, he'll fry like a pork rind!" she hollered, seizing the sunscreen out of Bethany's hand and giving chase.

Bethany could see that he was seated up to his belly now, and seemed to be looking down at the point where the water divided him up.

EATING

THE FATHER DRANK TOO MUCH at dinner and made the waitress cry. She wouldn't come back to the table and John had to get up and walk across the restaurant and talk to her and talk to the manager. She watched him standing there with them, grinning under his beard, gesturing in an open and accepting sort of way with his enormous hands. The girl was being charmed by him and the manager was being charmed by him in a different manner. She knew how he was charming the waitress, because she had been charmed like that too. How a big man like that could grin so open-handed and vulnerable. He could take your head between those two hands and pop it like a zit, but he was decent enough not to do that, not to even remind you that he could. He smiled, instead, and cajoled. He had no interest in bullying you — the easiest thing in the world for him to do. Everything about his demeanour said: *I am just a great big guy with a drunk dad and a new fiancée and nobody wants to feel like this, so let's not.* It was brave of him. It was exactly what made him so good.

Pretty soon the girl was laughing with tears still in her eyes and John was laughing and picking her up from the ground with a bear hug which made her shriek and laugh even harder. She could not have been more than seventeen, and was in love now. He sauntered back to the table, his mouth pursed in a comical sort of way.

"A little thing out there called PR," he said to his pink, smirking father.

"A little fucking thing called incompetence in the work force," the dad shot back. "If one of my girls had ever pulled any of that kind of shit back when I was running the Bluenoser ..."

"Boy, boy," said John. "Jeez, eh?" He went on making inarticulate noises of comfort and reprimand. The father made noises of declining outrage and increasing shame, as his awareness of the situation grew. But she could see that he wasn't going to acknowledge it, blustering about incompetence all throughout dessert and, while waiting for the bill, about teenager girls with earrings in their noses instead of their ears where God intended them. Blustering all the while but now drinking out of his water glass instead of the other one that was poised beside the wreckage of his meal. Bethany could tell he hoped to bluster until he was blustering on a different topic, one that made everyone more comfortable and jovial. Blustering wittily and cheerfully, no longer blustering at all — a benevolent father regaling the family with priceless and innumerable anecdotes from a rich and varied life.

The sister puked for what seemed like hours. Bethany in an agony because she thought she should go and see if she was sick, but on the other hand, John had said she used to be anorexic, and she knew that this was what anorexics sometimes did after big meals. It was an impossible situation. It was almost dawn, and she and John and the sister had made a deal — that Bethany would sleep with John for a little before slipping through the bathroom that joined their rooms and crawling into Ann's bed. This being the arrangement the parents would be expecting when they arrived from the other cabin to make breakfast. But now it was getting light and Ann was still in there, puking away, and Bethany was in an impossible situation. John snored.

Lying there angry, it took her a couple of seconds to realize that the retching echoes from the bathroom had ceased. The bedroom was now almost fully illuminated, and she flung the blankets away, fully awake, deciding she didn't care if Ann knew she had heard her puking or not. When Bethany didn't get a good night's sleep, it did terrible things to her body. It gave her indigestion, made her cranky and intolerant, red-eyed and snippy. She had to catch a good couple of hours in Ann's bed before the parents stormed in wanting to take pictures and see them splashing around in canoes.

"Ugh," said Ann as Bethany crawled in beside her.

"Are you okay?"

"The *dreams* I was having!"

Bethany licked her lips. She wasn't going to pretend she was stupid. "But you were throwing up, Ann."

"Before I was throwing up," she said. "Sick dreams. It has to have been the scallops. Sometimes my stomach doesn't welcome the shellfish."

"Hm," said Bethany, in a way she hoped sounded as if the explanation had been accepted and the incident forgotten about in almost the same moment.

"Ohg," moaned Ann some moments later. "Did you ever dream that you were *where you were?*"

"I don't know what you mean," Bethany said around a yawn.

"You're not supposed to dream about being where you are. It's not natural. I'm not supposed to be dreaming about being in this cabin with all of you. In my grandmother's house. Or in school, or in Halifax or something, or somewhere I've never even been. Nobody dreams literally, for Christ's sake."

"What were we doing?"

"Oh God, it was horrible. We were just doing all the things we've been doing all along."

She was snoring not five seconds later.

DRIVING

THEY DROVE ANOTHER FEW MILES, on their way to still more rented cottages. The father made a point of repeating all through breakfast he hoped these would be more amenable than the ones they had spent the previous night in.

"No TV, no radio," he kept saying. "Nothing but four walls and a goddamn bed. I can haul a cot into the closet at home, if that's what

I want. Charge people fifty bucks a night to use it."

"It's a *cabin*, boy," John said. "You're supposed to sit on the porch and watch the sunset. What do you need a TV for?"

"It's the principle of the thing. What if it rains? What if there's a ball game? Beds not fit to piss on — I can see plain as day that poor Betty didn't get a moment's sleep. I should have complained. I should have complained at that goddamn restaurant, and I should've complained the moment we showed up here. Reservations two jeezly months in advance and this is the best they can give us."

"You *did* complain at the restaurant," Ann reminded him, looking around to confirm that no one else was going to do it. "Don't you remember?"

"To the manager, not to that young one. Poor girl didn't know what I was talking about."

"You might have thought about that before you called her a useless twat."

"Well, goddamnit, I was mad!"

"Leave it now, Ann," said John. Bethany was beginning to see that this was the way they commenced most mornings. John saw her understanding this.

"All I wanted," rumbled the father, "was a good dry chip. That's all I wanted. What do they bring me? *Potato wedges!* What the Jesus? Greasy old potato wedges with some kind of crap sprinkled all over them. That's not chips. I asked for chips. I just wanted a *good dry chip!* Not that gourmet crap swimming in Christ knows what."

"Well, it's done with now."

"Well, I'm not letting them get away with that shit."

"Good, then, boy."

"You have to let them know, Johnny. You can't just let them keep on with that kind of shoddy service."

"All right."

"You have to remind them — I'm the customer. I'm payin' your salary. You need me. I don't need you." The father seemed to whisper to himself for an instant as if imagining some outlandish response, and then turned to Bethany and smiled suddenly. "You just ignore me, Betty," he said. "John here's the family dip-lo-mat. We'd get kicked outta where-all we went if the dip-lo-mat wasn't around."

"I guess to God," said John.

"I'm just an old boxer," said the father, manoeuvring his bulk from the confines of their picnic table. "I hit people. Don't take mucha the dip-lo-mat for that," he chuckled, moving off to examine the workmanship of the cabin's front step. Intermittently they heard quiet exclamations of disgust from his direction as they cleared away the breakfast things.

He wanted John and Bethany to ride with him to Dingwall because he felt as if he wasn't spending enough time with them. He told the mother to take the car with the other two. The mother announced that she would have to drive, then, because Hugh was a maniac and Ann had always been too stubborn to learn, and they couldn't expect her to go for very long because her nerves were bad. The three of them chewed at each other for a bit, but Bethany got the feeling that they were pleased to have been thrown together — a day off from the father's gruff bullying and the more genuine authority of John. Lachie was content to ride with herself and John and the father, however, because he didn't care either way. They were taking John's Escort, and that was the one he had climbed into immediately after breakfast, and so that was the car he was going in.

"Come on, come on, come on," he kept saying, watching them load the baggage. "Ding-Dong. Going Ding-Dong now."

They stopped at a lookout point, and Bethany climbed out of the car before the rest. In every direction she turned, she could see nothing but dark, fuzzy mountains. The ever-present ocean was nowhere in sight, and it disoriented her. She didn't know if this was beautiful or not. The green mounds sloped upward uninsistently, and then came together in dark, obscene valleys that reminded her of the creases in a woman's flesh — her own. Reminded her of sitting naked and looking down at the spot where her stomach protruded slightly over her thighs. She didn't like how these low mountains were everywhere, their dark rolling motion completely uninterrupted by a view of water, or patches of field. John suddenly moved past her and jumped up onto the wooden railing, framing himself against them.

"Get down. John, get down. Get down now," she said.

"What? Take my picture!"

"Get down," she hissed, queasy at the sight of him poised there, ready to disappear into one of the dark creases. Meanwhile, Lachie refused to get out of the car to look. She could hear the father's persistent cursing as he tried to yank him by the hand, then coming around to the other side of the car and trying to shove him out the opposite door. Lachie remained where he was, however, unmoved and only a little irritated with the father's proddings. All he wanted to do was go, to drive in the car. "Come on, come on, come on," he said, and, "No, no, no." With their arms around each other, Bethany and John watched him easily resist the father. Bethany was thinking that John could probably go over there and lift him out, but she hoped that he wouldn't. By this time the father was laughing with frustration. He said that they were going to stay there and see the view and Lachie could drive the friggin' car to Ding-Dong all by himself, if he wanted to go so badly.

The rest of the trip, the father told her the story of Archie "Fisher" Dale, a fine boxer he knew out of the Miramichi, "who some people called Tiny because he was such a little fella, in fact his manager had wanted to bill him as Tiny Dale, but Archie would have none of it. In actual fact, he wasn't all that small — five-six — but smaller than what you'd usually see hanging out at the boxing clubs and whathaveyou. Well this one — you wouldn't find yourself taking him too-too seriously to look at him, I mean, some of the fellas you'd see at those places were like Johnny here, great big bastards, and a lot of them figured they could fight simply by virtue of the fact that they were bigger than anybody else. But that's not always the case, you know, and there's nothing more pathetic than seeing some big lumbering bastard getting all tangled up in his own legs trying to keep up with some little lightning rod like Fisher himself who lands you a good right cross before you even see him in front of you."

Because, besides height and mass, this little fella had it all. John's father had never seen a fighter so well equipped for greatness. He fought single-mindedly. He often appeared vicious, but he never actually got angry — to get angry at your opponent was just foolishness, the quickest way to spot an amateur. He was fast, he was graceful, he had arms like steel cords lashed together, but for all that grace he was *tough*. You could just *hit* him. He didn't care. John's father and Fisher Dale would go drinking downtown in Halifax, and after downing a few, the little prick would just grin at him with his gap-filled mouth and say, "Hit me, John Neil. Hit me a good one, now." Well, John's father was never one to oblige in this respect, but there would always be one or two fellas nearby just chompin' at the bit to take a poke at Fisher Dale. You couldn't drop him. You just could not drop him. He'd weave and teeter, blood pouring out of his mouth, and, by Jesus, that grin would never leave his face. "Hit me again, why don'tcha?" was all he'd say.

"What would he do that for?" Bethany asked, genuinely mystified.

"Because," John's father told her with very precise enunciation to give the statement weight, "Fisher was crazy as mine and your arse put together. Everywhere except the ring. He was Albert Jesus Jesus Einstein in the ring. The drinking, you know. What it does to some people. Archie Dale was such a one."

"This is the saddest story I know," the father reflected, after having paused for some time. "Now that I think of it. What that boy couldn't have done. And he was one of the hardest working in them days too. The stamina. Fight in Halifax one night, under one name, hop on the train right after for one in Yarmouth or somewhere, callin' himself Wildman Dale or some such thing. You could only fight a certain number of matches in them days if you wanted to keep your licence, but the more ambitious and greedy of the bunch — Dale was both — would just hop from town to town, fighting under different names. Sometimes he'd go ten, fifteen fights a week. Outlandish, if you knew anything about the circuit. I could never go more than five.

"You know, the only time he had the boozin' under control was when he was fighting that way — hopping from town to town, sometimes going two a night. Kept him busy, kept him focused. See, he wasn't the type a fella could just fight a couple times a week, and then head down to the tavern for a couple of beers with his buddies, waiting for his manager to call about the next one. It was all or nothing with Dale. That was his problem right there. If he stopped fighting, he started drinking, it had to be one or the other. Manager shoulda just kept putting him up against one guy after another till he dropped dead of a brain clot — least he wouldn't've ended up a drunken failure."

"What happened?"

"What happened was that he got caught, they found out he was fighting illegally like that, and he got his licence suspended. And howls just went up all across the country, you know, with the gamblers and everything, because the boy was on a streak — he was winning every match he fought. He'd pounded me long ago, I don't mind telling you, not to mention pretty near every other fella on the circuit, and his manager was talking about taking him over to the States. "But that was that — suspension for a month."

"That's not so bad."

"Ach, no. Most boys'd take their winnings and go off on a tear. Well, that's what he meant to do at first, but, like I said, with Dale it was all or nothing. I went downtown with him the one night, we drank ourselves stupid, and the last I seen of him" — John's father began to heave and shake at this memory — "he was chasin' a cop down Gottingen Street at four in the morning. He was chasing the cop! Somehow he got his nightstick away from him, and he was chasing him down the street, waving it around his head like a lasso! Cop hollerin to beat hell."

"So what happened to him?"

"*That* happened to him. Like I said, it was the last of him I seen. Never fought again, I can guarantee you that much. Disappeared into the night."

"You saw him again, Dad," John's voice came from the driver's seat. It was as if he were repeating something by rote.

"Oh, yes, wait now, I did see him again. Eight or so years later, in Inverness, of all places, walking home from a square dance. This little frigger in a trench coat shuffling towards me with great deliberation, you know. I didn't know who it was, some queer or something, I was getting ready to pop him. Well, isn't it Fisher Dale. 'John Neil!' he shouts. 'Whad'llya have?' Then he yanks something from the pocket of his trenchcoat" — the father began to act out the role of Fisher Dale, now. "'A little *puck* a whisky? Or — reaching into his other pocket with the opposite hand — "'a little *puck* a rum?'" The father shook and heaved and gasped. He repeated the gesture a couple of times for effect, the yanking of one bottle out of the right-hand pocket upon the word "puck," and then another from out of the left. It was like Lachie wishing her Merry Christmas and Happy Easter in succession.

"This is all he has to tell me after eight years," John's father finished, jovial and refreshed from the story's telling. "Ah — Jesus, though. Lord save us if it wasn't a shameful waste of a beautiful fighter. Just a beautiful little fighter."

John told her later that he told that story to everyone. It was his favourite story. She would hear it a hundred more times in the upcoming years, he said. In the meantime, the road rose and sunk like a sea serpent's tail. Every so often they would come around a craggy bend, after miles of nothing but the low, fuzzy mountains, and all of a sudden it would seem as if the whole of the Atlantic Ocean was glittering before them, so big it eclipsed even the sky. And then the road would sink lower and lower imperceptibly, until they were trundling through some infinitesimal community and she'd see grey, half-demolished barns with black letters spelling CLAMS painted across the roofs and little stores with Pepsi-Cola signs from the early seventies in the windows, the red in the logo faded to pink and the blue now a sick green. She went into one of them to get lemonade and ice-cream bars for everybody, and the woman behind the counter was not nearly as friendly as Bethany had been expecting. The woman had a little girl sitting with her back there, and every time the little girl did something other than just sit there the woman would bark, "Whad I tell ya? Whad I tell ya?" at her — oblivious to Bethany's presence — so the little girl would place her hands at her sides and arrange her legs and sit chewing on her lips until the fact of being a child got the better of her and she would once again reach for something with absent-minded curiosity. Then the woman would bark again.

"You've got a lovely place here," said Bethany, and the woman regarded her with terror. She thought Bethany was talking about the store, and not the island, and therefore must be insane. She added, "This is my first visit," to make it more clear. The woman looked down at the little girl, as if hoping to find her trespassing again so that she could yell at her and ignore Bethany. But the girl was being good, so the woman ignored Bethany anyway, a confused and queasy look taking over her ruddy, mean face. "Six sevenny-five, wha?" she said. Bethany gave her a five and a two, hoping she had understood correctly. She gathered up her ice-cream bars without asking for a bag and staggered out the door and into the sunshine, cowbells clunking rude music behind her.

FIGHTING

SHE ATE BARBECUED BOLOGNA for the first time in her life. John was trying to convince her it was a delicacy of the area as he

23

slathered Kraft sauce onto it, splattering the coals. She kept telling him in a low voice not to lie to her, to quit lying to her. She made her voice low because if he was telling the truth, she didn't want the rest of the family to know she hadn't believed it.

"Listen here," he kept saying. "You haven't *lived* until you've scarfed a good feed of barbecued bologna."

"Shut up," she said, giggling and looking around. "Liar." She saw that Ann was nearby, sprawled in a sun-chair and drinking a beer. She had probably heard everything, and so Bethany took a chance and looked seriously at her for confirmation. Ann smiled and raised her eyes to heaven. She turned back to John.

"I knew you were lying!"

"What?"

"Ann says you're lying."

"Ann's not gonna get her share of barbecued bologna."

"Quit teasing the woman," said Ann. "You're always teasing her. How long do you think she'll put up with it before she kicks your arse?"

Bethany smiled at Ann. They were getting somewhere. Most of the time the sister had seemed too high-strung to even talk to, but Ann had started taking long, slow draughts of beer early in the afternoon, and now her movements were easy and fluid — nothing of the crow remained. She had been in the sun-chair most of the afternoon, letting the sun burn it out of her, while the rest of them played badminton and lawn darts. Her smiles became slow and amused instead of fleeting and anguished. Bethany sat on the grass beside her every once in a while to drink a beer of her own and together they would holler insults at John about whatever he happened to be doing at that moment. Hugh came over and capsized the chair at one point, but Ann simply rolled away from it and fell asleep a few feet away in the grass.

They must have eaten the red, charred flesh of every beast imaginable that evening, and the lot of them sat exhausted in chairs they had each pulled up around Ann's chair as if she had become some sort of axis during the afternoon. The father's face was the same colour as the meat they'd consumed, and bloated, and he blinked constantly as if a breeze was blowing directly into his eyes. While Ann had relaxed herself with long, slow, sunny draughts of beer, the father had done the exact opposite — disappearing without a word at steady intervals throughout the day in order to shoot rum in the kitchenette, the imperative of it seeming to make him more and more anxious. She knew he was doing that, because she had stupidly kept asking, "Where's your father gotten to? Isn't it your father's turn? Where's your father?" until John finally had to tell her. He said this was the only way the father had ever learned to drink — like a teenager sneaking swigs at a dance. He'd never sipped a cocktail in his life, much less enjoyed a beer during a fishing trip or something. John said that his father had never understood the purpose of beer. He didn't see the *point* of an alcoholic beverage with so little alcohol in it. Why something should take so long to do what it was intended to do.

"He's an alcoholic," said Bethany, epiphanic. They were walking along the beach when he told her this.

"Oh Christ," John said, then, letting go of her hand. "You don't know much." It hurt her feelings but she didn't tell him.

On the path back to the cabin, they saw the father coming towards them. The sun had set moments before and their eyes were used to the dark, but the father's weren't. They saw him first, walking with great clomps, his arms stretched out in front of him like Boris Karloff in *Frankenstein*. Bethany remembered hearing that, in *Frankenstein*, Boris Karloff had stretched out his arms before him like that because the filmmaker had at first wanted to have the monster be blind. They never followed up that aspect of the story, but they kept the footage of Karloff playing the monster blind anyway, and that was why the enduring image of Frankenstein ended up being this clomping creature with his arms stuck out in front of him. The problem was that this was what John's father looked like, coming towards them — a frightened, blind monstrosity. John made a sound beside her, before speaking to him in a loud, fatherly voice. She almost thought she'd imagined that sound. It could have been mistaken for a brief intake of air which would have been necessary before speaking so loud to the father. But it hadn't been that.

"Jesus, Jesus, Jesus, boy!" was what John said. "You stumbling around looking for some place to take a piss or wha?" Bethany jumped at the "wha." High-strung like the lady at the store.

The father tittered, focused in on their dark outlines, and came forward, blustering jokes about getting lost in the raspberry bushes and their having to send in a search party for him in the morning. He had just wanted to walk with them on the beach, he said. Was he too late? Were they on their way back?

"We'll have another walk," said John.

"No, no. Betty's tired. Are you tired, Betty?"

"No, no." So they headed back to the beach.

She couldn't remember what he said. All she could think about was Boris Karloff, clomping around confused and horrified, chucking a little girl into a pond. She pretended to be enthralled with the moon on the water. The truth was, the old man was incoherent. She could hear John mm-hmming in response to him. It seemed as if he had something very important to say, a zillion different things, none of which he could keep straight. He said that they were blessed. He said that they were lucky. He said that he would help them. He said that family was the only important thing. He kept saying that he was old, and that life could be difficult. He said wouldn't it be nice if people sometimes understood each other. Nobody had ever come close to understanding him in his godforsaken life. But at some point he'd decided that being understood wasn't as important as being good. So just because nobody gave a shit about him and had no respect for him and thought him a foolish old bastard — he'd decided that wasn't what was important.

"Boy, boy," John kept saying. "You need to get to bed."

At the cabin they shared with the brother and sister, they found the same two locked in violent combat, the worst Bethany had seen so far. The two of them laughed hysterically throughout, Hugh with a giddy and unrelenting "Huhn! Huhn! Huhn!" and Ann with an ongoing, high-pitched shriek. John was not in the mood for it. There was a broken glass on the floor and a lamp on its side. Hugh was trying to manoeuvre Ann into one of his paralyser holds, but Ann was resisting heroically. Bethany had never seen her quite so nimble — just as he managed to position his arm about her throat, or somewhere equally critical, she would slither away as though greased. "I've uncovered the secret!" she kept shrieking when she could speak. "I've uncovered the secret!" And Hugh would gasp, "Shut up! No you haven't! Shut up! No you haven't!" — so that for an instant Bethany thought there must be some hideous secret about Hugh that Ann was threatening to reveal. But Hugh was laughing too hard for it to be that. He seemed to be hysterical with disbelief that Ann was suddenly able to wrench herself out of his every grip.

"Settle the fuck down!" John was shouting.

"You just move ..." Ann sputtered, near to the point of being too winded to speak, "where *he* moves...." She dove around her brother and jabbed a fist into his solar plexus, Hugh howling pain and laughter. "You just move" — she threw her hands into the air and brought them down onto his ears — "*with* the hold! You move *with* the hold!"

"Shut up!" Hugh roared, holding his ears as if he couldn't stand to hear it. Giggling and panting, she scrambled for a phone book to defend herself from his next onslaught. John stepped forward and wrenched it out of her hands and hit his stampeding brother with it himself, which stopped both his laughter and his forward momentum at exactly the same time. Ann flew across the room, but might have caught her balance if not for staggering against an end table, which propelled her, arms like windmills, into Bethany, who caught an elbow in the mouth.

All night she lay wriggling the tooth with her tongue, tasting for blood. Everyone was deeply upset with Ann, but Bethany didn't care. She could hear them in the next room yelling at each other. She could hear Ann crying like one betrayed and broken-hearted. Tomorrow, Bethany thought, she would have to go up to her and assure her that she was all right, that it wasn't her fault and all that. But she didn't feel like doing it at the moment. Hugh had given her a 222 that he had been carrying around from the time he sprained his wrist, and now the pain had transformed itself into torpor. But she didn't feel as if she could sleep. She wanted to just lie, in the dark, away from the bunch of them.

Ann kept whining that it wasn't fair, Bethany could hear her. Whining and sobbing. "Just because you guys can beat up on anybody you want without actually hurting them!" she was saying. Then John crawled into bed and issued almost a formal apology.

"Everybody's fuckin' drunk," he sighed afterwards.

"I know."

"Well, again, I'm sorry."

"Again, it's all right."

She could feel him picking up a handful of her hair and pressing it into the centre of his face.

"I'm lucky to have you," he said. "I don't tell you that enough — I know it."

Bethany wriggled her tooth and felt pleasure at the sudden bit of power. She smiled involuntarily, separating her split bottom lip and receiving a thread of pain. Perhaps she would be mad. Refuse to say another word. Keep him up all night with worry, her very need for him in question.

◇

Ice-Cream
Man

◇

YOU THINK YOU MUST NOT LOOK the way you feel. People the same height as you are still sometimes place their hands on their knees and lean their faces into yours and ask: "And how old are *you?*" You must somehow still look like you're small, a child. To be a child is not necessarily good, because it means getting more attention than someone more grown and established. Children are the only people that other people just stare at without worrying about it. Children aren't supposed to notice, or care.

But you always cared, remember, because you never liked being the centre of attention, you were just like him that way. People used to come into the shop and compliment him on what a fine job he had done on their shoes, and he would just say, "No, no, it's not true," confusing them because it was obvious that he had. But pretty soon they realized that was just what he said if you were nice to him. Great heels you put on these, Danny — No, no they're not. That's a nice coat you're wearing — No, no it isn't. It was like: Please, please, don't remark upon me. People learn not to. When they like someone, someone quiet who does a good job at things, they put up with what's strange about them. You notice that. It was the opposite with her, when she was alive. Nobody liked her, she didn't do anything, any kind of work, so they wouldn't put up with what was strange.

Locking you out of the bathroom for hours in her big tub full of suds and oils. Thick perfume smells wafting through the keyhole. Let me in, Mother. Pee, pee, pee.

Go to the other bathroom. There is no other bathroom! She knows. You've all lived here for years. She pretends.

Tooralooraloora she sings. You peek at her through the keyhole. She fills up that whole damn tub.

That's why no one cared for her. Let herself go. Wearing the bright clothes to the Co-op when she was supposed to be hiding herself. You used to hear ladies in the store. You knew they were talking about her, because they always called her "Herself."

Oh, look, if it isn't Herself.

What's Herself into today?

Lord bless us and save us if she isn't into the make-up!

Oh my dear God!

It was funny, because she was so enormous. To them it was like washing down a banana split with a diet cola.

But the good thing was that nobody ever noticed you with her around. You were like him, hidden away in the shop, hunched over soles. Everyone likes him, hidden down there. Now that you're tall and she's dead and people see you, they don't mind you too much either.

It is probably important to keep it that way. You never used to have to worry about all this. When you were a child, you could be as weird and stupid as you wanted, but you never actually wanted to. You were practising to be like him, for when you got tall. Because you could see who they put up with and who they didn't. You can see it now, too.

You used to play with Paula Morin all the time because she lived next door and your mother called up and asked her to because you were "too stubborn" to go find anyone yourself. So she'd come over in the winter and ignore you and play with all your toys. It seemed perfectly natural, because she was three years older than you and didn't have any really good toys of her own. So the two of you would just sit on different sides of the living room, you building stuff with Lego and her in the middle of a circle of all these toys you'd forgotten about long ago that she pulled out of the cubbyhole. You'd sit like that in silence for hours. You thought she was great. You begged to have her come over after a while. When the weather got warmer you'd go outside and she'd involve you in all her imaginary games. You would be her baby, or her dog, or an evil arch rival who was not quite as powerful as she was.

She moved to the trailer park on the other side of the town to live with her dad. When she was next door to you, she was with her grandmother. Her mother was, for some reason, in Sydney. It didn't make much sense at the time. So she was one of those people you just forget about for a long time and then in junior high you see them again and you look at each other and say hi and just know somehow that it's as if you have been reincarnated as different people, and it would be in bad taste to act as if you've known each other in the past.

She had these boobs and a perm and wore tops that showed her stomach. The only difference with you was that you were tall. She hung out with the guys that stuck out their feet to trip you if you were passing them outside or in the hall. They were the worst kind of guys, because it didn't matter if you were someone like your mother or someone like you or someone like anyone, they'd trip you and laugh their holes out no matter who you were. One of the guys was Bernie Heany. You used to play skipping with him when you were around eight. He was the only boy who ever played skipping. He used to love it.

The point is that now Paula Morin can't leave her house, because she gang-banged and everybody knows. They used to call her "Paula More 'n' More" and sometimes "Ball-a," and laugh about her all the time, but she still was able to linger in the halls and the smoking area with Bernie and everybody, sticking out her foot right along with them and having a great time, but now she can't leave her house. She used to go to school but she can't even go to school any more. People were saying they were going to kill her. They left stuff in her locker and in her desk. One day when she was still in school, everybody knew about the plan to kill her. People were passing notes all over the place, because they wanted everyone to be in on it. Some girls were going to trick her into going outside behind the rink and then the guys were going to get her. You sat there reading the notes thinking: Why doesn't she call the police? It's against the law to threaten to kill someone. It's written all over her books and her locker. She's got proof. I would just call the police. All she has to do is call the police.

But nothing ever happened. A lot of people went to the rink, but there was nothing going on, the girls couldn't find her. She just stopped coming to school after that.

He feeds you soup every night for dinner and doesn't worry too much about anything. You have to keep reminding him he said he would drive you to the hockey game after you eat. He says he'll do things and then forgets. Oh my, I can't wait to sit and watch the news right after this. You said you'd drive me to the hockey game. Oh yes.... Well, now, I think I'll take another shot at fixing that zipper on Mary MacEachern's bag after dinner. You said you'd drive me to the hockey game. Oh yes.

It's because he never had to do it. She would always do it, if she wasn't in the tub. She loved doing it. Sometimes when you had nowhere to go she would invent stuff for you. She signed you up for step dancing because the lessons were in Antigonish and she enjoyed the drive. She'd get to fart around in the mall while you were dancing. You could never get the hang of it. You hated it. Toe-heel, toe-heel. People said you looked as if you were killing snakes. But she didn't mind one bit.

She'd drive you to the games and you'd sit with Peggy Landry and Gus MacPhail and she'd be standing around talking to the Mountie who took tickets or to Rory McKay who drove the zamboni, not even caring that they were trying to see who had the puck. You used to wish she would go so that you could concentrate and not see which people were looking at her, or what kind of face the Mountie had on him while she was talking. But it was better that she would drive you there and wait and drive you home again than having him taking off his shoes and picking up the newspaper when you're standing there with your coat on.

She'd anticipate the next bath in the car, shivering. Mmmm ... my warm bath calls, she'd growl. Mmmm, the pleasure of a hot bath after having to stand in that cold rink for hours. (You didn't have to stay.) Oh, but the longer I stay, the better it is. Mmmm, I can't wait. The simple pleasures. Pleasure is the absence of pain, Socrates says. All the little things you can indulge in to decrease the pains of living. Oohhhhh yes yes yes, my dear, if that isn't what it's all about, I don't know what is.

And the whole hallway saturated with the smell of lavender and honey and Jim Beam, still hanging in the air when you're getting up for school. Cookie crumbs under your feet as you stand brushing your teeth at the sink.

Gus MacPhail doesn't sit with you any more. Now he's on the ice. But he probably wouldn't anyway. It's just like it was with Ball-a More 'n' More. You used to go over to his house and listen to Bay City Rollers albums on his brother's turntable and he had posters of the Bay City Rollers all over his bedroom. Then you lost track of him and saw him again when you started junior high and the only thing you could think to say was, So, ya still like the Bay City Rollers? And Gus had said, The Gay City Blowers? And that had been the end of that. Now he's a goalie.

You still sit with Peggy, but there's all these other girls there who want to sit with Peggy too. You and Peggy glance at each other sorrowfully every once in a while, because you have less and less to talk about these days. You used to spend days on end together, completely content to be in one another's company. You used to be like the same person. Now the games are pretty much the only thing you have in common and both of you know it.

One of the girls is talking about Paula, that she saw her or something at MacIssac's Variety buying an ice-cream bar and Mr. MacIsaac shot a porno mag down on the counter in front of her and asked if she'd like that too. All the girls go, Oh my God, oh my God for a while, and then talk of other things. When you think about people gossiping, you think of them sitting around talking and talking about people until it makes everyone sick, but that's not really how it works at all. All it takes is one sentence every couple of days, a passing remark or joke. And then that person and all that is wrong with them is riveted inside your skull and if anyone ever says their name around you, it triggers all the remarks and the jokes in a flood — that's what you think of when you think of them. That's how it works.

It's getting hard for the girls to talk, because the game is getting exciting and the men all around you roar. Alan Petrie gets sent into the penalty box, and everyone wants to kill the referee. He's the most judicious and fair referee there's ever been, and most of the time they go around singing his praises, but when he calls against the team they all want to kill him anyway. He is the elementary school math teacher, and the only black man in town. You really hear about it with this sort of thing. Gus MacPhail's mother is hollering that they're going to melt him down and make hockey pucks out of him.

And it's one–nothing for them and the guys try and try to get a goal before the end of the first period, but they can't do it without Alan. When the buzzer goes off, everyone howls with rage and frustration, and then there's a crush to get at the canteen for the pop and chips.

For as long as you've been coming to the rink, the guy at the canteen has always thought it was funny to pretend to refuse to give you whatever it is you come asking for. He never cares how many people are waiting in line behind you, he has to get his joke in. He stands there smoking and grinning, the cigarette bobbing up and down as he talks.

"Chips."

"Chips? Nah, you don't want chips."

"Hot chocolate."

"Oh, no, I don't think so."

"Chips and hot chocolate!"

"I've never heard a more disgustin' combination."

"Just give her her goddamn chips and hot chocolate, Hughie, and stop flirting with the young girls!" some old guy hollers from the throng behind you. All the old drunks retching laughter.

"Wouldn't you rather have a nice ... cold ... ice-cream sandwich?" This same joke since you were seven years old.

"It's too cold!"

"What are you talking about, it's a sauna in here!"

"Give her the Jesus chips, ya pervert! Haw haw haw."

He winks and hands them over. You have to smile at this guy because it's nice to talk to someone who says and does exactly the same thing he's been doing and saying ever since you've known him, without exception. The canteen guy is the only person you know like that. This is a revelation. You'd like to crawl back there behind the counter with him and to hell with the rest of the game.

The nice feeling stays with you for the next two periods. Alan Petrie's back in the game. They score, one, two, three goals, and the other team can't score any. The final buzzer goes off and the surrounding crowd writhes and roars in ecstasy, filling up your ears and brain with nothing but them. You're in such a good mood you wave to the canteen guy from the middle of the stampede to get outside. He's lingering in the kitchen door with a smoke behind his ear and one in his mouth. He tells you come here with his finger and there's a look on his face like he's finally going to give you the ice-cream sandwich he's been talking about all these years.

◇

He's not there. The throngs have long since broken up into their cars and gone to their separate homes, the parking lot's empty, he's not waiting. He's at home examining the holes in his slippers. Baffled, probably. What on earth does one do when there's holes in one's slippers? Completely engrossed with the problem.

You're still standing there, too angry to walk when he comes up behind you. You're not surprised, because you listened to him slam and lock the arena doors, and you can smell his duMaurier.

"Still here?"

"He didn't come."

"Boyfriend?"

You actually giggle at this and instantly feel stupid. "No, no. Him, him — my father."

"Just left you here to freeze!"

"Yes."

"Well that's a frigger right there, now."

"I know," you say, feeling grateful.

"I can take you home," he says.

"Oh, good."

"Least I can do, isn't it?" You don't know what he means by that. "Have to be there right away?"

You picture him in the recliner with his slippers in his hands. Open mouth.

"Nope." And off you go.

◇

At ten to twelve, he's asleep in front of the late news, Mrs. MacEachern's bag on his lap. You're lucky he didn't lock the house and go to bed. After a couple of seconds of standing in the hallway regarding him, you walk back to the door, open it, and slam it harder and louder than when you first came in. When you get back to the hall, the bag is on the floor and his eyes are open and he looks about six years old.

"Frigger," you say.

"Now, now...." He picks up the bag and automatically starts experimenting with the zipper again.

"Left me up there to freeze."

"I thought you'd get a ride," he says, furiously yanking the zipper back and forth.

"You didn't think that at all, that or anything."

He stops yanking on the zipper and looks around, still fingering the bag's soft leather. "You have to understand. It never used to be my job."

"It's just common friggin' courtesy. Can't you think of it as just common friggin' courtesy?"

"I've never *had* to think of it."

You decide to go to bed now.

It occurs to him to call, "How did you get home?" when you're at the top of the stairs.

"Got a ride," you call back. "I'll get a ride all the time from now on."

You can hear him making pleased noises to himself down there.

You sit on the toilet across from the enormous claw-foot bathtub Herself had installed before you were born. It would be nice to dump a ton of smelly crap in there and sit in the steaming water, your bones are cold from sitting in his truck, your muscles stiff — but you want too much to go to sleep. It's dangerous to fall asleep in the tub, somebody told you that when you were six and you thought instantly of Herself and never forgot it. You crouched outside the locked door

39

night after night, peeking in the keyhole occasionally to check on her.

"You better not fall asleep in there!" you'd holler, if she appeared ready to nod off. Water would splash everywhere as she jerked up.

"Jesus Murphy! Go play with something and give me some peace."

"Well, you looked as if you were going to sleep."

"Git! Go with you!" You'd watch her sink back down beneath the froth.

You haven't sat in that tub since you were so little you had to be bathed. You always take showers downstairs, quick, without even giving the process a second thought. Him too, every evening after coming up from the shop smelling like dye and leather and polish and glue. It would no more occur to the two of you to sit in Herself's tub than it would to put on her clothes and walk around in them. Why was that?

The first thing to change is the hockey games. You feel foolish just going up and getting your chips and hot chocolate now, and you were afraid, because you didn't know if he might say something new, something that he had never said before, in front of the bundled, hockey-maddened throngs. So for the first little while you had other people get things for you if they were going, and then you'd go and see him afterwards, while everyone else was watching the ice.

"Where were you? I had your chips waitin' right here."

"I don't know."

"Well, here, have them now, eat them with me."

"Good, then."

You rip open the bag and the two of you pass it back and forth. He doesn't even care about the game. He is the only such person in the world. He gives you a hot chocolate and gives himself a coffee and he pours a bit of rum into both. Which tastes awfully good. You try his and you try yours, and yours is better. You're looking at his teeth. They're very long, and each of them is clearly outlined, almost framed by the brown nicotine stains between every one. Cigarettes seem to have given him all the character that is in his face. It's a yellowish colour and the most prominent wrinkles he has are the ones that show up around his mouth when he takes a long drag.

"How long have you been smoking?"

"Since I was ten."

"How old are you now?"

"Thirty ... two."

"Pretty old."

"Ya got that right. How 'bout yerself? Just kiddin'."

So this is what you look forward to more than the games themselves. You never would have imagined such a thing. Sitting in back of the canteen with the sound of coffee dripping into the pot louder than the wails and moans of the entire town every time a goal is scored or missed.

One dinnertime at the house in the middle of the soup, he suddenly looks up. "What about your chips?"

"Wha?"

"What about your chips? Don't you still get your treats up at the game?"

"Yah, I get em." You take a half-package of crackers and, holding them above your soup, demolish them into dust and salty fragments.

"Don't you need any money?" he asks.

"Where'd this come from all of a sudden?" you say, because it's been two months since you had to pay for your chips and hot chocolate. "You should be happy."

"It's a boyfriend or something," he says to himself. "Giving you the drives home as well, I suppose."

Two whole months, you think.

"Isn't that nice," he says after a little while. "That'd be your first, if I'm not mistaken." He looks directly at you and bobs his eyebrows. He's impressed with himself for possessing such intimate knowledge of your comings and goings.

It's different at school as well. Since you scarcely see Peggy at the games any more, there are almost no ties left between you at all. It used to bother you, but it now doesn't so much. Sometimes she looks like her feelings are hurt when you don't bother going up to her after French, and all the oh-my-God girls who try so hard to be with her as often as possible must think you're crazy.

Bernie Heany sticks out his foot and you leap over it like a ballerina. They laugh at you, but they laugh at you no matter what, and it's better than falling on your face.

✧

It just seems natural when it's spring and the hockey's all over for the season to traipse past the Kentucky Fried Chicken after school and visit him at the apartment. You have nowhere else to go in particular. Sometimes you just shove the beer boxes and dishes aside and sit at his kitchen table with a cup of tea and do homework and wait for him to wake up.

He says, "Why don't you ever bring me some chicken, you go right past."

"I didn't think of it," you say.

"Don't you think it would be a nice gesture?"

"I suppose."

He's smoking on the couch, watching TV, wearing a sweater, but no pants. "Every woman I've known," he says, "has always tried to do nice things for me."

You put your pencil down and sit there for a second.

"It's not like that with me," you say after a while.

"Well, obviously, eh?"

"It's bad?"

"No, it's not bad. I just think it's interesting, that's all."

A fat boy at school has been sticking notes in your locker. *I like you you are very prety.* That's the sort of thing he means. All that sort of foolishness.

◇

The grandmother used to come over and watch her swirling around the kitchen, her hair coming and going like a black tide. My Jesus, won't you cut that hair, she'd say. Letting it get all over the kitchen. Into the girl's food.

It was true. Every mealtime of your life spent pulling two-foot hairs from the plate.

"I just have to check the bird, and then I'll pin it back," she'd say.

It's hanging into the pot!

Grandmother would gag. Herself used to say that the grandmother spent her whole life making herself sick worrying about germs that would make her sick. When you were a baby, the grandmother would come to visit, and Herself would have spent a week preparing it, filling bucket after bucket with hot water and bleach, sanitizing the whole house. And then the grandmother would arrive and some sort of radar would kick in and she would head straight for underneath the sink and pull out the rag that had been used for cleaning. My good Lord, dear, what's this doing just sitting here? Throw it in the wash! Do you know how many germs could live in here?

It's full of bleach. There's no germs.

Well, it's filthy. The girl would have that in her mouth in no time.

Then, for no reason in particular, the grandmother would raise her head and peer at the light fixture. Herself would follow her mother's gaze, and the two of them would stand regarding the bodies of dead flies all around the bulb. Like they'd been laid there as sacrifices.

Dear, dear, dear, the grandmother would say. *Tch.* She'd wander off to find a bucket and rubber gloves.

But the worst thing, the dirtiest thing for the grandmother was always hair, and the house was always full of it. The kitchen, the bathtub, the laundry. The food. There is still quite a bit of it around. You had to untangle one from the button of your sweater just the other day. You still use one of her brushes, and there's no getting all of it out. You could hypnotize yourself if you think too long about the drain of the bathtub, of how much of Herself remains clogged down there.

Then later the old woman would say, Aren't you a little old for that sort of hair, dear? Couldn't you do something a bit more conservative with it? She was always saying a little, a bit: Oh, just a little wee drop, if you don't mind. I think I'll take a little nap. I think I've got a bit of a cold. Couldn't you stand to lose a bit of weight?

For the first few months after the funeral, she used to come over to the house all the time, thinking that you and he would have it in a shambles, unable to care for yourselves. But much to her surprise, it was in very good order. It remained so. It was like you didn't even live there at all. The grandmother was so impressed that she decided she was no longer needed and went away to live in British Columbia.

◇

It's late when you leave his apartment, hands greasy with chicken, and see Ball-a More 'n' More standing there in the hall. All around her is the smell of cigarette smoke and cheap clothes detergent, which wafts up from the laundry room downstairs. You don't know what to say to her so you just keep heading towards the stairwell, zipping up your coat. She calls, "Hello, hello," sarcastically at you, and you turn around and say that you didn't even recognize her. It is a reasonable thing to say, you think. The last time the two of you had a conversation, you were seven years old and she was making you scamper around on your hands and knees fetching sticks and rocks in your mouth.

She says, "I live just across the hall," but she is in her boots and jacket, and following you down the stairs.

"I didn't know that. Where are you off to now?"

"Out to get smokes. Wanna come for the walk?"

"I've got to get home."

"Fine, then." She's insulted, oddly. "Actually, I saw you coming in a couple of hours ago. I was walkin' right behind you."

"Oh yah," You don't say: *I thought you couldn't go outside any more.* But maybe people are finally starting to forget about Ball-a and how much they want to kill her.

"I know the guy that lives in there," she says.

"Yah, me too. He's nice."

"How do you know him?"

"Oh, I know him from the rink. I just brought him some chicken." Ball-a snorts, but it's not as if you're lying.

"Aren't you good," she says.

"Aren't I though."

"That's what the good people do, I suppose," she says. "The good people bring each other *chicken.*" There's so much hate in her voice that your instinct is to run. But abruptly she laughs and dashes across the field to the variety store, her boots crunching holes through the crust of the snow. You can hear her tossing words over her shoulder, and at first it just seems like an echo — *Chicken! Chicken!* — but then you realize she's calling you names. Just like when you both were little, and you wouldn't touch a cat that had been laying split open on the street.

Now all of a sudden he decides he wants you to go back to religion classes. You haven't gone since Herself stopped being around to take you. You give him a look as if he's crazy and stupid. You've just walked in the door and he's standing there at the table in front of two bowls of soup, one empty, one full.

"Look," he goes, "I remembered."

"Isn't that dandy."

"But you didn't."

"I didn't remember the *soup?* Is that what you're on about?"

"Well, where were you?"

"Eating chicken."

"With himself, I suppose." That's what he has dubbed the new "boyfriend." He has built up a whole mythology surrounding this person and you have at no time spoken one word about it to him. He turns around suddenly. You watch him execute one full circle around the kitchen.

"What in God's name are you doing?"

"You're getting a mouth," he says, squeezing his hands together. "You're eating chicken. You have to go back to religion."

So that's what you do. You don't like seeing him walking in circles, looking this way and that, so you just go. They hold it on Wednesday nights, and that's what it is now.

You come in late, and all the worst kids are there. The kids whose parents are the most strict about prayer and chastity — they automatically become the ones who smoke and drink and curse. You'd think people would see this connection. Bernie Heany is seated behind you with his feet on the back of your chair.

The nun is going on about Abraham and Isaac. God told Abraham to take his son up to the pyre and sacrifice him like a goat, just to see what Abraham would do. Abraham said, Anything you say, God, and hauled him on up there. Then God sent an angel to say, For Pete's sake, Abraham, we didn't really mean for you to do it. But Abraham's all set to go and the angel has to hold him back. Praise be, says the nun, and shows us a picture of a famous painting. There's Abraham with his knife in the air, all set to tear in, the angel trying to wrestle him away. Bernie Heany is snickering because Isaac isn't wearing any clothes and he looks like a girl, all tied up there.

You tell him you're not going back to religion, and you're not coming home for the soup, all the time, either.

"But I got it ready," he keeps saying. "You weren't even here, and I got it ready. I got the bowls down and I heated it up. I was thinking about you."

"I don't want to have soup every friggin' night."

He has to think about that for a moment.

"We can have something else!" It dawns on him: "We can order pizza." You're already stomping up the stairs, pulling off your sweater.

"I can get that when I'm out."

"But you should really have it with me," he says. You can tell by the way he says it that he doesn't even quite know why that is. He just knows that you should.

After a moment or so in front of the bathroom mirror, you holler, "Taking a bath now!" And he lets a couple of moments go by as well.

"What?"

"I'm going to have a bath."

"I wish you wouldn't," he calls immediately. So you turn on both taps at once and water thunders through the empty pipes, causing the entire house to shudder.

And for God's sake, it's great, once you get in there.

Batter
My Heart

YOU SEE IT THERE, every time on the way back to the old man's. Put up by Baptists or the like, about twenty miles or so from the toll-booths. What always happens is that you go away and you forget that it's there until the next time. Just when the fog and eternal drizzle have seeped deep enough inside your head and sufficiently damp-ened your thinking, it leaps out from the grey and yellow landscape — the same landscape that has been unravelling in front of your eyes for the last three hours. Lurid, oversized letters painted with green and red and black:

PREPARE
TO MEET
THY GOD

Then the bus zips past almost before you can be startled. And it makes you smile for a moment, just like it always has, and then you forget about it, until, presumably, the next time you've gone away and then come back again.

By the time it gets dark, you are driving through Monastery, so called because there is a monastery. You know when you're passing it because there is a large cross lit up by spotlights positioned on either side of the turn-off. Earlier in the day, the driver slowed down and the people oohed and pointed because a small (it looked small, in the distance) brown bear was scampering towards the woods. Just before disappearing, it turned around to glare. These are all the signs.

The monastery you remember from twice in your life. Once, a pious little kid with your family. You saw the crosses marking the graves of dead monks, you saw the building but didn't go inside that day. It hadn't looked like a monastery. Industrial, like a hospital or a prison. It had been built some time in the fifties. You drank water from a blessed stream.

Now they run some kind of detox program there, the drunks living with the monks. The second time, you were a less-than-pious teenager there to visit both your boyfriend and your history teacher. The two of them were actually related somehow — same last name. He had told you it was a disease that runs in his family. The history teacher, far worse than him, older, having had more time to perfect his craft. The monastery like a second home. Word was, this time it was because he had showed up at an end-of-the-year staff party at the principal's house and walked directly through a sliding-glass door. He had a Ph.D. and spoke fluent Russian. You walked into the common room with your boyfriend and the history teacher was sitting at a table playing gin rummy (ha, ha, ha,) with the other drunks. You and he chatted a moment, he condescending, as usual. But not nearly so much as when he was drunk. You can't remember why, but the last thing he said was that you would never make it in the big world. You could only agree, pliant. You still agree. What did that mean, though, *make it?* Did he think you would shrivel up like an unwatered plant? But at the time, you didn't care, you didn't care to defend yourself, you didn't care about any of it. It was liberating, that. It was almost fun. All of a sudden you didn't have to be nice to the boyfriend who used to seem so sad and fragile, who used to get drunk and then go and take a dirty steak knife from out of the dishpan and look at it.

❖

Now about Daddy, different people have said different things. He is the kindest man you could ever know. Well — he's got his own way. He's got his own opinions and, goddamnit, he's not afraid to express them. With his fists if it comes down to that. Quite the temper. Quite the mouth, if you get him going. A good man. The only honest man in town. A visionary. A saint. Would do anything for you, but if you disappoint him, I guess he'll let you know it. Stark raving mad. One mean son of a bitch.

You get home, and Daddy's throwing a man off the step.

"Mr. Leary, I implore you." The man is filthy, flabby, pale.

"Get offa my step, you goddamn drunk."

"Mr. Leary, I've changed. I've turned over a new Jesus leaf."

"And what d'ya know, there's a bottle of Hermit underneath it!" (a sometime wit, Dad.) "You're more full of shit than my own arse. I'm through wasting time with you, Martin. Offa my step."

"Another chance, Mr. Leary, that's all I ask." The bum straightens himself with boozy dignity.

The old fella has caught sight of you. "Hello, Katey! Martin, I'm telling you for the last time to fuck off. I won't have my little girl gazing on the likes of you."

Martin turns, he seems to bow, but may have just lost his balance. "Hello, dear. I'm sorry not to have a hat to tip at you."

Daddy steps forward with a no-nonsense air. His fists are clenched, his jaw is clenched. It should be laughable in a man this side of sixty, but here is the truth: he is terrifying.

"I'm not gonna tell you again," his voice breaks a little, as though any minute he's going to lose control. Again, it seems so put on that it should be ridiculous. You would think that, anyway. Martin is no fool. He retreats into the driveway.

"Mr. Leary," the bum says, actually resting his hand on his heart. "You were my last hope. I went around tellin' everybody who would listen, Jane at the hospital and them, I ain't worried, no matter how down I get, I know I can count on Mr. Leary to come through for me."

"Don't you try to make me feel guilty, you sick bastard!" Daddy shouts. "I broke my ass for you, Martin, I put my ass on the line!" But Martin is stumbling down the driveway. He has his pride.

"Jesus bum." Dad looks like he wants to hit something. He always looks like that. "Come in and have a bite of tea, now, Katherine."

❖

Daddy had done all he could for Martin. This is what you hear over tea and bannock and Cheddar. Put his ass on the line. Tried to get him straightened up. On his Jesus feet again. Martin lived in an old pulp-cutter's shack out in the woods with no water or electricity. His wife dead of a ruined liver. Both boys in jail for the drunk driving. His girl off living with someone. Dad spits, sickened.

Dad normally wouldn't have done a blessed thing for the drunken idiot, but there had been something rather enchanting about him when they had met over the summer. "Lyrical," Daddy says around a mouthful of bannock, surprising you with the word. Daddy had been on the river helping out a friend with his gaspreaux catch. This was etiquette — everyone who had a fish trap helped everyone else load their vats. Daddy didn't begrudge his friend this, particularly because his own catch, brought in last week, had been larger.

Dad had been sitting on the edge of the trap once the last vat was filled, wiping sweat from his pink, hairless forehead, when Martin Carlyle appeared from out of nowhere and greeted him. The two men had never actually come face to face before, but, as both had attained a kind of notoriety within the community, they recognized one another, and each knew the other's name. Now Daddy puts on a show, acting out the two parts:

"Good day, Mr. Leary, sir!"

"Hullo, Martin."

"By the Lord Jesus, it's a beautiful day!"

"Yes."

"Did you catch a lot of fish today?"

"One or two, Martin, one or two," Dad says, squinting up at the man, who had a terrible matted beard and pee stains on the front of his pants.

Now Martin stands in silence, weaving just a little bit, and appears to be thinking very deeply about something.

"Mr. Leary," he says at last, "I put it to you. Would this not be the perfect day to be bobbing along down the river in one of those vats with a big blonde in one hand and a bottle of Captain Morgan in the other and a pink ribbon tied around your pinocchio?"

Daddy concludes the performance, sputtering bannock crumbs from his laughter. "Lyrical," he says. "That's what you would call lyrical, isn't it, Katey?"

There you were in the monastery, once upon a time, a walking sin.

Defiling the floor tile upon which you tread. A sin taking life in your gut. No one can see it, which is good. Being a girl is bad enough, in a monastery. The drunks turn and stare.

Martin Carlyle among them at the time. A pink ribbon tied around his pinocchio. Sitting on the bridge that crosses the blessed stream as you and the boyfriend traipse by along the muddy path. Spring. Grimy, miserable season. You irreverently spit your gum out into an oncoming mud puddle, and he shoots you a dirty look. Impiety. He's religious now, after two weeks among them. Martin is on the bridge with a fishing pole between his legs. He calls:

"Hey-ho, Stephen, boy!"

"Martin!" Raises his hand.

"Whee-hoo! You got a little friend!"

"How are you, Martin?"

"Ready to break into the vestry, that's how. Get meself a little taste of wine!"

"Don't do that, Martin, don't do that now."

"No —"

Together, you walk up the hill to look at the stations of the cross. He is insistent that you pause at every station. The women clamour at the feet of the suffering Christ. He keeps telling you about how different he is. He keeps saying things like: "I pray now. I honestly pray," and, "Everything seems right. Like all my problems were meaningless."

And you say, "Of course it does," and he says, "What?" and you say, "You get to be in a monastery."

He tells you, "The monastery doesn't have anything to do with it. You just have to learn to pray. I mean really pray. What that means is accepting God."

Well, you are certainly too much of a hardened and worldly wise seventeen-year-old to go for that. "No way," you say.

"Why?" He gives you a gentle look, and you see that he thinks he is a monk. Wise, wizened. Sleeping in a narrow bed, in a little cell, humble. But when you spit your gum out onto the path, and were impolite to Brother Mike, he wanted to hit you. You could see that. Any fool could see that.

"Nothing to accept," you say.

"You can't believe that," Misguided woman. Is there no one left to condemn you? No one, Lord. Then I will condemn you.

"Belief," you say, "doesn't come into it."

He attempts to look at peace with himself yet disappointed with you all at once. Then: "Do you want to go see the shrine to the Virgin?"

Why not? Very nice, very pretty. Easily the prettiest thing here in man-land, white stones and plastic flowers all about. He tries to hold your hand, to create some kind of moment, sinner and saviour. He looks over: "Do you want to kneel?"

"No, I don't want to kneel!"

❖

He smiles when you leave, all benevolence, alongside of his favourite monk, Brother Mike. He had wanted you to talk to Brother Mike for some reason, but you said no. He was disappointed, but he said he understood. He thinks that you're making the wrong decision, going away, but he understands that too. He understands everything. He and the monk stand side by side waving goodbye.

When you first arrived, it was Brother Mike who intercepted you. You had gone into the chapel instead of the main entrance, and stood overwhelmed by the height of the ceiling, the lit candles, the looming statues of saints looking down from every corner, the darkness. For want of something to do while you waited for someone to come and find you, you went over and lit a candle for your dead Gramma.

Brother Mike had been kneeling up front, but you didn't even see him, it was so dark. He was standing right beside you before you noticed him. He spoke in a natural speaking voice, not a whisper, which in a church seemed abnormal. "Are you Katherine?"

He led you to the common room, and that was when, watching your feet hit the grey industrial floor tile, it occurred to you what a desecration your presence constituted. Every heartbeat, every snoutful of sanctified oxygen you took went blasphemously down into your bellyful of sin to give it strength. Brother Mike looks around to see if you are still following and gives you a kindly smile.

"Well, the boy had a lot of anger when he came here. A good deal of anger with himself and the world. I think you'll see a big difference."

Now, a few years gone by, the phone will ring late at night. Not often, but every now and again. Bitch. Heartless, stupid …. Just like old times!

The day after you arrive is Sunday, and it is clear that he expects you to accompany your mother to church. No argument. *My, hasn't Katey changed.* Because then it used to seem like there was some kind of moral imperative to jump up and down on the backs of their sacred cows. Isn't it, you used to argue into Daddy's pulsating face, more of a sin to be sitting there thinking the whole proceeding is a pile of shit than to just stay at home? And now you don't care if it is or not, sins and moral imperatives alike being figments of the past.

But when the choir isn't present, ruining the peace, church can be nice, the sun coming in through the fragmented window. You can sit alone among everybody, enjoying your mild hangover. Everybody murmuring responses to the priest in unison. You do it too and are not even aware. That's nice. The powdery smell of clean old men and old ladies all around. The feel of their dry hands when it comes time to extend the blessing to one another. You love the sight of old men in glasses, kneeling, fingering their beads.

But one of the last times you were to mass, also sixteen, Mommy insisted for some reason on going to the early one and there you are with the worst hangover in the world. Ever, in the world. Mother, God love her, with no idea. You say in the car: Hm, Mom, I'm not feeling so good this morning. She says, Yes, Margaret-Ann's kids are all coming down with the flu.

Inside, everything makes you nauseous. You remember that your Gramma had this bottle of perfume that she only wore on Sundays, for mass. She said that she had been using the same bottle for thirty years, and only on Sundays and for weddings and for funerals. You remember that because it smells like the old women sitting on all sides of you must do that too — don thirty-year-old scent for mass. Everything smells putrid. You think that the old man in the pew ahead must have pissed himself a little, as old men will. The priest waves around incense. You stand up, you sit down, you stand up, you sit down, you mutter the response to the priest. You turn to tell your mother that you need to go outside for air — dang flu bug. Halfway down the aisle, bile fills your cheeks.

Outside, you run around to the back of the church where no one will see you because it faces the water. It's February, the puddle steams. Your breath steams. You eat some snow and gaze out at the frozen strait, mist hanging above it. Hm, you think.

Today, it's not like that. You feel pleasant, dozy, as soon as you take a seat beside your mother in the pew. You pick up the Catholic Book of Worship and read the words to the songs. You've always done that, every since you were small.

Sadly, the choir will be singing today. The well-to-do matrons with sprayed, silver hair and chunky gold jewellery. Most of them are members of the Ladies Auxiliary. You don't know what that is. Mrs. Tamara Cameron approaches the microphone and tells everybody that the opening hymn will be "Seek Ye First." This is the one where they all try to harmonize one long, high-pitched "ALLLLL-LEEEEE-LOOOOO-YAAAAA" with a whole verse. They think it sounds ethereal. The organist is a stiff, skinny fifteen-year-old outcast who appears to be scared out of her mind. You lean over to ask Mommy where the real organist is, Mrs. Fougere, who has been there for as long as you can remember, and your mother whispers that she is dead, as of only two weeks ago.

The first chord that the fifteen-year-old hits is off-key, causing Mrs. Cameron to glower. The girl is going to cry, maybe. No — the song begins.

The congregation has always liked the choir because it means they don't have to sing. They are content to stand there, holding their books open in front of them. But Mommy always sings, choir or no, and she holds her book at an angle so that you can see the words and sing too.

A wonderful thing happens now. You notice Martin Carlyle, shuffling unobtrusively into the back row of the choir box. He is wearing the same clothes as you saw him in yesterday. He blows his nose quietly, with deference, into a repulsive piece of cloth and then tucks it back into his sleeve, where he got it. He picks up a hymn-book, flips it open to the correct page after peeking at someone else's, and decides to join in on the high-pitched "Alleluia" rather than the regular verse. Except that his voice isn't high-pitched, like the ladies'.

> Seek ye first the Kingdom of God
> And his righteousness
> And all these things will be offered unto you
> Allelu, alleluia.

Mommy says into your ear, "There's Martin," unsurprised, which must mean he shows up for this every Sunday. That is why Mrs. Cameron has failed to glower, and only looks a little put out. What can she say? They are all God's children.

◇

After you've been around for a while, Martin seems to turn up everywhere. He's the town drunk, is why, and the town is small. Every Sunday, you see him at church, singing in the choir, his voice even more off-note than the ladies'. Half the time he doesn't even know the words and sort of yah-yahs his way through. One day you do an experiment and go to the nine o'clock mass instead of the later one. There Martin is, singing away.

He never recognizes you, even after the time on the step. One time you see him at the bar bumming for drinks and you are so pissed that you say to the assholes you are with: "Look! It's my soulmate," and you go over and fling your arm around him and call for two scotches and sodas. You remember him blinking at you with reservation and saying, "Thank you, dear. Thank you, Miss."

Another day you go to the bar — even though you have been saying to yourself all along: I probably shouldn't go to the bar — and of course on that day you see him there and he comes and sits down at the table you're at. So then you go and sit down at a different one but then he comes and sits down there too. All he does is look at you and smoke. It is the first time you've been face to face in two years. At a third table, he sits down right beside you and tells you, in a number of ways, that you are a terrible person and why. The assholes you are with examine their drinks. If one of them would at least move, you could get up from the table.

◇

For a long time, nothing much happens.

Then, word comes around that Martin has shot himself in the head. Doctor Bernie, a second cousin, calls from the hospital and informs Daddy that the patient has been asking for him.

"Holy shit!" says Dad.

"Yes,"the doctor replies. He has an implacable, sing-song voice which has always annoyed you and your father equally.

"He's been asking for you ever since they brought him in here, Alec."

"Well, holy shit, Bernie, is he going to live or what?"

"Oh yes, he's sitting up having a cup of tea."

Dad has to get you to drive him to the hospital because he is "so Jesus pissed off I can't see straight."

"Holy shit," he keeps muttering, and, "Stupid bugger."

In the hospital, you hang around the reception desk listening to his voice resound in the corridor. It is a small hospital. Nurses rush past to silence him, not understanding that their pasty, wrinkled faces and harsh, hushed voices and fingers pressed against their lipless mouths are just going to make him angrier. You remember this from all your life. Shrinking down in the front seat of the car while Daddy yells at a careless driver. Shrinking down in the wooden desk while Daddy yells at your math teacher. Shrinking down into the chester-field while Daddy yells at the television. Everything making him angrier and angrier and nobody getting it right.

But when Daddy emerges, trailing flustered and ignored nurses, he is laughing.

"Leave it to Martin," he says. "Shoots himself through the head and even that doesn't do him a bit of good."

"So are you going to help him again, Daddy?"

"Well, Jesus Christ, Katey, what are you gonna do, you know?"

He doesn't really know what to do any more, he's done so much already. He used to drive Martin to AA meetings (much as he had hated them himself in the old days) but was soon informed by such-and-such that Martin took advantage of the trips into town to visit the liquor store and drop in at Buddy's Tavern. And everything ended up like that. Daddy had badgered social services into boosting Martin's allowance so that he could buy some soap and deodorant and Aqua Velva and clothes to get himself cleaned up for the job Dad had managed to get him sweeping up at the mill. Then, when Dad heard about the new public housing units that were going up, social services found themselves duly annoyed into putting one aside for Martin, even though they were being clamoured for by single mothers and the like.

So Daddy drove out to Martin's shack in the woods, which had no water or electricity, and laid all of this at his feet.

"By God, Martin," he said, "you'll get the new place all snugged up nice and pretty soon you'll be having your daughter over for Sunday dinner."

"No, Mr. Leary, my daughter wouldn't come over so she could spit on me."

"Well, goddamnit, you can have me over to dinner!"

"Proud to, Mr. Leary."

Daddy handed him the keys and, looking around at the differing piles of junk that served as Martin's furniture, told him to just give social services a call once he got everything packed away and ready to go. They'd come and get him moved in. "By the Jesus, I'll come and help too," he added.

"God bless you, Mr. Leary,"

"Aw, well, what the fuck."

Dad left, feeling good, stepping over Martin's sick, emaciated dog, King.

But months went by and social services called up: "Mr. Leary, there is a list of people as long as my arm who are waiting to get into that unit, and it just sitting there...." Dad barks something that shuts the sarcastic little bastard right up, and then hangs up so he can phone his buddy at the mill. How has Martin been getting along? Martin Carlyle? He didn't show up, Alec, and I wasn't expecting him to.

Outside the shack with no water or electricity, Daddy found Martin asleep on the ground while King sniffed daintily at the surrounding vomit. Martin's drinking friend, Alistair, was leaning against the side of the house, taking in the sunshine. A beautiful spring day. He was not passed out, but cradled a near-empty bottle of White Shark against his crotch, serene and Buddha-like. He squinted up at Daddy and said that himself and Martin had been having "a regular ceilidh" all month long with the extra welfare that Martin was now getting. Daddy kicked the dog into the woods and threw the bottle of White Shark in after it. This having been the incident that preceded the throwing of Martin Carlyle from Alec Leary's step, where you came in.

Daddy has a sore knee. It makes him hobble when he walks, and it makes him angry. You have to go out and help him bring the wood in because none of your brothers are about. If you were one of them, it would be a bonding moment between you and he. It might be anyway. He likes you when you work. Here is one thing you know: Men love work. You might not know anything about what women love, but men love work.

You can always tell when it's Martin phoning, because Daddy's tone will become reserved. You hear him say things like: Well, I'll do what I can, Martin, but I'm not making any promises, you hear me? I can't just give give give. Then Dad will hang up and turn to you.

"If that Martin Carlyle ever comes around when I'm not here, don't you let him in."

"No."

"Do you know what he looks like?"

"Yes, I've seen him a million —"

"A big fat hairy ugly bastard and he's got a hole in his head" — Daddy points to a spot above one of his eyebrows — "where the bullet went in."

Daddy is busy these days with Little League. The head of the recreation department called him up and asked him to coach. "Nobody else wanted to do it, I suppose," he grunted into the phone. "Selfish whores."

And your mother, observing that you never seem to go out any more and have absolutely nothing to occupy your time, ever so delicately suggests that it would be nice and he would like it if you attended the games. So you do, even though you have no understanding of baseball and don't know when to cheer or when to boo and are the only woman there who isn't somebody's mother and almost get hit on the head with a foul ball twice. You watch him hobbling back and forth in front of the dugout, hollering at both teams and causing the little guy at bat's knees to knock together. At the end of every game, win or lose, he takes them to the Dairy Queen and buys them all sundaes. You get to come along too. You have coffee. The little boys look at you and ask you questions about yourself. Are you married? What grade are you in? They can't quite figure out where you fit. You answer every question as honestly as you can, but it doesn't help them any.

Soon, you're attending the practices. Maybe you are the unofficial mascot. Dad gets frustrated with them one day and steps up to the plate to show them how it's done. He can't throw any more because his arm cramps up when he raises it above his shoulder, and he can't run because of his knee, but he gets the best pitcher on the team to throw him one so they can see how to hit. The clenched fists and clenched jaw all over again — overweight, balding man clutching a child's tool in his large, pink hands. When he swings the bat, it makes a sound that frightens you and you look up from picking at your nails and see that all the little round faces are turned upward in awe.

❖

Jesus Christ,
Murdeena

❖

HER MOTHER WOULD TELL YOU it started with the walks. Just out of the blue, not too long after she got fired from the Busy Burger and had been kicking around the house for a few days. Out comes Murdeena with, "I think I'll go out for a little walk." Margaret-Ann was just finishing up the dishes and hurried to dry off her hands when she heard it, thinking Murdeena was being sly about asking for a drive somewhere.

"Where do you want to go?" asks Margaret-Ann.

"I don't know, I'm just going to walk around."

"Where are you going to walk around?"

"I'll just go down by the water or somewhere."

"Here, I'll take you down," she says, reaching for the keys.

"Pick me up a Scratch and Win!" Mr. Morrisson calls from the couch, hearing them jingle.

"No, no, no," goes Murdeena. "I'm just going for a walk, to look at the water."

"I'll drive you down, we can sit in the car and look at it," says Margaret-Ann. She doesn't know what her daughter is on about.

"I want to go for a *walk*," says Murdeena.

"Who goes for *walks*?" points out Margaret-Ann. She's right, too.

Nobody goes for walks. The only people who go for walks are old women and men who have been told by their doctors that they have to get more exercise. You can see them, taking their turns around the block every night after supper, looking none too pleased.

"What's the matter with you?" asks Margaret-Ann. She's thinking Murdeena is feeling bad about getting fired and wants to go mope.

"Nothing, Mumma. It's a nice night."

"Go sit on the porch, you don't have to go traipsing about."

"I *want* to."

"Go on, I'll bring you a cup of tea."

"I don't want to drink any more tea. I want to walk."

Thinking of the seniors, it occurs to Margaret-Ann that walking is a healthy pastime, and maybe she should encourage it.

"You're on some kind of new health kick, now, are you?"

"No."

"Well, if that's what you want to do," she says, doubtful. "Are you going to be all right?"

"Yes." Meanwhile Murdeena's digging around in the porch, trying to find something to put on her feet.

"Do you need a jacket?"

"Yeah, I'll put on my windbreaker."

"Maybe you should wear mine," says Margaret-Ann, fidgety about the whole performance.

"No, I'll be all right."

"What do you got on your feet?"

That's a bit of a problem. Nobody walks, so nobody has any walking shoes. Murdeena settles for a pair of cowboy boots she bought in Sydney back when they were in style.

"You can't walk in those."

"They're *made* for people to walk in. Cowboys. They walk all around the range."

"They ride around on their horses," protests Margaret-Ann.

"Well, they'll do for now." Murdeena puts on her windbreaker.

Then Ronald pipes up again. "She's not going out by herself, is she?" he calls from the couch.

"Yes. She wants to go for a *walk*."

"Where's she going to walk to?"

"Jesus Murphy, I'll bring you back a Lotto!" Murdeena hollers before the whole rigmarole can get under way again, and she clomps out the door in her boots. So there's Margaret-Ann left to do all the explaining.

Margaret-Ann will tell you that is where it all started, although it didn't seem like much of anything at first. Murdeena walking. By herself, in the evening. Perhaps it was getting fired, that's what Margaret-Ann thought. Murdeena had never been fired before, although the Busy Burger was only her second job — before that she was a cashier at Sobey's, for four years, right up until it closed down. She was great at it, and everybody liked her. She liked it too because she got to visit with everyone in town and catch up on their news. The Busy Burger wasn't so much her style because most of the people who came in were high school kids and Carl Ferguson who ran the place was a big fat shit. She used to get along so well with her manager at Sobey's, because they'd gone to school together, but Carl Ferguson was just this mean old bastard she couldn't relate to who didn't like girls and treated them all like idiots. He picked on Murdeena especially because she couldn't count. Even with the cash register there giving a read-out, she never gave anyone the right change. Murdeena could never do math, none of the teachers at school could figure her out because the math teacher assumed she was borderline retarded while the rest of them were giving her A's and B's. There must be some kind of condition where you can't do math, just like the one where you can't spell, and that's what Murdeena had. If you asked her anything having to do with numbers, she'd change the subject. If you asked her how many people lived in her town, she'd say, "Oh, quite a few," or else, "Oh, it's about the size of Amherst, I'd guess. Maybe more." If you'd try to pin her down on a figure, she might say something like, "Oh ... maybe ... a ... couple of hundred." It was a good way to get her back in high school. We'd all laugh.

But her mind just didn't work that way, some people's minds don't. It didn't make her a moron, but Carl Ferguson treated her like one anyway. She was always careful to check the register and count out the change meticulously, but sometimes the bastard would stand there watching her making slow calculations as she moved the change from the register to her palm and he'd wear this disgusted smirk and make her all nervous. So one day, right in front of him, she handed Neil MacLean a twenty instead of a five. Neil said he could see her hand shaking as she did it, and he tried to nod to her or something, let her know in some way that the change was wrong. Before he could do a blessed thing, though, Carl Ferguson tears the twenty out of her hand. "For Christ's sake, woman," he goes. "You trying to make me go broke?" And Murdeena cried and Neil, probably trying to help out, told Carl he was an arsehole, but that's when Carl told her she was fired — probably just to shut Neil up and prove that he could do or say whatever he damn well pleased in his own establishment.

Everyone hated Carl after that because everyone liked Murdeena. Whenever she gave people back the wrong change at Sobey's, they'd just say, "Oops, dear, I need a bit more than that," or a bit less, or whatever, and then they'd help her to count out the right amount, and then everyone would have a big laugh together.

So then she was on UI again and there was talk in town about a big bulk-food store opening up, and Margaret-Ann kept telling her there was no need to worry.

"I'm not worried anyways," says Murdeena.

"Then why all the walks?" This was after the fourth walk of the week. Murdeena was going through all the shoes in the closet, trying to find the best pair for walking. Tonight she had auditioned a pair of her brother Martin's old basketball sneakers from eight years ago.

"I'm not walking because I'm worried about anything!" says Murdeena, surprised. And the way she says it is so clean and forthright that Margaret-Ann knows she's not lying. This makes Margaret-Ann more nervous than before.

"Well for the love of God, Murdeena, what are you doing stomping around out there all by yourself?"

"It's nice out there."

"It's nice, is it."

"Yes."

"Well, it seems like an awful waste of time, when I could be driving you anywhere you wanted to go."

Murdeena has never gotten her driver's licence. This is something else about her that's kind of peculiar. She says there isn't any point because she never goes anywhere. Margaret-Ann and Ronald like it because it means that she still needs them to do things for her from time to time.

"If I wanted to go for a drive," says Murdeena, "I'd go for a drive."

"It just seems so Jesus *pointless!*" bursts out Margaret-Ann, wishing Murdeena would quit fooling with her, pretending everything was normal. People around town were starting to make remarks. Cullen Petrie at the post office:

"Oh, I see your girl out going for the walks these days."

"Yes, it's her new thing, now."

"Well, good for her! I should be getting out more myself."

"Yes, shouldn't we all," says Margaret-Ann, officiously licking her stamps.

"Isn't she tough!"

"Yes, she is."

"Every night I see her out there," marvels Cullen Petrie. "Every night!"

"Yes." Margaret-Ann gathers up her mail in a pointed sort of fashion, so as to put Cullen in his place. "Yes, she's tough, all right."

Cullen calls after her to have Murdeena put in an application at the post office — he'd be happy to see what he could do for her. Margaret-Ann would like to kick him.

"You don't *need* a job right now, in any event," Margaret-Ann keeps telling her over and over again. "Your UI won't run out for a year, and you've got enough to keep you busy these days."

"That's right," agrees Murdeena, clomping around in an old pair of work boots to see how they fit, and not really paying much attention. "I've got lots to keep me busy."

Murdeena is always on the go, everyone says so. She plays piano for the seniors every weekend and always helps out at the church teas and bake sales. She'll do the readings in church sometimes, and plays on her softball team. It used to be the Sobey's softball team before it closed down, but they all enjoyed the games so much that the employees didn't want to disband. They ripped the cheap SOBEY'S logos off their uniforms and kept playing the other businesses in town anyway. Nobody minded. For a joke, they changed their name to the S.O.B.'s.

Some people are concerned that she doesn't have a boyfriend, but Margaret-Ann and Ronald are relieved, they like her where she is. She went out with a fellow in high school for three years, and it looked as if things were pretty much all sewn up for after graduation, but didn't he go off to university — promising they'd talk about the wedding when he came home for the summer. Well, you don't have to be a psychic, now, do you?

So Murdeena hasn't been seeing anyone since then — almost five years now. She has her own small group of friends, the same ones she had in school, and they all go out to the tavern together, or sometimes will take a trip over to the island or into Halifax. There are a couple of young fellows that she spends time with, but they're all part of the group, one with a girlfriend and one married.

So no one can think of anyone Murdeena might end up with. Murdeena knows everyone in town and everyone knows her. Everyone has their place and plays their part. So it's hard to think of changing things around in any sort of fundamental way. Like starting something up with someone you've known since you were two. It doesn't feel right, somehow.

✧

"To hell with it," she announces one evening after supper. She's got every pair of shoes in the house lined up across the kitchen floor.

"What is it now?" gripes Margaret-Ann, even though Murdeena hasn't said a word up until now. Margaret-Ann always feels a little edgy after suppertime, now, knowing Murdeena will be leaving the house to go God knows where. "What's the matter with you?"

"None of these are any good." She kicks at the shoes.

"What do you mean? Wear your nice deck shoes."

"No."

"Wear your desert boots."

"They're all worn out. I've worn them all. None of them feel right."

"Do they hurt your feet? Maybe you need to see a doctor."

"They don't hurt, Mumma, they just don't feel *right*."

"Well, for Christ's sake, Murdeena, we'll go out and get you a pair of them hundred-dollar Nike bastards, if that'll keep you quiet."

"I'm going to try something else," says Murdeena, sitting down in one of the kitchen chairs. *Thank God!* thinks Margaret-Ann. *She's going to stay in and drink her tea like a normal person.*

But Murdeena doesn't reach for the teapot at all. What she does is take off her socks. Margaret-Ann just watches her, not really registering anything. Then Murdeena gets up and goes to the closet. She takes out her windbreaker. She puts it on. Margaret-Ann blinks her eyes rapidly, like a switch has been thrown.

"What in the name of God are you doing now?"

"I'm going for my walk."

Margaret-Ann collapses into the same chair Murdeena had been sitting in, one hand covering her mouth.

"You've got no *shoes!*" she whispers.

"I'm going to give it a try," says Murdeena, hesitating in the doorway. "I think it'll feel better."

"For the love of Jesus, Murdeena, you can't go walking around with no shoes!" her mother wails.

Murdeena makes her lips go thin and doesn't ask her mother why, because she knows why just as well as Margaret-Ann does. But she's stubborn.

"It'll be all right. It's not cold."

"There's broken glass all over the street!"

"Oh, Mother, there is not."

"At least put on a pair of sandals," Margaret-Ann calls, hoping for a compromise. She follows Murdeena to the door, because she's leaving, she's going out the door, she's doing it. And she's hurrying, too, because she knows if her mother gets hold of that windbreaker, she'll yank her back inside.

"I won't be long," Murdeena calls, rushing down the porch steps.

Margaret-Ann stands on the porch, blinking some more. She thinks of Cullen Petrie sitting on his own front porch across the street, taking in the evening breeze.

Murdeena Morrisson has been parading all over town with no shoes on her feet, everyone says to everyone else. They marvel and chuckle together. They don't know what she's trying to prove, but it's kind of cute. People will honk their horns at her as they go by and she'll grin and wave, understanding. "You're going to catch cold!" most of them yell, even though it's the middle of summer. The only people who are kind of snotty about it are the teenagers, who are snotty to everyone anyway. They yell "hippie!" at her from their bikes, because they don't know what else to yell at a person without shoes. Sometimes they'll yell, "Didn't you forget something at home?"

Murdeena hollers back: "Nope! Thanks for your concern!" She's awfully good-natured, so nobody makes a fuss over it, to her face anyway. If that's what she wants to do, that's what she wants to do, they say, shaking their heads.

Margaret-Ann does her shopping with a scowl and nobody dares mention it to her. Murdeena won't wear shoes at all any more. She'll go flopping into the pharmacy or the seniors home or anywhere at all with her big, dirty feet. The Ladies Auxiliary held a lobster dinner the other night, and there Murdeena was as usual, bringing plates and cups of tea to the old ladies, and how anyone kept their appetites Margaret-Ann could not fathom. Murdeena stumbled with a teacup: "Don't burn your tootsies, now, dear!" Laughter like gulls.

❖

"I don't want to hear another word about it!" Margaret-Ann announces one evening at the supper table. Murdeena looks up from her potatoes. She hasn't said a thing.

It is obviously a signal to Ronald. He puts down his fork and sighs and dabs his lips with a paper napkin. "Well," he says, searching for the right words. "What will you do in the winter? They're'll be snow on the ground."

Margaret-Ann nods rapidly. Good sound logic.

Murdeena, still hunched over her plate — she's been eating like a football player these days, but not putting on weight, as she tends to — suddenly grins at the two of them with startling love.

"I'll put on *boots* when it's wintertime!" she exclaims. "I haven't gone crazy!" She goes to shovel in some potatoes but starts to laugh suddenly and they get sprayed across the table.

"Oh, for Christ's sake, Murdeena!" complains her mother, getting up. "You'd think you were raised by savages."

"That's politically incorrect," Ronald articulates carefully, having done nothing but watch television since his retirement.

"My arse," Margaret-Ann articulates even more carefully. Murdeena continues to titter over her plate. This quiet glee coming off her lately is starting to wear on Margaret-Ann. Like she's got some big secret tucked away that she's going to spring on them at any moment, giving them instant triple heart attacks. "And what's so Jesus funny inside that head of yours, anyway?" she stabs at Murdeena suddenly. "Walking around grinning like a monkey, like you're playing some big trick on everybody, showing off those big ugly feet of yours."

Offended, Murdeena peers beneath the table at them. "They're not ugly."

"They're ugly as sin!"

"Since when?"

"Since you decided you wanted to start showing them off to the world!"

"Why should anybody care about seeing my *feet?*" queries Murdeena, purely bewildered.

"Exactly!" shoots back her mother. "Why should anyone care about seeing your feet!"

It ends there for a while.

◇

She had always been the sweetest, most uncontentious little girl. Even as a baby, she never cried. As a child, never talked back. As a teenager, never sullen. She was their youngest and their best. Martin had driven drunk and had to go to AA or face jail, and Cora had gotten pregnant and then married and then divorced, and Alistair had failed grade nine. And all of them moved far away from home. But Murdeena never gave them any trouble at all. *Agreeable* was the word that best described Murdeena. She was always the most agreeable of children. Everybody thought so.

Gradually, however, she takes to speaking to Margaret-Ann like she believes her to be an idiot.

"Mother," she says, slow and patient, "there's things you don't understand right now."

"Mother," she murmurs, smiling indulgently, "all will be explained."

Margaret-Ann rams a taunt, red fist into a swollen mound of bread dough. "Will you take your 'mothers' and stuff them up your hole, please, dear?"

"Ah, Mumma," Murdeena shakes her head and wanders away smiling, her bare feet sticking to the kitchen linoleum. Margaret-Ann fires an oven mitt at her daughter's backside, and feels around the counter for something more solid to follow it up with. She can't stand to be condescended to by Murdeena. The world seems on its head. She can hear her in the living room with Ronald, solemnly advising him to turn off the TV and listen to her tell him something, and Ronald is trying to joke with her, and play round-and-round-the-garden-like-a-teddy-bear on her hand to make her laugh. She won't give him her hand. Margaret-Ann can hear her daughter speaking quietly to her husband while he laughs and sings songs. Margaret-Ann feels dread. She goes to bed without asking Ronald what Murdeena had tried to say.

It is reported to Margaret-Ann later in the week. The folks at the seniors home were enjoying a slow and lovely traditional reel when the entertainer abruptly yanked her hands from the keys and slammed the piano shut. The loud wooden *thunk* echoed throughout the common room and the piano wires hummed suddenly in nervous unison. A couple of old folks yelped in surprise, and one who had been sleeping would have lurched forward out of his wheelchair if he hadn't been strapped in.

"Murdeena, dear, are you trying to scare the poor old souls out of their skins?" gasped Sister Tina, the events organizer, and Margaret-Ann's informant.

"There's just so much to tell you all," Murdeena reportedly answered, staring down at the shut piano, which looked like a mouth closed over its teeth. "And here I am playing reels!" She laughed to herself.

"Are you tired, dear?" Sister Tina asked in her little-girl's voice, always calculated to be soothing and inoffensive to those around her. She moved carefully forward, using the same non-threatening gestures she approached the seniors with.

With unnerving spontaneity, Murdeena suddenly cried, "There's so much news!"

"What's wrong with her?" barked Eleanor Sullivan, who loved a good piano tune. "Get her a drink of rum!"

"Give her some slippers, her feet are cold," slurred Angus Chisholm, groggy from being jolted out of his snooze.

"I have some good wool socks she can put on," Mrs. Sullivan, the most alert and officious of the bunch of them, offered. "Run and get them for her, Sister, dear." All of a sudden, all the seniors were offering to give Murdeena socks. A couple of them were beckoning for Sister Tina to come and help them off with their slippers — Murdeena obviously had more need of them than they did.

"I haven't been able to feel my *own* goddamned feet in years," Annie Chaisson was reasoning, struggling to kick off her pom-pommed knits.

"For the love of God, everyone keep your shoes on," commanded Sister Tina. "You'll all get the cold and there won't be enough people to look after you!"

"I don't need your footwear!" hollered Murdeena. "I need to be heard! I need to be believed and trusted and heard!"

It was an outlandishly earnest thing to say, and the old people looked everywhere but at the piano. Murdeena had swung around on the stool and was beaming at them. What came next was worse.

"I take it you've heard," says Murdeena to her mother. She'd gone for a walk after her time with the seniors and stayed out for two and a half hours. Margaret-Ann stands in the middle of the kitchen, practically tapping her foot like a caricature of an angry, waiting mother. You would think Murdeena was a teenager who had been out carousing all night. Ronald is sitting at the kitchen table looking apprehensive because Margaret-Ann told him to and because he is.

"I take it you have something you'd like to say," Margaret-Ann shoots back. "You're father tells me you've already said it to him. And now that you've said it to a bunch of senile incontinent old friggers, perhaps you can say it to your own mother."

"All right," says Murdeena, taking a breath. "Here she goes."

"Let's hear it, then," says Margaret-Ann.

"I am the Way and the Light," says Murdeena.

"What's that now?"

"I am the Way and the Light," says Murdeena.

"*You* are," says Margaret-Ann.

"I am."

"I see."

Ronald covers the lower part of his face with his hands and looks from one woman to the other.

"Now what way and what light is that?" asks Margaret-Ann with her hands on her hips.

"What — ?"

"What way and what light is it we're talking about?"

Murdeena swallows and presses her lips together in that stubborn but uncertain way she has. "The way," she says, "to heaven."

Margaret-Ann looks to her husband, who shrugs.

"And the light," continues Murdeena, "of — well, you know all this, Mother. I shouldn't have to explain it."

"Of?"

"Of salvation."

Murdeena clears her throat to fill up the silence.

They are up all night arguing about it.

First of all, the arrogance. It is just plain arrogant to walk around thinking you are "the end-all and be-all," as Margaret-Ann insisted on putting it. She would acknowledge it in no other terms.

"What you're saying is you're better than the rest of us," was Margaret-Ann's argument.

"No, no!"

"You're walking around talking like you know everything. No one's going to stand for it."

"Not *everything*," said Murdeena. But she was smiling a little, you could tell she thought she was being modest.

"People aren't going to stand for it," Margaret-Ann repeated. "They're going to say: 'Murdeena Morrisson, who does she think she is?'"

"Oh, for Pete's sake, Mumma!" burst Murdeena with uncharacteristic impatience. "Don't you think back in Nazareth when Jes — I mean me, when I was telling everyone in Nazareth ..."

Margaret-Ann covered her ears.

"... about how I was the Way and the Light back then, don't you think everyone was going around saying: 'Humph! Jesus Christ! He must think he's some good! Walking around, preaching at people.'"

"This is blasphemy," hollered Margaret-Ann over the sound of blood pumping through her head. She was pressing against her ears too tightly.

"That's what they said back then, too."

Margaret-Ann was right and Murdeena was wrong. Nobody wanted to hear it. Everyone liked Murdeena, but she was taking her dirty bare feet and tromping all over their sacred ground. Word spread fast.

Pouring tea for Mrs. Foguere in the church basement, she leans over to speak.

"Once upon a time, there was a little town on the water...." she begins.

"Oh, please, dear, not now," Mrs. Fouguere interrupts, knowing by now what's coming and everybody looking at her with pity.

"No, it's okay," says Murdeena, "I'm telling you a story."

"I just want to drink my tea, Murdeena, love,"

"There was this whole town of people, you see ... and they were all asleep! The whole town!"

"I don't believe I care for this story, dear," says Mrs. Fouguere.

"No, no, it's a parable! Just wait," Murdeena persists. "This whole town, they were all asleep, but the thing is ... they were sleepwalking and going about their business just as if they were awake."

"I don't care to hear it, Murdeena."

"Yes, for God's sake, dear, go and have a little talk with the Father, if you want to talk," Mrs. MacLaughlin, seated at the next table and known for her straightforward manner, speaks up.

"But it's a parable!" explains Murdeena.

"It doesn't sound like much of a friggin' parable to me!" Mrs. MacLaughlin complains. The women nearby all grumble in agreement.

Murdeena straightens up and looks around at the room: "Well, I'm only starting to get the hang of it!"

The ladies look away from her. They take comfort, instead, in looking at each other — in their dresses and nylons and aggressive, desperate cosmetics. Someone snickers finally that it was certainly a long way from the Sermon on the Mount, and a demure wave of giggles ripples across the room. Murdeena puts her hands on her hips. Several of the ladies later remark on how like Margaret-Ann she appeared at that moment.

"To hell with you, then," she declares, and flops from the room, bare feet glaring.

Murdeena has never been known to say anything like this to anyone before, certainly no one on the Ladies Auxiliary.

Sister Tina comes to the house for a visit.

"Seeing as I'm the Way and the Light," Murdeena explains, "it would be wrong for me not to talk about it as often as possible."

"Yes, but, dear, it wasn't a very subtle story, was it? No one likes to hear that sort of thing about themselves."

"The point isn't for them to *like* it," spits Murdeena. "They should just be quiet and listen to me."

At this, Margaret-Ann leans back in her chair and caws. Sister Tina smiles a little, playing with the doily the teapot has been placed upon.

"They *should*," the girl insists.

"They don't agree with you, dear."

"Then they can go to hell, like I said."

"Wash your mouth out!" gasps her mother, furious but still half-laughing.

Sister Tina holds up her tiny hand with all the minute authority she possesses. "Now, that's not a very Christian sentiment, is it Murdeena?"

"It's as Christian as you can get," Murdeena counters. Scandalously sure of herself.

The next day, the Sister brings the Father.

"I hate the way she *talks* to everyone now," Margaret-Ann confides to him in the doorway. "She's such a big know-it-all." The Father nods knowingly and scratches his belly. The two of them, he and Murdeena, are left alone in the dining room so they can talk freely.

Crouched outside the door, Margaret-Ann hears Murdeena complain: "What are dining rooms for, anyway? We never even use this room. Everything's covered in dust."

"It's for *good!*" Margaret-Ann hollers in exasperation. Sister Tina gently guides her back into the kitchen.

The Father's visit is basically useless. Afterwards he keeps remarking on how argumentative little Murdeena has become. She would not be told. *She simply will not be told*, he keeps repeating. The Father has little idea how to deal with someone who will not be told. He makes it clear that his uselessness was therefore Murdeena's own fault, and goes off to give Communion to the next-door neighbour, Allan Beaton, a shut-in.

"Everyone's too old around here," Murdeena mutters once the priest is gone. She's watching him out the window as Allan Beaton's nurse holds the door open to let him in. The nurse is no spring chicken herself. The father is mostly bald with sparse, cotton-ball hair and a face like a crushed paper bag.

"You're just full of complaints, these days," her mother fumes, hauling a dust rag into the dining room.

So now Murdeena is going around thinking she can heal the sick. She figures that will shut them up. In the parking lot at the mall, Leanne Cameron accidentally slams her seven-year-old boy's finger in the car door and Murdeena leaps from her mother's Chevette and comes running up, bare feet burning against the asphalt, a big expectant grin splitting her face. This scaring the piss out of the little boy, who starts to scream at the sight of her, twice as loud as before. Murdeena tries and tries to grab the hand, but Leanne won't let her anywhere near him. It is a scene that is witnessed and talked about. Margaret-Ann vows never to take Murdeena shopping with her again, or anywhere else, for that matter.

Margaret-Ann declares that she has officially "had it." She experiments with giving Murdeena the silent treatment, but Murdeena is too preoccupied to notice. This hurts Margaret-Ann's feelings, and so she stops experimenting and quits talking to her daughter altogether. Her days get angrier and quieter, as she waits for Murdeena to take notice of her mother and do the right thing. See to her.

"See to your mother," Ronald pleads with her at night, lowering his voice so that the television will keep it from carrying into the kitchen. "Please go in and see to her."

Murdeena's head snaps up as if she had been asleep and someone had clapped their hands by her ear. "Did she hurt herself? Is she bleeding?" She wiggles her fingers eagerly, limbering up.

She starts lurking around the children's softball games, hoping someone will get a ball in the face or sprain their wrist sliding into home. She hovers like a ghoul and the children play extra carefully all summer long as a result. Murdeena watches toddlers waddling away from their parents, toward broken bottles and the like, with her fingers crossed.

By now, though, people know to keep their kids away from Murdeena Morrisson. In the space of a couple of months it has become the community instinct. She stalks the adult softball games too, even though she has long since stopped playing for the S.O.B.'s.

❖

No one can very well tell Murdeena to stop coming to play piano, since she has been doing it since she was thirteen and on a volunteer basis — Margaret-Ann thought it would be a good way for her to get some practice and do something nice for the senile incontinent old friggers at the same time. So Murdeena headed over every Sunday after supper, and for the next ten years there never arose any reason for her to stop. It was a perfectly satisfactory relationship, if somewhat stagnant. The seniors asked for, and Murdeena played impeccably, the same songs, Sunday night after Sunday night. "Mairi's Wedding" and "Kelligrew's Soiree" and such. Some of the seniors who were there when she first started playing had died, but most of them were still around — living out the final years of their lives while Murdeena was experiencing practically the whole of her own, a bland and inoffensive local girl for them to tease about clothes and boyfriends, sucking up her youth.

But Murdeena will no longer be teased. Her friends have abandoned her in response to the "high and mighty" tone she's adopted with them, her mother is angry, and her father has never spoken to her much in the first place. The seniors are the only captive audience she has. For the first little while after the night she slammed the piano shut, she'd make a slight pretence of being there to play for them, but the tunes would usually trickle off after a few minutes. She'd stealthily start making inquiries about Angus Chisholm's knee, Annie Chaisson's hip, Eleanor Sullivan's arthritis.

"If you'd just let me hold your hands for a couple seconds, Mrs. Sullivan," she'd plead.

"My dear, I'd love for you to hold my hands, but not in the spirit of blasphemy."

They listened, though. The seniors are the most tolerant of the town, for some reason neither threatened nor scandalized by what Murdeena has to say. They don't tease her about the way she looks either — they don't mention her feet. Murdeena's lips are now always thin, and so is her body — she has finally lost all her baby fat from walking the streets for hours into the night and sometimes forgetting to eat supper. It's October, and there's no sign of shoes as yet. The seniors decide it's her own business and they don't say a word.

And so, stymied by the town, she gradually turns all her attention and efforts to the attentive oldies, stuck in their chairs every Sunday night until the nurses come along to help them to bed, waiting to hear Murdeena. Sister Tina — who writhes and jumps like she's being jabbed with hot pokers at every word out of Murdeena's mouth — soon realizes that she needn't be worried about the girl giving them offence. The seniors greet the blasphemy with more good humour than anyone else in town. Born in farmhouses, raised up on hills or in remote valleys, where to come across another human being, no matter who they were or what they had to say, was a deep and unexpected pleasure — therefore humble, charitable, and polite — the old folks listen, lined up side by side in front of the piano.

It's like Murdeena figures that the seniors represent the front lines — that if she can just plough her way through them, everything else might fall into place. The world will become reasonable again. So Sunday after Sunday, she abandons the music in order to plead. Sunday after Sunday, now, she pleads with them until dark.

And they're good about it. They let her talk and hold out her hands to them. They don't complain or interrupt. They smile with their kind and patient old faces and refuse to let themselves be touched.

◇

Look,
and Pass On

◇

Inferno, CANTO 3, 1.51

THE THING WAS EIGHTEEN and she wore her dead grandmother's underpants.

"I like them," she enunciated to him over and over, because he would not let up about it. "They are comfortable."

They didn't bunch?

"Bunch where?"

Up her ass?

"I don't notice."

He was always leaning back and looking at the sky in a theatrical prayer for her. He drove a car with a window for a roof, could see the clouds fly past, if there had been any clouds. He said he was going to buy her some different ones.

"I don't need any."

But he would like to buy her some different ones. Her bare feet were up on the dashboard of his mother's car, dirty. She squinted, thinking about discomfort.

"Not those ones ... not the ones with no arse ... with the little bit of material that goes up your arse...."

Thongs, Thing. Lots of women wear them.

"I don't like them."

She would like them.

"No, no. I don't think I would."

He saw her underwear at night in the hotel. He hooted and yanked at them, like diapers. The elastic waistband came up almost underneath her breasts, her whole lower torso obscured by white cotton. One time when she turned to go to the bathroom, he grabbed a cushion from the chair and shoved it in there, and there was plenty of room left. She had reached behind herself and removed it and put it back down on the chair. Fifty other women would have thrown it at him. She was eighteen, however, and she did not have a playful bone in her body.

But he wanted to buy her some. He had all sorts of money. It was no problem. He could buy her all sorts of things. Whenever they pulled into an Irving for gas, she would wordlessly try to hand him twenty dollars like her father had told her to do, and he would say, in the phlegmy Cape Breton accent he used to mock her with, to take that thing and shove it up her hole. At this she would laugh. Hole-humour was big where she was from. She did not insist about the money because, he was aware, she was too young to know that she should insist.

It was late August and stifling in New Brunswick. They drove past the long Saint John River with boats on it and she said that the sight of water made her sad, because she always wanted to be in it. He said they could stop somewhere and swim but they shouldn't make a habit of it, if they wanted to make it to Guelph in good time. Anyway, they would go for good swims in the Georgian Bay once they arrived. He would have a long weekend to show her the sights before she had to be at the university, to start her first year of school. Alan was excited about this. He would take her to his parents' cottage on the bay, show her the beauty. He would take her to bars where his best friend Trent's band was playing for the Labour Day celebrations. His friends would see her and she would see them.

She wanted to stop at everything that was big. They had to stop at the big blueberry and the big potato. She insisted. The blueberry was friendly, but the potato was an evil-looking thing. She took a picture of him cringing before it. This was the kind of thing she enjoyed.

She enjoyed the hotel rooms for different reasons than him. The father had not agreed with the hotel rooms, with her blithely factoring them into the travel itinerary. The father had looked Alan in the eye and made it clear that he did not see any reason for hotel rooms. They could make it straight through without stopping if they got an early start, didn't take too many breaks. Alan was agreeing with him, but she vetoed them both without looking up from the map, spread out across her family's kitchen table with the innocent bechickened tablecloth. "I *want* to stay in a couple of hotels," she had said. Her father silenced by her lack of shame, hands placed palms-down atop the chickens, as if to keep him from falling into them. It was clear she scarcely noticed him any more. In all likelihood he hadn't agreed with any of her travel plans to begin with. To get this *friend*, six years her senior, to drive her out to school.

What had he said when she told him this? Alan wanted to know.

"What could he say?"

What had *she* said?

"I said I'm eighteen." Smiling at her dirty feet. Not really smiling at all. "He can't say too much these days. Right numb."

She insisted on the hotels the way she insisted on her grandmother's underwear. It was what she liked. It turned out that it was actually the old man's own fault, this particular penchant in the thing. He used to take them on vacations all the time. It reminded her of being on vacations with her family, she said. Mother, father, sister, brother. At their first motor inn, she had shocked him by making a beeline to the bed and jumping furiously up and down on it. "This is how we always used to christen the room." she said, voice hiccuping from the bounces. She didn't really smile or look as if she were enjoying herself. But she did it every time, no matter what, he would come to know, bouncing, looking straight ahead.

They'd spent time together before, but not time like this. Car time. He could talk to her about whatever came to mind. Books he'd read. Music she should listen to. Interesting ideas he sometimes had about things — what he liked to call his "little philosophies." She enjoyed listening. They stopped at a beach and he got to see her in a shiny pink bathing suit. It was a one-piece, but he could see the unstable protrusion of her little stomach, from a year ago. And there were still stretch marks on the backs of her thighs, making them strangely dimpled. There was a pleasant layer of fat — although diminishing — all over her and he thought to himself, *like baby fat*, and then he tittered when he realized it literally was. He read somewhere, later, that stretch marks never went away. The stomach reminded him of pictures and statues of the Catholic Madonna, her abdomen always prominent, the flowing robes moulded around it, emphasizing. He saw why they made them like that now — the pictures, the statues. He told her at one point that he thought a prominent abdomen was sexy.

"Oh, good." she said, serious. "How about stretch marks?"

They sped on through the haze. It was his mother's Lexus. She gave it to him for the summer, for his great trek through Maritime Canada. He had not planned on going back to Bridget's town, where he worked for not quite a year before having to flee the sulphurous egg smell of the pulp mill and his sodden-eyed, violent co-workers, coming to work hungover and beaten every Monday, always asking why he never went "out on the town" with them on the weekends, did he think he was too good? But in the end he placed a call from Smooth Herman's in Sydney after three pints and said perhaps he could drop in on his way back to the causeway. And she'd said without any ado, why didn't he take her with him. She had a train ticket but it wasn't too late to cancel.

So she was leaving? he'd kept repeating. She was finally leaving?

"'Bout time, wha'?" she said.

He agreed that it was. It sounded as if she were becoming more illiterate by the second. She replied something about her hole, to kiss it or play it like a fife or something. He hung up the phone, surprised to be euphoric.

He remembered her then. Tar-eyed thing in a Woolco dress, sitting at a chair and table set up outside the high school auditorium, vacantly accepting his admission to see the Swedish fiddlers. He had said, "I can't believe I am paying money to see Swedish fiddlers. I wonder what is happening to me," and she'd looked up as if he had introduced himself as an angel of the Lord. Later she came up to him to say that she had learned the Swedish word for cheese and it was *oosht.*

Pregnant then but nobody knew it. All he had thought was *what a body for a kid.* It turned out those changes had occurred only a couple of months before and she was exasperated with them. He was the first person she told about it. He had been flattered, but not really surprised. The people in the town were like hornets in the hottest part of the summer, flying drunk, bashing their prickly bodies into one another, buzzing enraged. He'd asked her about *programs, supports,* and she'd said, Programs? Supports? He had wanted, in a fanciful part of his mind, to take her away, but nothing about the situation allowed for it. She was seventeen then. He had someone who had been his girlfriend for three years, finishing up her BA in film in Toronto. Before all of that, however, he knew he needed more than air to get away from the sulphurous hornets' nest where she'd spent her whole life. So she went to Halifax alone in her sixth or seventh month, and, apparently, came back alone, too, but by that time he had gone.

They hit a strawberry just before the Quebec border, at George's Famous Fruits. He rolled his eyes and pulled over without a word. Stepping out of the air-conditioned car, the heat threw itself over him like a quilt. She said, "Foo," and pushed her hair back. He could see on either side of her hairline that a good quantity of it had fallen out and was only now returning, tentatively. You didn't notice that when it hung down on either side of her face. He wanted to say, *My Christ, how many other things does it do to you?* but he didn't. She strode up to the strawberry, uncharacteristically purposeful. When she got there she did nothing but loiter in its presence, peering upwards, getting sun in her eyes. After a couple of minutes she said they could go.

There was nowhere to buy a thong in Quebec, not along these endless rural roads. They would have to go through Montreal, and they could stop there, but it could take forever, once they got in, to get back out again. He did not know the city well. But he was interested in the idea of a thong, in Montreal.

There is no reason to buy a thong, she had said in the hotel. I can just pull me underwear up to me chin and it'll go straight up me arse like so. She demonstrated. She was doing the big hick-voice now because she did it whenever they discussed her body.

Ach, she said at him. He was telling her that he would be worried about her, up in University all by herself — driving after the first hotel, when the underwear had made its appearance and he'd almost died — and all she said in reply was "Ach."

Something else she must've gotten from her grandmother. He didn't remember hearing it last year, except for when Bridget imitated her, but now she used it all the time, now that the old woman was dead. Bridget used to come to his apartment and lie on his floor last year, clutching a glass of wine, and she would tell him all about cleaning up her grandmother's defecate.

He thought it a wonderful word. The retch of it embodying pure disdain. Complete dismissal.

"Acccchhhhh," he repeated, relishing the cat-hiss feel in the back of his throat. "What do you mean, '"ach'?"

"It's just school. And you'll be close by."

"I can come see you on the weekends."

"Sure."

"Make sure those university boys don't step out of line."

"Ach," she said, smiling.

They drove in silence for a couple of minutes, during which time Alan was thinking, What am I talking about?

"We're friends," she said. "We've always been friends." She said that about a half-hour of Trans-Canada later.

"Oh, yes," he said, trying a bit to sound ironic. *But I have been acquainted with your underwear and what about that?*

A while later he proposed they get a room in Montreal. It was completely gratuitous. They could be in Guelph at a reasonable hour if they kept on at a steady click. The little thing opened her mouth at the prospect of a just-for-the-hell-of-it hotel room.

So he talked the rest of the way, in good spirits. The first hotel hadn't been perfect — they had both drunk too much beer and were road-tired, but Montreal would be better. It would be Montreal. He talked about CBC Radio and what his favourite programs were, which was what he always did when he was in a good mood. They listened to some of them, Alan greeting every announcer by name. She was reading a book that her English teacher had loaned her but she never gave back, and he had read it before, so he told her what he thought about it. It occurred to him that she might like to know about some other books he liked and it flattered him when she dug a pen out of the glove compartment and began compiling a list on the back page of the English teacher's book. She was going to take general arts for her first year, of course. He told her the key to university was to just read all the books and go to all the classes. There was no way you could fail. She laughed, but he said it wasn't as easy as it sounded: Listen to me, I know what I'm talking about. He told her that she would be kicking herself in a few years if she spent all that money only to have it come to naught.

"Ach," she said. "Government's money anyways."

"You're going to have to pay it all back, Bridget."

He could tell she didn't believe it.

He didn't know what world she lived in. Sometimes the words out of her mouth could be diamonds of the purest common sense. But most of the time she gazed around herself, never meeting anyone's eye and retreating into her accent and monosyllables. The casual observer might dismiss her as retarded — exasperatingly quiet and unfathomably stubborn. She was the only girl he knew who didn't insist people think she was smart.

"I never worry about going to hell," said Alan at some point. He had been talking books at her for the last half-hour. "Ever since reading *Inferno.*"

"Uh? Why? It doesn't sound so bad?" Like she'd been shaken out of sleep.

"No, it's bad. But it tells you how to get out."

"It tells you how to get out?"

"Oh yeah, it's a fucking road map."

"That doesn't sound right," she said. "I wouldn't think they'd just let you walk out."

He said nothing for the next ten minutes because she was right. Alan thought about the winged demons poking the souls back beneath bubbling pitch; and liars sunken up to their mouths in shit, and she was right. Dante had only been visiting. They were compelled by You-Know-Who to let him pass. The remark about not being afraid to go to hell was one he had often made in the company of well-read friends. Now he knew he couldn't make it any more, and was embarrassed at having said it so many times already. Because of her and her common-sense Catholicism. He pictured her mind at work, trying to reconcile the image of Alan taking a leisurely stroll through the pit — Dante under his arm to be consulted every now and again for directions — with what had been seared into her brain since childhood. That hell is not for tourists.

On the bypass they sat watching heat rise from the pavement, from the hoods of cars. He was telling her they weren't going to be staying anywhere fancy. It wasn't going to be the Ritz, or anything. She didn't care. He had sunglasses on, but she didn't and the glare made her blind. She talked to him from behind her fingers.

Traffic crawled, and he saw other drivers panting out their windows, end-of-the-summer arms like cured sausages. Cursing and practically weeping at their lot. Alan kept the windows shut tight, air-conditioning at full blast. "It won't be fancy," he repeated to himself, out loud. "But there will have to be air-conditioning. I will spring for an air-conditioner," he said.

"And beer," her voice came faint from behind the fingers. He thought she had fallen asleep.

"And thongs!" He tried to shout this, lustily, but something about the permeating swelter would not allow it. "Mountains of thongs," he croaked. Her sleepy titters muffled by the fingers. He was thinking about the last hotel and how he could make this one better. Maybe not so much beer — if he let her have her way, she would drink the world. And the air-conditioning at full blast this time. He had turned the air-conditioning off at the last one, because it was one of those air-conditioners where the sound drowned out everything else. But now he knew it would be just as well to have it on, so heat would be no excuse and he couldn't hear the noises she never made anyway. Alan was a planner. He had always been a planner. By the time they escaped the bypass heat prison it was dusk, the city was cooling, and he knew exactly how their evening was going to go.

They would go to the Peel Pub because it was the one bar he went to the last time he was here, her age, with the Varsity rugby team. He and the rest of them had done shooters, thrown up and lit farts on the street. He kept in touch with none of them now, but remembered them fondly. Alan knew he was a rarity because he had always enjoyed this kind of idiocy with men, but never understood the alternating fear and indifference towards women of some of them. Alan grew up running to the drugstore to buy tampons for his many sisters, picking up another's birth control while he was there. Certain male acquaintances were horrified at the fact that Alan had also lit farts with more than one girlfriend. Nothing was a mystery to him.

They found a Quality Inn, showered, and went out. There were prostitutes and pornography all over the street, which Alan didn't even remember from last time. He put his arm around her as they walked. They found the place, ordered chicken wings and Caesar salads and a pitcher. Alan told her they would have to go back to the room if they were really going to drink, because he probably should start being a little more careful with his money.

"Save it for the thongs," she said.

"Goddamnit, I forgot to ask someone where the thong warehouse is!"

"Are you really going to get one?"

He looked around him, thinking of the sex shops all up and down the street. "I could pop out and get one right now. It wouldn't necessarily be Victoria's Secret. I could get a few other things, while I'm at it."

"Like what?"

"Dog collars. Nipple-clamps. Two-foot pronged dildos!"

"People don't have those."

"They do, Bridget." He delighted in contradicting her about this sort of thing.

"No."

"Remember that girl I told you I went out with?"

"Yeah, but, just her."

"You are aware that you're not the most worldly person out there?"

"I don't care."

"I could show you."

"No."

"We can go outside and I can show you right now."

"Don't."

"If you don't know what's out there, you'll never know what you like."

"I don't want to like anything," she said.

◇

The next day on the road was hotter. At 7:00 A.M. they sat at a picnic table outside of a Shell station (Irving Bigstops left behind with all the oversized produce) and struggled to get their coffees down before the heat made it unthinkable. Bridget could scarcely open her eyes, but he had maliciously insisted they get an early start. All of a sudden something fast and loud buzzed near their heads and Bridget leapt away from it, splashing coffee everywhere.

"Jesus Christ, Bridget!"

"What was it?" She looked around her in horror. If it was a bug, then it was a bug approximately the size of a golf ball. A black, clicking, whirring golf ball blur. She assumed a stance of readiness, waiting for it to come back. It did, and stopped directly in front of them, whirring and blurry. Alan realized that it had come up alongside some sort of water container, hanging from the roof of the garage.

"It's a hummingbird," he said.

"What? What?"

"It's a hummingbird. See?"

They watched it for a while as if a tiny whirring deity had appeared. The cautious, hovering motions as it jerked away made it seem as if it were watching them also, monitoring them for movement.

"Jesus H. Christ, I guess I'm awake now," she said, heading back to the car.

The morning was silence but for CBC Radio. He was thinking of the different things he could say to her. He felt like his fourth grade math teacher must've felt, drilling the simple concept of fractions into his brain, over and over again, Alan staring with complete incomprehension. He had eventually mastered math, but he would never forget the slow forward rolls his stomach had begun to perform once the world started breaking the numbers up and putting them on top of each other. This had seemed like sheer perversity to Alan. It was funny, he thought, how things like that affect you when you're small. His doctor and mother feared ulcers. The inside of his little boy's stomach all raw.

He began by asking her slow, gentle questions about what she thought, and about himself. Tender, like how the patient math teacher used to explain things. Like Alan back then, something within the thing wasn't willing to cooperate. She was irritated by the necessity to answer. She pushed her feet into the dashboard, wanting more room as the questions became more insistent. He had decided somewhere along the way that he wasn't going to let up, he wasn't going to let her drift away like she always did. The night had been a farce, him hovering above, not knowing what to do, what was good and what was bad, Bridget offering nothing. He didn't think it was fair. There was no way he could let himself continue like this, hovering, in doubt. But instead of drifting away, she shut down. Her answers became as meaningless as she could possibly make them, and he felt himself getting angry. Deliberately. She was like this on purpose. It was not emotional laziness, as he had once supposed. Her mind was constantly in action, behind the heavy eyelids, forming strategies of avoidance. It was like trying to grab hold of a goldfish. Finally he said, "Your feet are fucking filthy," and she put them down.

"I didn't mean you had to put them down."

"That's okay."

"All I want to know is" — he wanted to kill her for just putting them down like that — "I mean, I always try to help...."

"But you don't have to."

God. God. God. "Well, I thought we were friends."

"Well, we are."

"Well, it seems like I'm the one who's doing all the giving here. Don't get me wrong, I'm not saying I'm in love with you, but it just seems like —"

"I'm eighteen," she said abruptly. His entire train of thought halted at once.

"Right," he said, listening. He meditated on the road.

"I just wanna get to school," she said.

◇

She did not fit in with anybody at the bar, but they loved her anyway because they were accepting, friendly people like himself, and because of her youth and supposed shyness. Alan's friend Trent tenderly brought her a Chocolate Monkey like a nurse bringing a patient a wee cupful of pills. It was a Polynesian bar, the kind of campy place a band like Trent's was perfectly at home in, stuffed full of youngish Labour Day partiers. There she sat, never having drank anywhere that wasn't called a tavern, looking around at the umbrellas and plastic hula dancers. He knew that she thought it was a bunch of foolishness, if she was thinking anything at all. That was something he would not have known about her a week ago. She sat alongside of Trent's delicately tattooed girlfriend wearing a Jack Daniel's T-shirt, once the property of the shit-kicker who had impregnated her, he imagined.

Everyone paid him compliments on Bridget whenever they caught him alone, because she was so adorable. No one knowing about the nastiness of the thing, or suspecting what the previous eight hours might have done to him.

"Sexy in that wholesome kind of way," said Trent's green-eyed girl-friend Quentin, who took art photos and wrote haiku and had been known to like girls sometimes, according to Trent anyway. Alan understood entirely why she said that and wanted to tell her that it wasn't true, that she wasn't wholesome at all. He was feeling cynical, as though in the last few days he had learned enough about the world to make him not want to know any more. He had used to feel impervious with knowledge, "existentially at ease," he used to tell his friends — when he wasn't being pretentious about Dante and espousing his indifference towards hell. He knew they envied him, using their fabricated traumas to add substance to their lives, turning to him for the advice of someone capable of accepting the world for what it was. Now he felt like a fraud. But he did not feel like a fraud. He felt like a dupe. He felt a way he had not felt since being introduced to fractions.

He saw her watching the band and thought that all she ever did was wait for everything to be over. It was grotesque. It was grotesque to think about the car and doing things with people who didn't care if you did them or not. They who practically said Ach when you asked your gentle well-thought-out and carefully worded questions. Like, *What do you need from me? What do you need me to do?* The *ach* palatable in the air, all over them like sweat. Impervious. Contagious. Dangerous to have this kind of realization on a highway in the middle of Canada. He had wanted to drive into an oncoming truck, and the thing, he knew, would not have spoken as he did.

A Great Man's
Passing

PEOPLE WHO DIDN'T KNOW, and that was mostly tourists, thought that the Sloane house, about a hundred feet backed up from the main road, had to be deserted. They didn't even think this in a conscious way. They processed it the way drivers process the things they see on a long, empty country road. House. Cow. Mailbox. Deserted house. It never occurred to anyone that such a place could be inhabited.

But it was, and the truth is, it had become so decrepit precisely because of how inhabited it was. This never occurred to anyone either. No one thought that a house could gradually be destroyed by how lived-in it was. People passed the Sloane house and thought: deserted. That house has no one looking after it. The people who drove by the Sloane house and thought that were the kind of people who assumed that if there was somebody living in a home, it was automatically being looked after.

But it wasn't, because the overriding concern of the Sloane family was looking after itself. And if the passing tourists had been aware of the size of the Sloane family, they would understand why there was no time for looking after anything else.

Bess never thought that the Sloane house was deserted because she had always known better. In the summers, when she and her parents would drive by on the way to Gramma and Grampa's, Bess would shout, There's the Sloane house, because it was a landmark that told her they were almost to the farm, and also because she had been in it before, and, in her little-girl consciousness, this fact made the house hers.

She knew the Sloanes, too, she knew the name of every single child living in that house. So they were hers, too. The youngest was Terry, then Margaret, then Mary Catherine. Then came some boys, Robert and Angus and Roland, who was Bess's age. Then they started getting older than her. Dougal and Jn'-Pat. Ann Rose. At that point they reached an age where the names came easier than the faces. Elizabeth. David. Ian. Joseph. Carrie and Stephen. That was it. Bess bragged to her friends about knowing so big a family.

We go down there every month, almost, she would say. We bring them our old clothes and other stuff. Mary Catherine always gets my old clothes and whatever toys I'm sick of. There's babies and clothes everywhere, in every room. And one of those boys has a weird eye. It doesn't go right. He wears glasses a hundred feet thick. His name is Angus but they call him Cookie 'cause his eyes make him look like the Cookie Monster.

At that point, Maureen MacEachern would always try to steal away a little bit of Bess's spotlight. I know! she'd say. 'Cause my mom is always filling up garbage bags with all of our old stuff and giving them to your mom to give to them.

Yeah, but you've never been there. I've been in the house and I know them. Dad says they're my third cousins. So I've got fifteen third cousins.

It made Bess mad because Maureen had so much to brag about already, why did she have to take what Bess had. She had lived in the nicest house in town and her dad was deputy mayor. Bess's dad was on the town council. Their families went on vacations and camping trips together. Plus, Maureen had five brothers and two sisters. That was a pretty big family, too, but it wasn't the same.

Bess had never known what Mr. Sloane did, and she hardly even knew what he looked like. He was never there when they came in to drop off their garbage bags, or maybe he was, but had just been obscured by children. Mrs. Sloane was always there, her stomach perpetually large because it never had a chance to get small again. She and Mom would talk. She would say, Thank you so much, Ellen, you are always thinking of us, to Mommy. The little girls would follow Bess around and ask her questions and try to show her things while the boys would yell at her and make fun of her and try to get her to chase them. Sometimes she would and sometimes she wouldn't. One time she was chasing Cookie, and he scrambled up onto the trunk of one of the rusted old automobiles that were sprawled alongside of the house. So Bess had reached out and grabbed Cookie by the belt of his pants, and down the pants came, and Cookie's underwear had the silliest patterns and most lurid colours on them that Bess ever could have imagined. Embarrassed more by the shorts than by the fact that she had pulled a boy's pants right off him, she turned away and pretended to be interested in what the little girls had been trying to tell her ever since she'd arrived. When she looked back, Cookie was returning, hoisting up his pants with a little smile. He didn't care. He wanted her to chase him some more.

When Bess got older, and it began to seem like less of a treat to go see Gramma and Grampa on the weekends, it also became less of an adventure to drop bags off at the Sloanes', which had been par for the course during such visits, just as it had been par for the course to do things like swinging on the thick rope with the hook on the end of it in the barn, which Grampa said never to do and Dad always said, Oh, go ahead and do it anyway. Like attending mass on Sundays at the small Catholic church down the road where you would always see Mrs. Sloane with what Daddy called "her litter" and Mom would say in the awed, quiet voice that she used when saying prayers with Bess,

That woman makes it to church every Sunday. All this was part of the adventure. But when Bess got older it became part of the routine. That's the problem with getting older, Bess thought.

And now, living here in her childhood vacationland, everything was different altogether, and it was strange that she had seen more of the Sloanes when she was a child and living in town than she did now that she was an adult and living only a few miles down the road. Every once in a while Mommy would say to her something like, "Jn'-Pat Sloane's supposed to be getting married. A little girl from the Forks, Cameron, I believe."

And Bess would have to think for a minute before honing in on his identity. "He's the dark one?"

"They're all dark, Bessie. Except for Angus and Ann Rose."

"No, I know which one you mean. Which Cameron girl?"

Dad would say, "Pregnant, I suppose."

"Oh, let's not be cynical," Bess would reply.

And every time Mommy would share some Sloane tidbit of news with Bess, she would always bring the topic to a close with the words "Poor Mary Kate." Which was Mrs. Sloane's first name. Every time something happened to one of the Sloane children, Mommy always spoke as if it had in some deeper, more significant way, to Mrs. Sloane. But as far as Bess knew, Mommy hardly ever saw Mrs. Sloane any more. And there they were, just a few miles down the road.

Mid-fall, Bess had a job. There had been no getting around it. It had fallen into her lap, such a rare thing that to refuse would have been like showing your middle finger to God just when he was in a good mood. The man who owned the Bonnie Prince Inn was an American named Rufus Bank, who asked that you call him Ruf. He had come to Daddy in the summer wanting to know where he could catch trout, and so Dad asked the man over for dinner and took him behind the house and down the side of the hill and they fished about a mile upriver from where Dad's gaspreaux trap was set up. Everyone but the American knew there wouldn't be any trout, but they also knew that he would be just as satisfied if he caught even one bony gaspreaux, which he did, and he was. They came back up to the house and fried the fish up for Mr. Bank's dinner. With it, he drank one of Bess's beer.

"You people have a paradise here, do you know that?" said Ruf, looking around at them all with good-hearted reproach, as though perhaps they were guilty of not knowing it. "I've wanted to live here all my life. When the Bonnie Prince came up for sale, I said to myself, there's my retirement. Right there. Couldn't believe my luck." He looked at Bess and told her that she couldn't have picked a better spot to raise her little boy. Then he looked at Dylan, chomping on a pork-chop bone in his high chair. Bess looked at him too.

In the winters, Ruf had to close the Bonnie Prince, but he left the lounge open for the locals. The previous owner hadn't done that, and if you wanted to get drunk, you either had to drive to Inverness, or go to one of the dances in the South-west Hall, or stay home. Bess had gone to one of the dances, once, in the early summer, with her second cousin, Meg, who was trying to help her to feel welcome. When they arrived outside the Hall, Bess said to Meg, "Is it an outdoor dance in this weather?" Because it looked as though everyone had gathered out in front instead of inside. Then Bess saw that the crowd was standing in a circle and in the middle one young man was jumping up and down on another man's head. Meg parked the car close by and the two of them sat in it, passing a bottle of rum back and forth until the fight was over.

"That was Dougal Sloane," Meg commented, capping the rum and dropping it back into her purse.

"Who?"

"The guy who won."

"He's gotten big," Bess said after a moment.

◇

But now there was Ruf's lounge to go to, and he had painted it, and installed a full-time DJ and every other week a band from Blue Mills called Ryder would play there. Also, Ruf had changed the name from the uncomplicated "Bonnie Prince Inn Lounge" to "Red Ruf's" because, he said, he used to have red hair and he noticed that everyone "around here" had nicknames and that was one of the things he loved about the place. Bess was to learn that the best way to endear yourself to the American was to refer to him affectionately as Red Ruf, as often as you could get away with.

Red Ruf had offered Bess a job because Daddy had asked him to during one of their fishing trips. Daddy wanted Bess to be clear about that.

"There we were in our hip-waders and Ruf's going on about the lounge and how there'll be people coming in from as far away as Whycocomah once he gets his whaddayacallit sound system installed and he's pretty damn sure he's going to be needing some extra staff to help serve the liquor up, and I say, 'Well, goddamnit Ruf, our Bessie's been looking for a job ever since she landed here and the little fella started getting more independent. I know she'd appreciate getting off the welfare. It's been hard on her, you know, what with the little guy....'"

Lies. Bess hadn't minded the welfare so much at all. It had kept Dylan clothed and fed all summer long, and she earned her own keep by working at home and helping with Gramma and Grampa. Best of all, it allowed for her to be with him every moment, and so Bess, although she heard things on the radio about Welfare Queens, and talk that the government would no longer tolerate her kind of inertia, could not feel guilty about her own reluctance to enter the work force. She knew this was a great sin in her society, but didn't quite understand why. She saw men on television who said that all they wanted to do was work. They would do anything, clean out toilets, mop floors, but they could not stand the ignominy of welfare. They said they felt degraded.

All Bess knew was that Dylan was being fed and that she was able to spend as much time with him as she needed, which was all the time. It seemed to her that if there had to be a government, this was the kind of thing it was supposed to be doing for people. Daddy said that this was naive.

"You have to participate. You can't just live off the sweat of honest, working people."

"I'm an honest working person, too."

"You're a hippie that thinks the world owes you something...." She saw him stop himself, and filled in the rest. Going around having babies, thinking the government's gonna look after them. Free love and all that. He's talking about himself, him and me, Bess thought, smouldering as she always did when she thought about the two of them, playing tug-of-war, and if one person lets go of the taut rope, the other will suddenly go flying. As if I'm not cleaning up your mother's pasty yellow poo every night, spoon-feeding her curds and potatoes. As if I have not conceded to raise my boy in a funeral home, with the two corpses propped up in front of the TV set, one saying a rosary, the other smoking a cigarette. As if I couldn't have stayed away if I wanted to. As if I still couldn't go.

Ruf didn't know about any of this. All Ruf knew was that he was giving a job to someone who needed it.

"That's very nice of you, Mr. Bank," stunned Bess had said into the phone when he called up with his offer.

"Oh, well," said Ruf. "It's nice to know that I can do some good around here, what with the unemployment situation and everything. It's nice to know that I'm not just here for myself, that I can make a little bit of a difference to some of the people — if you know what I mean. You know — you people are my neighbours now, and I want to help you in any way I can."

"That's very nice of you," Bess said again, beginning to panic, looking down at Dylan who was on the floor in front of her playing with her shoe. How long will he want me to work, she wondered.

How many hours out of the day? Then there was the fact that she had always thought that the last job she would ever choose for herself would be that of a bartender.

But there was no saying no, there simply wasn't, and she didn't. While she had been talking on the phone to Ruf, the members of her family had all quietly materialized, and when she looked up they were standing there with smiles, as if she had just opened a gift from the three of them.

"Who was that, now?" asked Daddy, smiling most of all.

So now Bess had a job, and even though that was more than could be said for the rest of the family, they still seemed to possess a sort of moral high ground that she would never be able to attain. She thought that it was probably because they were old, and had all worked in the past. A million years ago Aunt Marg was a nurse and Dad had done a lot of different things before having enough money to buy a hotel/restaurant, and becoming the kind of upstanding citizen who sits on town councils, and then losing the hotel/restaurant a few years later and not being that kind of citizen any more. Then Daddy became disillusioned and didn't do much and said that if he couldn't do things his way, he wouldn't do anything at all. And then he lost the house and he said that it was just as well because Mumma and The Boss were getting on and needing someone to take care of themselves and the farm full-time anyway. Plus, moving to the farm meant no mortgage, no rent. "Now I do what I goddamn well please," Bess had heard him say to Red Ruf Bank.

But Bess was young and had to work. It was, Dad said, "a shame" for her not to work, and worse for her not to want to. After Red Ruf's phone call, Bess had been cranky all day and drank all the beer that was in the fridge. She looked outside at the dead, empty field which no snow had the decency to come and bury yet. In a way, the job had come at a good time, she supposed, with winter on the way and the snow piled up at the doors and windows and no way for her and Dylan to escape down to the river for a swim or even out to the field because

Bess hated snow and the idea of plodding along in the wet cold stuff just for the hell of it made no sense to her. So that meant more time spent indoors, but more time spent indoors meant more time in the funeral home, so maybe it would be a good thing to have somewhere to go. Mommy had said, "It will be good for you to get out."

What irked her, though, was the momentousness of it all. Mommy making a special Bess-got-a-job dinner that night, and Daddy telling the stories of how he had wrangled the offer out of Red Ruf, reeling him in as they stood in the middle of the river with the pathos of Bess's "situation." Bess having to think about what she was going to wear for the first time in months, and everybody happy for her, happy that she was going to be serving up Moosehead to head-stomping pulp-cutters and cod-jiggers. And it wasn't even that. Just happy that she was going to be doing something. Not understanding that time is going to go by and that days are going to pass whether you are doing something or doing nothing. And when you are doing nothing, they go by just as quick, if not quicker — a fact that people who are always doing something will not believe if you tell it to them.

The first two shifts she did for Red Ruf, she had to go to and sit in the employees' bathroom and cry because she was wondering what Dylan was doing. She imagined Mommy and Aunt Marg gleefully following him around with aprons full of cookies to be offered in case he fell down and hurt himself or threw some kind of tantrum. It's like being in love, she thought to herself, rubbing her eyes unrestrainedly because she was unused to wearing make-up and forgot that she would be smudging black mascara and blue powder all over her stupid face. Washing she thought. It is, but it isn't.

The next couple of shifts she did were on the weekend, and Bess got her first taste of culture shock, the shock of someone who has been in hiding for over a year and suddenly finds herself at the centre of a large, oddly unsociable party where people seemed to expect more from her than drinks. They wanted to banter, they wanted her to smile and chat and learn their first names and tell them where she was from and who her father was. It seemed most of them would rather talk to her than the people they were there with.

Sometimes, Red Ruf would show up with the intention of helping her at the bar, but most of the time he forgot about that and ended up perching on one of the stools and holding a sort of court among the locals. Most of the locals loved him. He was afforded the status of "a character" because he was rich and American. This was something you could tell Red Ruf had always longed for but had never been able to attain when he had lived among other rich Americans.

There were awkward moments, like when she noticed her second cousin Meg there with all of her brothers and didn't know if she should speak to the brothers, who were virtually strangers in the way people are expected to speak to relatives that they haven't spoken to for ages, or, if she should just behave towards them the same way as she did to everyone else in the bar. She prayed that Meg would come up to the bar with the brothers in tow and initiate some kind of dialogue that would take the onus of Bess, but things never happen that way. The first time Bess noticed that her cousins were in the lounge, Meg hadn't even seen Bess working the bar and they went right past her, to a table. Then, a little later, one of the older brothers who, Bess was pretty sure was called Findlay, came up to get beers for everybody and looked right thought her. Bess took his order, began setting the beer down in front of him, and, watching the beer bottles very closely, said, "Do you remember me, Findlay?"

When she looked up, she saw that his gaze had focused in on her a little, even though his face hadn't changed.

"Of course I do, Bess," he said, and then he took his beer and returned to his table. Bess thought about it for a while before coming to the realization that she had forgotten all about the completely familiarizing power of gossip. Findlay had probably been hearing so much about Bess all throughout the summer from his sister Meg and father Alistair — who liked to talk about anything as often as possible — that it was impossible for him to have lost track of her existence in the way that she had of his, and of so many other people that her parents insisted she knew, and remembered fondly.

When the Sloanes began popping up, Bess had been expecting pretty much the same treatment she'd received from Meg's brothers, who, she could tell right away, had listened intently to every opinion their father Alistair had espoused regarding Bess. She had a pretty good idea as to what these opinions were, because he had also espoused them to Bess numerous times over the summer when he would be sitting across from her at the dinner table tossing back some of Aunt Marg's whisky after he and Daddy had come up from the trap. In any case, Bess was not bothered with what Alistair's sons thought, she was only relieved to know that she wasn't going to have to be friendly towards them as she had at first feared. As the weekend shifts went by, she came to see from their constant sponging of drinks and groping of randomly passing arses that they were only slimmed-down, less shambling versions of Alistair, and this made it easy to be unconcerned by them.

But late into one evening, Findlay came weaving up to the bar to have a rare word with her. "How's she going?" he initiated.

"Good, Findlay. How're you?"

"Well, well, well. She's talking to me."

"And you're talking to me."

"I never thought you'd lower yourself."

"Say hi to Alistair next time you see him."

"Don't you say nothin about Daddy."

"Okay."

"Okay. Some good, you."

"What — Findlay — what's the problem?"

But Findlay gave her a look as though to say that it was hopeless trying to talk to her, she was too low, or too high, or something ignoble like that, and he shambled away. Whoo, big confrontation, Bess thought, mopping beer up off the counter. But she was grimacing because it hadn't been good. You people are my neighbours now.

The first night she noticed the Sloanes had begun to frequent Red Ruf's was one time when somebody hollered, "Foit!" and everybody in the lounge bolted for the door.

"Oh my gosh," said Red Ruf, gazing out one of the windows. "Maybe you'd better call the police, Bessie. I don't think I want this kind of thing going on."

"What's happening?" said Bess, having to stay behind the bar.

"Some young lad's kicking a man's head in out there."

At that moment Cookie Sloane hurried in from outside. Bess thought that he had only grown about a foot since the time she had pulled down his pants. Otherwise he looked completely the same, peering though his thick glasses like they were fog.

"Don't call the Mounties," he said, rushing over to the bar. "Okay, Bessie? Please? The guy was a fucking arsehole. Dougal will finish up in just a bit. Okay?"

"Okay," said Bess, forgetting to consult with Ruf.

Cookie smiled, all dirty teeth — "God love ya, dear!" — and ran back outside.

Dougal and Cookie sat on bar stools beside one another, Dougal with his head down, looking at his beer, smiling very happily at all the things Cookie was saying to Bess about him.

"He's just a big idiot," Cookie was saying. "Stupid as mine and your arses put together. That's what he is. Doesn't know how to do anything except pummel the shit out of some poor bastard who doesn't know how to keep his tongue in his head. Isn't that right, you hopeless fucking dummy?"

"Yes," said Dougal, smiling.

"How you been, Bessie?" Cookie went on without blinking. When you looked into his freaky eyes through the thickness of those glasses, you expected his voice to sound like it was coming from a mile away. "Are you good? Mummy told me you was living down here now, up at Iain and Lizzie's place. Said you got knocked up and have a little boy now. That can be tough, eh? Same thing happened to Ann Rose and Elizabeth, but they're living together in town and doing okay. Sort of a joint effort. Still, it gets me cross. I'm saying to Mary Catherine all the time, 'Now don't you fuck! I don't care how bored you get, don't do it.' It's not all that much fun anyhow and it gives a lot of stupid bastards something to talk about and a person to feel superior to. But I suppose the girls've gotta get their rocks off somehow, too, that's only fair. Somebody told me that girls don't like it, and I used to think that was true but then I had a girlfriend and — Jesus, Mary, and Joseph — how we used to go at it. It was always her wanting to. She's gone now, though, up to Halifax to study the nursing. She wanted me to write letters but I'm no damn good at it. How's your Grammie and Grampie, Bess? Christ Almighty, they must be getting up there, eh? Your mum's helping to take care of them, my mum was saying. My mum says your mum's a saint, did you know that? She's always saying what a saint your mum is, and how you guys always used to help us out. I always remember, we'd see you and your mother driving up in the station wagon and it was just like fucking Christmas. The girls would go into hysterics and Mary Catherine would always have to have a lay-down after you left. Anyways, I know I talk too much, but someone's gotta make up for the wordless idiotic wonder over here. I'll have another beer, Bessie, me mouth is pretty dry. That was a good fight, though, you have to admit. The guy didn't look too bad. Listen, Bessie, how are you, though, dear, how are you really?"

With Cookie — and it hadn't been like this with anyone else since she had arrived in the late spring — it was just like picking up where they had left off. Like any second he would jump up and pull her hair and say, blah-blah, dumb old ugly old stupid old Bess, there she is, and she, delighted, would jump up too and chase him all over the yard until they got so tired that one of them would gasp, "Times," and then, after they had rested, Bess would abruptly scream, "Off times!" and pounce on him. She had not felt as if she could feel like that again in a very long time.

◇

Bess saw Cookie at Red Ruf's almost every weekend, usually with Dougal in tow. Although they caused no more fights, Red Ruf sometimes frowned in a worried, slightly disappointed way when he came in to hold court and spotted Bess haunched over the bar, straining to hear one of Cookie's observations, blatantly ignoring an older patron down on the far end, one of Ruf's own courtiers.

"You know those boys?" he wondered to her one day, in an almost laughingly casual tone. Bess had been watching Cookie with glee, out on the dance floor with one of the local girls. Cookie was, by his own admission, "a dancing fucking fool," and whenever he wasn't huddled on a bar stool beside Dougal, he would sweep into the crowd and descend upon any one of the girls, every one of whom loved him, and lead them, shaking their hips and clapping their hands, out onto the floor where Cookie would commence to stomp up and down in his work boots, shaking his frail blond head in ecstasy and pausing every now and again to adjust his glasses.

"Which boys?"

"The boys who started that fight," Ruf said pointedly. He referred to it as "that fight" because it was the first one ever to occur at Red Ruf's and there was no doubt in his mind that if it hadn't been for that first fight, none of the other ones that broke out regularly each weekend would ever have come about.

"Cookie and Dougal. They're great guys, Red Ruf. Look at Cookie out there. I don't think you'd get any women in here if it wasn't for him."

Ruf squinted out at the dance floor with all the ill-concealed befuddlement that all big men demonstrate when they see women obviously enjoying themselves with the kind of man that Cookie was.

It made Bess laugh out loud, which made Ruf jump and stare at her. As if Cookie was a man at all and not a sexless little sprite who made you feel as if he valued your company over everyone else's and told you everything as though it were the greatest of secrets and talked dirtier than anyone you've ever met, yet with an absolute innocence.

"You like that little fella, Bessie?" Ruf asked, turning his squint her way.

"He's adorable."

"I don't know," said Ruf, his big white head swivelling back towards the dance floor. "The first time I saw him and his lunkhead brother in here I kinda figured he was what your dad would call a shit-disturber."

Bess folded her arms coolly and gazed off in the same direction as Ruf. "They're my cousins," she said.

"Oh, Bessie, dear," he said, jumping again. "Why don't you set yourself up with a beer, dear."

Bess smiled, setting herself up with a beer. Ruf had yet to understand that everybody was cousins.

One night Bess arrived from work to find the funeral home minus one ghoul. Gramma sat on her side of the room, rocking in time with her prayers to the Virgin, and Mommy sat close beside her on a chair she had brought out from the kitchen, nodding at the garbled prayers and watching Dylan play with trucks. The television was on, babbling news. Bess came in and leaned against Grampa's empty chair, the stink of ancient smoke and piss emanating from its fibres. On the floor beside it sat the emptied stewed tomato can which he used to hork his old-man's juice into. Beside that was a pack of matches. Dylan came up and wrapped his body around Bess's leg.

"They took him to the hospital, did they?"

"Yes, God love the poor soul."

"When was this?"

"Around suppertime."

"Poor Iain," said Gramma to nobody. "*Croc a nian, scat a nean*" — which was a song about salt cod that she recently had been mistaking for the Our Father.

Saturday night she made a mistake that fated Sunday morning into being a bad one. She had been setting herself up with beers during most of her shift, as Red Ruf often invited her to do so, and when the time came to take off her apron and accept a lift home from him, Cookie, instead, instructed her to sit at a table with himself and Dougal, down a few, and they would take her home in a bit. Loving Cookie and Dougal as she did, this seemed at first a reasonable idea, but once she got out from behind the bar and into the centre of the crowd, the culture shock resurfaced and everything was terrible again. All of Cookie's many friends approached the table to talk to him, and when they saw Bess there, they tried to talk to her too. Sometimes Cookie went off to dance, but the friends stayed, talking to Bess and asking her questions. She knew them all remotely from working the bar, but now felt that this pleasant remoteness had been ruined. There would be no more of these people coming up, smiling at her, asking for a beer and saying please, and no more of Bess obliging them with another smile and their going away.

Cookie, indicating the dance floor, said to her at one point, "Let's get on out there for Jesus' sake," and she thought that she might as well, but once Bess found herself standing there across from Cookie doing his sweaty work-boot stomp, she felt very large and vivid with the lights flashing on her and the music all around, and so she reached over to pull on Cookie's sleeve and tell him that she was going to sit back down again. He nodded and bounded off towards the tables to get someone else.

And it was terrible because she had no way home except for Cookie and Dougal's father's fish truck parked outside. When she had told Ruf, no thanks, she'd be staying, he blinked at her in a kind of lost way and then said, All right, pulling on his jacket. She saw now that she should've gone home when Ruf offered his customary lift, like she always did — that would've been the right thing to do because now she was trapped with all these people and the road home was three miles long, unlit and lined on either side with woods. And, this was what always happened, the more nervous she got, the faster she finished her beer. Dougal, who sat always at the table, smiling, never getting up to dance or do anything except go to the men's room, looked over at her accumulation of empties and commented that she was "quite the Jesus partier."

Cookie bounded over, sweaty, and sat down. He leaned over and punched Bess on the shoulder: "Wouldn't even gimme a dance!" He laughed like it was a joke, which was a trick of his Bess had come to know. He used it when he sensed someone was uncomfortable. Just saying things and laughing at them, but making you feel as if you were actually the funny one, the clever wit. She smiled and shrugged and told him she was sorry as though what she had done was natural and excusable. They all pretended this. On the other side of her, her second cousin Findlay thumped into a chair.

"Findlay, ya crazy cocksucker," Cookie yelled above the music.

"Meg's wonderin' how you're doin'," he said, leaning towards Bess.

"Oh, is Meg here?" Bess stretched her neck and peered into the crowd.

"Oh, is Meg here?" Findlay repeated, pretending to look desperately around.

"Oh, for Christ's sake," Bess, who was now drunk, said.

"Now what's that supposed to mean, eh? We been here all night, looking y' right in the eye. I wonder what yer dad would say, hearing you turnin' up yer nose at Alistair's kids."

"Here's a beer for ya, Findlay," said Cookie.

"I don't suppose you'd lower yourself to dance."

"No thanks," Bess answered helplessly.

"Turned me down too, jeezless teaser!" shouted Cookie, still holding out Findlay's beer. "Walked right off the dance floor, me standing there with my dick in my hand! Trying to make me look silly or something is my guess."

"That's about what I figured." Findlay attempted to stand up, and, after a few minutes, succeeded at it, finally accepting the extended bottle. "Cookie," he said, pointing with it, "you don't talk to me, you little fairy bastard."

Dougal stood up, still smiling.

"Oh, no, no, no," Bess shouted, shaking her head extravagantly.

But Findlay had already lumbered hastily off towards his table, wherever that was. And Bess got up and went behind the bar to use the phone. She called her father who said that they hadn't even known where she was and here's the poor little fella squalling for his mother and nobody knowing what the Jesus to tell him, had to let him cry himself to sleep and Mommy pacing the floor half in tears and everybody worried sick to death about The Boss until finally he decided to give Ruf a call: "Oh my! She's out drinking with the Sloanes, Alec, didn't you know? Didn't she even call?"

"Daddy, won't you come get me, please?"

So Sunday morning was fated to be a bad one. Bess woke at around six in the morning, the sun still pale, and stayed awake even though she had several semi-dreams which were about ridiculous things like walking across the yard with the dumb chickens that her grandparents used to keep, scurrying behind her thinking she would feed them and then turning abruptly around and running at them, causing them all to cluck and scatter hysterically. On the other side of the room, the little boy breathed with comfortable steadiness. Bess tried to convince herself that, because of the dreams, she was really asleep, unaware of any headache.

At around eight o'clock, the house came awake, the first stirrings taking place in the bathroom down the hall and then extending into the kitchen downstairs. Bess had a brief dream about their dead black steer, Uncle Remus, who tried to kill her in the summer Daddy and

Alistair had to shoot it. In the dream she got Uncle Remus mixed up with Candy, their pony, and she was standing alongside of Uncle Remus out in the middle of the field, stroking his nose and feeding him a carrot. Uncle Remus chewed on the carrot thoughtfully before looking up at Bess and saying, Well, of course you must understand why. And Bess was embarrassed for him and stroked his nose furiously. Of course, of course, don't give it another thought.

Downstairs, the phone rang. It was their line, one long and two short, and she heard Marg scurry to answer it. Dylan turned over, sighing, would be awake soon wanting Bess to play and watch the sparse Sunday morning cartoons. Things were quiet downstairs for a little while, maybe a half an hour, and then Bess could hear Mommy clear her throat, get up from the chair, and cross the floor. Then Bess heard her feet on the staircase, *creak, creak*, and she cleared her throat again. She was coming very deliberately, to wake up Bess. Bess heard her coming down the hall, pushing aside the already half-open door. Dylan turning over again and probably opening his eyes and looking at her as she sat down on the edge of Bess's bed. Mommy touching her shoulder and clearing her throat a third time and then leaning over to kiss Bess soft on the cheek, which was the way she had woken up Bess since the beginning of everything.

"I have some bad news."

"Grampa's dead."

"An hour ago. Daddy says we're going to wake him here."

Bess sat up. "Jesus Christ." Dylan was awake and smiling at her.

Mommy ran her thin hands through her short hair. "I know," she said. "We're going to have to start the cleaning today, as soon as you're dressed."

Mary Kate Sloane brought six plates of sandwiches and two large bowls of potato salad. She also brought a banana bread and a cinnamon loaf and two tins full of biscuits. She also brought a bottle of rye and a bottle of scotch, which she presented to Aunt Marg.

"I couldn't remember, Margaret, was it the Jack Daniel's you liked? Or the Johnnie Walker?"

"It's the Johnnie Walker, dear, God love you. It all goes down the same hole, in any case."

She had pulled up wedged between Cookie and Dougal in her husband's fish truck. When they got out, Bess saw that the back was full of boxes with food in them, and her daughter, Mary Katherine, had ridden back there too, partly to hold the boxes in place but mostly because there was no room in the front. She sat primly on top of a box, wearing a jacket that certainly couldn't have kept her warm enough during the ride, and high heels, and smoothing down a black skirt. Bess was very pleased to see her, for some reason, and wanted to stay close to her the whole time she was there and ask her questions about how she was doing in school and whatever else she was up to these days.

"We're here to help, not as guests," Mrs. Sloane said. "Not that we don't want to pay our respects to Iain, God love his soul, but anything you need done, you tell me or one of the boys or Mary and we'll see to it. Now you get back to your guests and we'll serve this here food up."

"Don't be so foolish, Mary Kate," Aunt Marg protested.

"No, no, no," said Mrs. Sloane, picking up one of the boxes that Dougal had hefted from the truck. "Let me see. This is the pickles. I'll need some little bowls, unless you'd just like to serve them in the jars."

Daddy had hired a fiddler to sit in the corner with a drink at his feet and play mournful Scottish tunes. He had not actually been hired, Daddy had called him up with the request and offered to pay him for it, but because he was an old friend of the family, the fiddler refused. The fiddler was actually a celebrity of sorts and most of the guests considered it something of an event, having him there. He was an old man in a wheelchair, with a sagging pink face and pure white hair and black, fifties-style glasses. He had a deep, resonating voice and was known to be a storyteller. Someone from Ontario had once included him in a book of Maritime folklore, and now he was widely considered a sage. He remembered Bess's father as a little boy, he'd told her once.

Bess was in a state of nervous irritation. She had never seen so many people in the house at once. For the last three days the place was full, morning and night, as many of them were relatives from Boston and Ontario with no other place to stay. The corpse was laid out in the living room, the first thing she saw in the morning when she got up and the last when she went to bed at night. She worried about Dylan, about his psyche and all that, even though he appeared to be having the time of his life, and it was all Bess could do to keep him away from the coffin, from poking philosophically at its contents. It was Cookie, usually, who would intercept him at just the last minute, sweeping him up and away just as the baby was about to experiment with one of Grampa's eyelids. Cookie would take him off into a corner somewhere and bounce him up and down on his knee, singing,

> A deedle deedle dump
> diddle dump diddle dump.
> A deedle deedle dump
> deedle dump dump dump!

And on the last "dump," he would abruptly open his legs, dropping Dylan through the gap. Dylan loved this.

There were relatives like most people had flies in the summer. Cousins and uncles. No aunts except for Marg and a couple of great-ones, arriving with a child or grandchild supporting either arm, wearing black fur coats purchased over forty years ago, and freakish little black hats with veils that had to be pinned into their webby hair if they were to remain in place. The aunts sat in a corner on either side of Gramma's chair, fingering black rosaries, and guiding her through the correct number of Our Fathers and Hail Marys. The procession stopped by her chair to kiss her before heading to the coffin.

"God bless his dear soul, Elizabeth."

"Well, he's in a better place now, God love him."

"Yes, God love his soul."

"He's happy now, dear. No need to cry for poor Iain."

"No, God bless him."

Bess had never in her life heard Gramma so lucid, let alone so gracious. Something had come back to her. The procession moved away from her chair, murmuring, "My God, what a woman."

Daddy and the uncles sat in another corner of the living room, drinking coffee and looking extremely sober. Some were Dad's uncles and some were his bothers. They were all reformed, watching the youngsters soak it up with pity and contempt, the contempt, of course, for the young, and the pity for themselves.

Uncle Roddie's children, for instance, were something of a mess. They had all grown up in Ontario and visited as children in the summers. They were all older than Bess, and she could remember worshipping them with their clothes and cigarettes. They had been young in the sixties, and so the girls were very independent, one wearing a brushcut. They drank beer and were exotic.

Most of Roddie's kids were in the civil service, but one had gone to art school and now worked in the Museum of Civilization. They were still the way they had been, independent and open-minded, arguing with Daddy about the French. Whenever they visited, they would do things like buy a case of Alexander Keith's and go to square dances and Judique on the Floor Days and all the other festivals. They would come back to the house and sit in the kitchen with their Keith's and start all their sentences with "Jesus, Mary, and Joseph," and "Lord t'undering Jesus." They would play their Rankin Family and Rita MacNeil tapes.

But now they were a mess because Grampa had died and they remembered things about him Bess didn't, or so she supposed. One of them plunked down beside Bess on the couch and asked her how she was holding up and she said fine.

"You were with him right up until the end?"

"Yes."

"Last time I was down was five years ago, I think. God, maybe more. I never had a chance to get down. At home, we always would talk about it, spending maybe a month out of the summer, visiting all the relatives just like we used to. What was he like?"

"He wasn't like much of anything. I mean, he was pretty old."

"Ah, Bessie, you don't remember him like I do. What a man. What a great man. The stories he used to tell. But a simple man, you know?"

But I've lived with him all my life, Bess wished to say. Then she felt she was being callous all of a sudden and got up to get Aunt Marg, very dignified and controlled with her hand around her glass, because she would be able to talk to the cousins the way they wanted to be talked to. Bess penanced herself by fetching drinks for everybody and bringing the more distracted ones plates of food.

"Sit down, sit down, Bessie," said Mary Kate Sloane. "Mary Katherine and the boys are taking care of all that."

"No, no, no," said Bess.

Cookie, in fact, was sitting at the dining-room table with a scotch alongside of him, picking at a tray of squares. "Sit down, for the love of Christ, Bessie. Wait, fix yourself a drink first."

She sat down, feeling a tingling in her legs. He didn't say anything while she took her first sip.

"That's a nice buck your dad's got hanging outside," Cookie finally remarked. "Got it on the weekend, did he?"

"No, just the other day," she said, thinking for the first time about the gutted deer, swinging in the wind upside down from the big, leafless maple, with a red, open gash down its front. Everybody had forgotten about it. She thought that it probably wasn't a thing to have outside a wake, but she wasn't sure. Nobody had said anything until now.

"Season finished Saturday," Cookie pointed out.

"I know," said Bess. "But there was nothing to be done. Daddy looked out into the field early the other morning and it was just standing there."

"No shit!"

"Yes, he nearly killed himself going for the rifle."

"Were you there? Did you see it go down?"

"Oh, yes. Alistair was asleep on the couch because he had passed out the night before and Daddy was hollering for him to get up."

"Did he get up?"

"He got up just in time to see Daddy shoot it."

It had been just like the time with Uncle Remus. Men running to and fro, hollering to each other. Except Uncle Remus had been crazy and the buck just stood there the whole time, in the morning frost.

"Well, I'll be jiggered," said Cookie leaning back.

"Do you think anybody noticed it, Cookie?"

"The deer? Jesus, yes, she looks great."

Daddy wandered in and put his coffee cup down on the table. He examined the trays for something good.

"I was just saying to Bessie that's a hell of a nice deer you got out there," Cookie told him.

"Thank you, Angus," Daddy said, picking up a square. "You tell your mother to sit down and have a bite to eat, now. There's no need for her going to all this trouble."

"She don't mind at all, but I'll see if I can bring her a bite." Cookie got up apologetically and went to find his mother, and Daddy sat down in his spot.

"Glad to see you're enjoying yourself," he said, indicating Bess's drink.

"I'm taking a break, here."

"What's all this with the little Sloane fella?"

"Cookie's nice."

"Cookie's nice, is he? Weird little eyeball bastard. Ruf says you're just as thick as thieves, you and the Sloane boys. I said to him, 'I hope that's not right, Ruf, I honestly do.'"

"What's wrong with the Sloanes?" she said to him pointedly.

He held up his hands. "Mary Kate's a saint and I'd never say a word against her, now."

"Well, what the hell?"

"Don't let me hear about you running all over hell with those boys, that's all I'm saying."

"I don't. I never do anything."

"Drunk till all hours with The Boss on his deathbed."

And what was there to say to that? There was nothing to say. The times when Bess was angriest were always the times when there was nothing to say. When Daddy told an unfair truth and made it so there was nothing to say. She got up and went to find Cookie so that she could make a joke out of it.

Later, she was to feel sorry, getting angry and getting up like that so that she could be away from him. She felt sorry watching him move among all the people that he was so unused to with nothing to defend himself but an empty coffee mug and a napkin with a brownie on it. He wore a grey wool sweater that stretched out over his belly, and a tie stuffed down inside of it, so you could only see the knot. His father was dead. The problem was, Bess kept having to remind herself of that, that today was an especially bad day for him, and that all of his anger was justified today. And it was basically her fault. She knew that he was the angriest man in the world and that it was her fault. That his father had died and that he was poor and then not poor and then poor again, that he had been an alcoholic but then got to a point where he had to quit, and so quit, all by himself, without any help from AA or anyone. It was her fault because she had done nothing the right way. She had done nothing in her life to make any of it worthwhile.

Red Ruf Bank, looking like a large, grey baby in his dark suit and with his combed-down hair, got on well with Leland MacEachern when both of them put in an appearance on the last day of the wake, Leland and his wife and daughter Maureen in tow, Maureen probably having been dragged along because she was closest in his family to Bess's age, and since they had played together on all the camping and fishing trips that their families had gone on all those years ago, both families assumed that they were friends.

It was rather an awesome thing, Leland coming to pay his respects, because he was now an MLA in the Conservative government and you sometimes saw him on television. After he had spoken quietly to Gramma, holding her hand all the while, and knelt down beside the corpse to pay his respects, he stood chatting with Ruf and Daddy and all the men, and his wife and Maureen stood with the women, Bess trying to think of something to say to Maureen, who had grown very sleek and stylish, in a conservative kind of way.

"How's your little boy?" Maureen wanted to know.

"He's very good."

Mrs. MacEachern turned her head and said, "Oh, that reminds me, Ellen. We brought a bag down for those people you used to help, remember?"

"The Sloanes."

"The Sloanes. But I was just thinking that there may be one or two things in there to fit Bess's little one. David's boy, Peter, outgrows things faster than we can buy them, so everything's practically unused!"

And, before Bess had time to think about it, she had answered enthusiastically, that this was great, and she couldn't wait to look through the bag. She was momentarily enchanted by the thought of Dylan in new clothes, which he needed, but after she stood there listening to the women talk for a little while, the feeling wore off. She had just turned to resume her search for Cookie, when she realized that he was approaching with Dylan in one arm and fresh scotch for Bess.

"Do you want to know something funny?" she said to him, relieving him of both Dylan and the drink. "Every now and again I find myself having a good time."

"It's all this free booze," said Cookie. "Do *you* want to know something funny? You know that wire fence in the playground of the Forks school?" Bess shook her head and reminded him that they hadn't gone to school together. "Oh, yeah. Well, there's this fence in behind the school that they put there to keep all the little bastards from running off into the woods at recess. Anyways, every day at recess and lunch, I used to go and talk to the fence."

"Talk to the fence?"

"Yes, that fence was my Jesus best friend. And I gave him a name too. Jaimeson."

"Oh, yeah."

"Maybe if little Dilly here goes to school at the Forks, he'll take to talking to Jaimeson too."

"I hope to God he doesn't."

Maureen MacEachern, Bess saw, was observing them for lack of anything else to do. Bess looked at her and said, "Oh, this is Dylan," jostling the boy in her arms to draw Maureen's attention.

"What a sweetie," said Maureen, "oooh, what a sweetie." She poked at his nose. Cookie stood there, smiling, trying to see through his glasses.

"This here," added Bess, hastily pulling her free arm around Cookie and towering over him, also spilling a little bit of her drink, "is my husband."

"Is that right?"

"His name," said Bess, "is Red Angus John Dougal Sloane McFelly."

"But he doesn't even have red hair!" said Maureen.

"No, I know. They call him that because his great-uncle once had an Irish setter."

Bess put Dylan down and let him run.

A moment, later she explained to Cookie, who hadn't even questioned, "Daddy figures you and me are going to run away together."

"Actually, you can't blame me, most men are afraid of that," he said, looking thoughtful. "Me running off with their women. I'm a known snatch-sniffer."

Bess couldn't believe it, this at the poor old bastard's wake. She had to run to the bathroom, it was so funny.

◇

Big Dog
Rage

◇

EVEN THOUGH I WAS ONLY FIVE or something, I can remember the first time I met him because I was brimming with hatred and rage and despair. Being a child, I'd never felt such things before, not all at once. His dog had killed my dog in front of me, picked her up in his teeth, shook her once, and broke her neck. We'd collided in the woods behind my house and had been having a pretty amiable chat for a couple of kids when his Lab went crazy. It was on a leash — he'd been taking it for a walk. Mine wasn't, because I had just wandered down into the woods to play and she followed me like she always did. I don't remember much about it. I just remember being in the vet's with my mother and his parents and my dead dog having been carted off somewhere and his about to be put to sleep, and he was crying and hating me as much as I was hating him and his dog was wagging its tail and trying to put its nose up my crotch.

We got to be friends after a while because my mother was after his parents for compensation or something and would drag me over to his house and we'd go off and play spaceman while they had it out. Spaceman was his own game and entirely original. He would pull all the pillows off the chesterfield and chairs and we would bounce around on them pretending to be on Mars or somewhere.

If a monster came, we would both jump in his father's recliner chair and recline rapidly, launching ourselves out into space. He vowed he would never get another dog, and so did I.

We whined to go over to one another's houses every single day for the next five years. My mother thought I was crazy because she was the kind of person who identified people immediately as being either good people or bad people, no one was in between, and it was always based on how other people's actions affected her. She thought Germans were bad, for example, not because of anything they had done historically, but because some Germans had bought up all the property in Dunvegan that used to belong to her family. The Newhooks had killed our dog, so they were bad also. That was how we met them. It made them our natural enemies, she thought.

And then she would talk about him like he was my boyfriend. He's going to break your heart, she would tell me. He broke your heart once, he'll do it again. She meant because of the dog, but I had gotten over it, and it irritated me that she never would let me forget.

Gerald and I made a game of it. The vet had said *Big dog rage*, and it was three words we never forgot. Big dogs see small dogs and become infuriated by their very presence, the vet told us, their very *being*. Big, friendly dogs, like yellow Labs — a breed I can't see to this day without hyperventilating — dogs who would normally never hurt a fly. Out of the blue they will jump on a little dog and kill them.

Big dog rage! he would suddenly shout in the middle of a cartoon, and lunge at me, teeth and claws.

His mother told me years later that when Gerald was a baby, she had left him with that same Lab, the Yellow Labrador of Death, in the living room while she went into the kitchen for something. She heard the Lab make this gurgly, pleading sort of noise that he'd never made before. She glanced back into the living room and saw that Gerald had stretched out his chubby hand and grabbed hold of the yellow Lab's scrotum, and the Lab was just sitting there, waiting for Gerald's mother to do something about it.

He could stop himself from biting the kid's arm off, she said to me, *but he couldn't stop big dog rage.* Gerald's mother always got weepy when she talked about that dog. I think she actually loved him more than Gerald ever did, more than any of my family ever loved the black poodle. My mother always said it was the *principle* of the thing, referring to all the grief she put Gerald's parents through afterwards, insisting the Lab be put to sleep or else she would call the police and get them to do it. *Imagine what could have happened to the little girl,* she said, meaning me. That's what she told them she was going to say to the police. So in the end Gerald's parents gave in and put the dog to sleep. His name had been Harvey, after the imaginary rabbit. It was Gerald's mother's all-time favourite film.

We played spaceman and big dog rage. We dressed up as Siamese twins at Hallowe'en. We decided we were going to be exactly the same person when we grew up. We would dress alike and have the same haircuts. We would talk at the same time when people asked us questions, and say precisely the same thing. We would be the same person, so we would just be able to talk like that. We would have the same job and live in the same house. Many of our days were spent practising for it, trying to find clothes that looked exactly alike, trying to talk simultaneously to his mother. We played on the same teams, and even though I was better than him at sports, I made it so that I wasn't. He quit Scouts because they wouldn't let me join.

His father made Gerald become an altar boy, however, because Gerald's father had been an altar boy when he was a kid, and my mother would not let me be an altar girl because she thought it was against the Pope. That's how it started. So he was up there serving mass on Saturday evenings and Sunday mornings, and I would watch him, agonized and inwardly raging against the Pope, while Gerald puttered around the altar, ringing the bell and carrying around the host.

"It's stupid," he said.

"But I want to do it because you're doing it."

"I know, but it's better if we figure out a way for me to get out of it, because it's stupid."

"I can write to the Pope." My mother had me believing that writing letters was the best and only way to change anything. I believed I could just write to anyone I wanted and they would read it, because that's what she believed. Even if they never responded, even if nothing ever changed, deep in my mother's heart she trusted that every recipient would be deeply shamed and chastened by her words. She wrote to newspapers, MLAs, businesses, lawyers, all the people who had wronged her over the years, on a regular basis.

"No," he said. "The Pope will never change his mind. I have to get out. I have to show I'm not worthy to serve the mass."

"How?"

"I can sin. " His face lit up, epiphanic. "I'll become a sinner."

"No! Just pretend to be a sinner."

"If I pretend to be a sinner, than I'm still sinning because I'm lying," he insisted.

"But you won't have sinned in your heart."

"But I will have if I lie! There's no escape. I've got to sin."

I floundered. It was a theological quagmire, but Gerald wasn't interested in negotiating it with me. I could tell he was excited about it, about having no choice, about circumstances conspiring against him like this. He had decided on his course of action.

Mass became suspenseful, torturously so. Gerald kept testing his boundaries, and I never knew how far he was willing to push it. He started digging at the interior of his left nostril one day while the priest gave the homily, but this was commonplace boy-behaviour as far as the congregation was concerned, even if it did occur on the holy altar. His father merely smacked him one on the back of the head and told Gerald not to let him catch him at it again. And the priest had had his back turned the entire time anyway.

"It's gotta be the priest," Gerald reflected. "He's the only one who can kick me off the altar. The priest has gotta catch me at something."

The whole thing made me uncomfortable because it looked to me as if Gerald was getting ready to do to the world one of his favourite things to do to everything else: take it all apart. Unscrew all the teensy imperceptible screws, and start tinkering around inside.

Gerald held the round, golden tray underneath the priest's hands as the latter fumbled the host towards the waiting tongues and hands of the congregation. He waited for it to be my turn to receive so that I could get an up-close view of what he was going to do. He simply dropped the tray onto my foot and then picked it up again.

"You old slut," he said to the tray. He breathed on it and then polished it with his sleeve.

If the host had not melted onto the roof of my mouth I would have choked on it. I thought the priest would reach out and knock our heads together — I was certain he would have assumed that I was involved in Gerald's blasphemy somehow, that the word *guilty* would have appeared on my forehead in blistered, red script.

But the priest was cool. He knew it was important to correct Gerald, but more important was the necessity not to make a scene. So he glowered for only a split second, and waited until after mass to give Gerald a brief, kindly-but-stern talking-to. He told Gerald that God didn't appreciate that kind of language, and that was that. Say an act of contrition and try to be good. Gerald was disgusted.

"It's no use," I told him, hopeful.

"It didn't work because the only people who saw and heard it was you and the priest," said Gerald.

The next Sunday when it was time to ring the bell before communion, Gerald just kept ringing and ringing it until he was sure the priest and everyone else was looking at him and then he did this little dance to the bell-music that he used to do for me which he called the Dirty Boogie, and which basically involved just waving his pelvis around. He made a face at the two other altar boys, and they cracked up, and so did all of the less-pious parishioners, of whom there seemed to be quite a few. But I was frozen in my seat. My mother punched me hard in the arm because she was wiser than the priest — she knew I was, at the very least, guilty by association.

When Gerald was allowed to appear in public again, he was as giddy from the crime as if it had occurred moments ago. He would climb up to the top of the monkey bars and perform the Dirty Boogie for everyone, and everyone on the ground would cheer and do it with him. Then he would leap onto the ground and lead everyone in a Dirty Boogie dance-line. He was the most popular boy in town. Meanwhile, everybody's parents had started making dire predictions about Gerald. To be kicked out of the altar boys apparently did not bode well for a young man's future. It was taken as the worst sort of omen.

I was disturbed for all the obvious reasons. To serve the mass was sacred, but Gerald had acted like it was any other foolish thing your parents would force you to do, like violin lessons. Something to be weaselled out of at all costs. When I was very young, I never suspected it was the altar boys who rang the bells before communion. I always thought it was God. I'd hear the sound of bells suddenly echoing throughout the church and would look around wildly, in a panic. I started to get nervous and fidgety every Sunday before communion, waiting for the disembodied bells to sound, until finally my mother grabbed my swivelling head and forced me to watch the altar boy reach unobtrusively down beside his chair to give the bells a shake. It was one of the first religious anticlimaxes of my life, but I still thought ringing the bells at mass had to be one of the holiest things a kid could ever hope to do, and Gerald treated it like doing the dishes.

And Gerald had committed all these sins to be with me, but now that he was such a big shot he wasn't with me as much any more. Other boys began to take an interest in him because he was bad. Gerald loved it. He waved his pelvis around every chance he got, at teachers, girls, and parents. Boys followed, and imitated him like monkeys. When people got tired of that he had to think of something else to do.

He clamoured to be in the Christmas play. And not just as a haystack or donkey, he wanted to be something right up front, a wise man or an angel, if he couldn't be Joseph. He wanted to be Joseph, but at this point, with his reputation, it was laughable. He managed to get himself positioned as Balthazar, all decked out in a bathrobe and a big bedsheet-turban, and when it came time for him to present the frankincense to the Baby Brenda doll they had sat in a pile of straw, instead he opted to shout, "Go long!" and punt the doll across the stage with his foot, in front of all the parents. One of the shepherds in back instinctively raised his tinfoil-wrapped hockey stick to keep the baby from flying off into the wings, and the effect was as if some kind of spontaneous sporting event had broken out. I was an angel, told to stand at precisely the opposite position on the stage from where Gerald was supposed to present his offering. I'll never forget the floppy, swaddled body of Christ shuttling towards me like that.

So practically overnight Gerald had turned himself into the kind of boy who doesn't get chosen to be in Christmas pageants any more, or any pageants. Who isn't trusted to carry the milk money up to the office and is followed around the schoolyard relentlessly by the recess monitor. My mother was filled with satisfaction. In the later, wet winter months, somebody left a naked Baby Brenda doll with tits drawn on it on my doorstep, like an orphan. I took it in and washed it and dressed it up in clothes and put it to bed, but after a while it started giving me nightmares, so I threw it in the closet. Then all I could think about at night was the doll lying in my closet, so one morning I got up and put it in my mother's closet.

In the wintertime, the backyard of my house, sloping down into the woods, got turned by local kids into the beginning of a long, meandering sled-hill. They would pour buckets and buckets of water all along the whole thing until it was so unbearably slick that the moment you set foot on it, you would find yourself propelled into the woods at breakneck speed and there would be no way on earth you could slow yourself down. You would shoot past trees and bushes and screaming kids until finally you would find yourself rapidly approaching "the hill" — the steepest part of the whole ride, full of bumps and kid-made ramps. This was the climax of the ride, the only problem being that the bottom of the hill gave way to the Trans-Canada Highway, where pulp trucks went barrelling past on their way to and from the mill, making their loud and angry farting noises. There was a pretty deep gully which kept most of the sliders from shooting right out into the highway, but I had seen a couple of the speedier ones come so close my heart jumped. Even so, it didn't stop me, or anyone else, from spending entire twelve-hour days repeatedly hurtling ourselves towards the speeding traffic.

I remember the queer frenzy of those times, the bright snow against the grey sky, how the snow seemed like this cushion that would come between you and any harm, even though we were constantly almost breaking our necks and braining each other with snowballs, and kids would leave crying and dripping and come back in different snowsuits half an hour later, all memory of past offences having dried up as well. Nothing could keep us from the speed.

The only place I saw Gerald on a fairly regular basis then was the hill, shooting past me, loaded up on a sled with five or six other screaming boys. In the summer we used to sit on the top of the hill and watch for a pulp truck to go by and as soon as it made its noise, Gerald would jump up, make a face, and wave his hand in the air — "Oh my God! Hold your breath!" — and I would pretend that it was too late and I was already dead.

I had seen his mother around town and her face would melt like it always did when she saw me, because she associated me with the tragedy of dead dogs and childhood. She would hold my face in her hands, with her eyes all dewy, and ask why I never came to visit, and I would curse Gerald for having the sweet, soft mother that I wanted, and for cutting me off from her. I missed the whole decent normalcy of his entire family — the sweet, soft mother, the remote, joking father, and Gerald completing the triangle. They struck me as being wholesome and complete in a way that me and my suspicious, letter-writing mother could never aspire to. No matter what my mother said about the Newhooks, I always understood that they were better than us in a very fundamental way, and later I grew to understand that this was the reason my mother hated practically everyone.

But I wanted to be with people like that, those my mother said would break my heart. I wanted to be friends with my mother's enemies and prove that I was not like her, but like them.

On the top of the melting hill, I saw Gerald was scarcely two feet away from me, hands on his hips, yelling orders at a bunch of boys sprawled down at the bottom. He was screaming his head off so that they could hear him and his face was red under his blond hair, and I thought he looked like a Viking and I wanted him to belong to me again. I lobbed a lightly packed snowball at him and he spun around as if to say: *Who dares!*

"Nice doll," I told him.

"What?"

"Nice doll."

He cocked his head. "Nice dog?"

"Nice *doll*," I said.

"Nice doggie," Gerald said. "Good doggie." He panted at me and threw himself, stomach first, down the hill. I sat down.

He returned, pulling behind him a very lovely new sled I had seen before in the Christmas Wish-book, black, like his snowsuit, and sort of designed to look like a cross between a speedboat and a motorcycle. He was excited.

"Did you see that?" he said. "I came *this close* to the highway and I was only sliding *on my stomach!*"

"Where'd you get that?"

"Someone gave it to me." He glanced down at the sled. "On this thing I'll overshoot the gully, no problem. I'll be completely killed."

"Let me go on with you," I said like nothing had ever happened. "More weight will make you go faster."

He looked skeptical.

"We'll end up right in the middle of the highway!" I enthused. "Death will be instantaneous! We'll just be one big blot on the road."

"When I come back," he promised, flinging himself down onto it and flying away.

The Devil's
Bo-Peep

WELL, IT BEGAN. The family were given a wheelchair to bring her in with, and Ramona watched from behind the desk as this wild-eyed, rotten apple of a woman was brought into the lobby howling as if her entire family — who were in fact all around her, patting her hand, kissing her cheek, reassuring — had been killed in some kind of big disaster. The kind of all-annihilating disaster Ramona was always dreaming of, which would be, in her imagination, like God blowing a candle out.

"You are going to leave me here to die," the woman was saying. She had a thick near-Scottish accent, like most of the senior citizens of the area, and was winding a clunky set of ancient rosary beads into the flesh of her hands so insistently that soon her hands were actually bound together by the beads, but she didn't notice. The man, the son, was in control and stubborn. The son's wife looked as if she needed to be checked in herself — Ramona guessed that she had been doing most of the work where the old woman was concerned. The daughter, the son's sister, was the most sprightly of the bunch. She must be from away, thought Ramona.

"Nobody's leaving you to die, Mumma."

Ramona had done the intake on the old woman, and she thought the entire situation was foolish. The family merely wanted to go away for a week. A son in a far-off province was getting married, they wanted to attend, but had no one to look after the mother. The senior's home, on the other side of the parking lot, didn't take people as decrepit as this woman was; it was really more of an apartment complex for the elderly but self-sufficient. The woman needed around-the-clock care, however, so dear old Doctor Joey, the administrator and apparently an old friend of the family, took it upon himself to offer up one of the hospital's rarer-than-gold empty beds.

The sprightly daughter smiled at Ramona. "I'll be visiting her every day, making sure she doesn't get too lonely."

"We'll be back in a goddamn week!" the son was hollering at the wailing wheelchair.

"I'm staying up at the house while they're gone," the sister offered. "So I can come every day."

So, thought Ramona. The son's family had been caring for the woman into her extreme dotage, but the daughter wasn't even willing to put up with her for a week. No wonder she looked so fresh. She was about thirty years older than Ramona.

There was a sullen-eyed teenage girl poking around the waiting area, one of the family but trying to pretend she wasn't. Ramona used to have to run home from school every day and take care of her own grandmother, so she allowed herself a trickle of sympathy for the sulky thing, even though she did not approve of her enormous earrings and foolish clothes. If Ramona had a daughter, she would force her not to dress like an idiot until she was nineteen at least — then the girl could walk a tightrope in the town square wearing a G-string, for all Ramona cared.

The old woman was now wailing for the granddaughter, whose unfortunate name was Cassie Ann — "Cassie Ann! Cassie Ann! Where is my Cassie?" — and the girl tugged on her earrings and shuffled over, looking around to see who else might be in the lobby watching. I would teach her not to care what anyone thinks, thought Ramona. Like myself.

"Take off my handcuffs!" the woman begged, holding her hands out pathetically to the granddaughter, finally figuring out that they were inextricably bound.

The old could be dramatic. Ramona had noticed it before. She watched the girl blink three quick times before attempting to unwind the rosary beads. Soon she was yanking. They wouldn't come. The woman started wailing again, as though she took this as some sort of horrible cosmic portent. At last the family stared helplessly at Ramona, the authority figure, who came over to examine the bonds. She'd never seen such a thing before. The old woman shrieked at the sight of Ramona's big body in her white, blank uniform as it advanced.

"What in God's name kind of rosary is this?" Ramona demanded. It was enormous, a caricature of the real thing.

"We got her an extra big set," the wife answered, quiet and guilty.

"She's half blind, so she can't see the beads," the son interjected. "We needed big ones so she could tell the Our Fathers from the Hail Marys!" He glared at Ramona, daring her to question further. Ramona sized him up and decided to back down for the time being.

The mother was thrashing in her chair. "Why am I in chains?" she shrieked at Ramona. "Why have you done this to me?"

Oh, thought Ramona, this is lovely. This is just the cat's tit.

"We'll have to get some scissors," Ramona stated, heading back towards the nurses' station before there could be any argument.

The sullen granddaughter was shocked into speech. "You can't cut up her rosary!" Apparently she did fine wearing some kind of heavy-metal T-shirt with a skull and a 666 plastered across it, but the thought of cutting her grandmother free of the Our Fathers and Hail Marys offended her religious sensibilities. Ramona returned with a big pair of desk scissors and peered at the girl, who was standing protectively in front of her grandmother's chair. The grandmother had somehow deciphered the logistics of the situation and as a result quieted down and began paying attention. She knew only this: Someone she loved was standing between her and the big, unfamiliar person in white. It comforted. And Ramona was going to have to wreck it, having no time for such indulgences.

"I remember you, dear," Ramona said to the girl all of a sudden. And she did. The teenage girl had been brought in at seven in the morning some time last year with a stomach full of pills. Ramona had stuffed the tube down her nose and pumped green and black out of her stomach, barking at her all the while just what kind of foolish nonsense was she trying to perpetuate? Now Ramona smiled, and the girl stepped out of the way.

Perhaps Ramona shouldn't have raised the scissors quite so high as she approached the old woman, brandishing them, really, as it only served to send her into new fits of terror. As the family watched, the wife with her hands together and the son chewing on the inside of his face and the girl with her back to them all, Ramona ignored the wails and thrashing, slashed the rosary to pieces, and got the woman free. Oversized beads with bits of string attached clattered to the floor and rolled crazily off in every direction. Ramona hollered down the hall for an orderly.

"Well!" said the sister, standing apart from them all, a few feet away. "That's done." She wiped her palms on the front of her skirt.

Ramona saw at once that the old woman, whose name, it turned out, was also Cassie Ann, was going to have to be given her own room because she was so disruptive. The waste of hospital resources was appalling, and she thought Doctor Joey a politicking twit. She understood it all. The soft-hearted son could not bear the notion of putting dear Mother in a home, and so, early in her agedness, when she was still dear old Mother and not a gibbering banshee, he committed himself, and his entire unwitting family, to her eternal care in the bosom of home and hearth. Ramona knew the scenario so well because her own goddamn mother had done it to her, although perhaps if they had had more money and a few helpful relatives living nearby, it would not have been such a trial, and Ramona would not have been relegated to primary caregiver from the ages of twelve to eighteen while her mother worked at the fruit stand. She knew she had to have a career because it didn't look as if anyone was going to marry her, and she needed a reason to move the hell out of the house by the time she finished high school. She despised children, so being a teacher was out. The only other possible alternative was to enrol in nursing school, and considering she already had so much hands-on experience emptying bedpans and dispensing pills, it seemed the natural thing to do.

Of course, two months after Ramona had settled into the nursing program at Saint Mary's, her grandmother died. It was typical.

But she continued on with the program anyway and did well, and then eventually moved back home to work in a hospital also named after Saint Mary — the hospital in which she had been born. This was a practical decision, because here she could look after her own mother, who had given birth to Ramona late in life and was getting on. Ramona prided herself on the fact that she did not live with her mother out in the sticks, but had her own little house here in town, the mortgage paid with her own money. And when her mother could not get along on her own any more, Ramona would have no qualms. None. She had enough to do, enough old, sick people to take care of.

It was true that most of the patients in the hospital were old. Not a lot happened on this corner of the planet, so there was usually little to arouse excitement, the only youthful faces appearing whenever some kid flipped over his ATV while tearing around the hills. And sometimes people ran right into stately, immovable moose with their cars. The most exciting thing had been a few years ago when the mine was still operating and one of the shafts gave way. Miraculously, nobody was killed, the shaft was fairly close to the surface, so they were able to haul everyone to safety eventually. For weeks following, the wards were filled up with men of all ages, shapes, and sizes. Ramona tried to treat them with the brisk irritation she displayed towards her regular patients — an attitude that said: Who do you think you are, taking up all my time with your foolish ailments? — but found that she couldn't. The men were so lively and full of jokes. They knew they wouldn't be there for very long, and enjoyed themselves to the fullest. Ramona was so unused to people having fun in the hospital that she was completely disarmed. They shouted at the TV news and ate all the meals with gusto and then complained about them to Ramona with equal vehemence. They talked about the lives they couldn't wait to get back to, their wives and children. At visiting hours the halls were full of wives and children, all young, arms full of flowers. Some of the men even talked about the mine itself as if it were some kind of glorious haven. Indeed some of them loved the mine, the very mine that had dropped tons of rock on top of them only a few days before.

But soon the healthy male bodies knit themselves together, as was only natural, and Ramona was left once again with the old and the sick. All those who kept coming back, the terminally ill, the terminally old, taking up all of her time.

Today was more interesting than most, not because of the shrieking old woman, which was par for the Jesus course, but because Ramona was having lunch with a friend. This was a complete anomaly for Ramona — typically she just strolled down the street to her house, a mere five-minute walk away, and had some soup and a roll by herself. But this was a special occasion because Tamara Rutledge was in town, and she and Tamara had gone to nursing school together and been friends. It was one of those queer situations where they had lived in the same tiny part of the world for years and not said boo to each other, but once they were both alone in the same city, they sought each other out like sisters. Tamara was home to see her parents, because her father was dying of leukemia. Ramona had done his blood count up at the hospital a hundred times, and soon he would check in for good.

Ramona had enjoyed having Tamara as a friend in the last couple of years before graduation, because Tamara was a bit strange, and it was funny to show her to the other friends Ramona eventually made. At one point, Ramona had a good deal of friends. They would go to the Misty Moon and the Palace together on weekends and get drunk and dance with each other. During the week they would study and drink tea in one another's room and look at magazines. The friends were all inevitably from small towns like Ramona, and they banded together.

But Tamara was like someone from away. She sat in her room playing guitar and singing songs she made up in her terrible voice, but if you asked her to play one of the songs for you, she wouldn't do it. She wanted to travel all over the world after graduation, working for free in places like the Philippines, where you could catch a disease, or the Arctic, where you would freeze to death. One of her favourite songs, the only one she would sing out in public, was "Leaving on a Jet Plane." She could play it very well. She had several boyfriends and brought them to her room, which Ramona thought was vulgar, but, as many of the girls had pointed out, she wasn't able to hold on to a single one of them for more than a couple of months, so what was the point.

All those girls were married now, except for Ramona and Tamara. Everyone knew that Tamara couldn't keep a man, and Ramona could care less about them to begin with — she trusted her friends understood that much about her.

"Did you ever see anyone get all tangled up in their own rosary beads?" Ramona said to her friend. They had finished embracing and looking each other up and down.

"Are you speaking euphemistically?" asked Tamara with her bright, open face.

It was an irritating beginning, typical of Tamara. She didn't know enough to answer no, and wait for the story.

"Of course not," said Ramona. Before Tamara could interject any other comment, she launched into the story of the old doll in the wheelchair who checked in that morning, and what a trial it all had been. She embellished with a description of the comically oversized beads, a lament for the well-meaning ineptitudes of Doctor Joey, and finally a description of the sullen teenaged girl with her stomach full of pills last year and her earrings like two daggers.

"So then doesn't the devil's Bo-Peep enter into the fray," she was saying. "She does fine with the six-six-six emblazoned on her chest everywhere she wanders, but, dear God, don't cut up Nana's rosary in front of her!"

Tamara was twiddling her hair like a five-year-old, her mouth slightly open. "The devil's Bo-Peep, my Jesus, I haven't heard that in years."

Ramona was gratified. "I don't know where I heard it, it just came to me out of the blue, thinking of that thing with the Satan-shirt on her."

"My father used to call me that," said Tamara. Leave it to her to turn the conversation back to herself. "When I was a teenager going out with the boys. I think he would have been happy if I stayed a spinster my whole life."

But you *are* a spinster, Ramona stopped herself from pointing out. She was too polite. "What does he think about your travelling all over Kingdom Come?"

"Well," said Tamara, "Kingdom Come is pretty much the only thing on his mind these days as it is, he's not too interested in my goings-on any more."

Ramona was irritated again. "But when you started out on your travels, he wasn't too pleased, as I recall." Ramona knew all this already, but she wanted Tamara to remind her of it.

"Oh, he figured I'd catch some exotic disease." Tamara blew at her bangs with scorn. "Then, when I went up North, every time I called home it would be: 'Now don't you ever show up at this house with some big Eskimo in tow!' *Eskimo*, he calls them."

"Well, what do you call them? Inuit, I suppose."

"Actually, I was working almost exclusively with the Dene."

Tamara looked as if she wanted to talk about the Dene some

more, so Ramona said, "And is there a man in the picture these days?"

"Now I'm in Indonesia. Hm? Oh." Tamara smiled and blew at her bangs again and Ramona wondered why she didn't just go for a trim. "Yes, yes, isn't there always a man in the picture."

"A different one every time I talk to you," added Ramona. "You must like the variety."

Tamara's face registered pain, and Ramona was reminded of why she enjoyed spending time with her. Tamara was always blurting things out, leaving herself open, and it confirmed for Ramona how glad she was to know that she was nothing like her friend.

She returned from the luncheon buoyant and revitalized, having not visited with anyone except for her mother in months. She extracted a promise from Tamara to come over and see the house some time during her visit home and Tamara said she would do her best and Ramona replied for her not to put herself out, thus ensuring the visit would take place.

"Bring your guitar and sing "Leaving on a Jet Plane" for me," Ramona called when they parted.

The old woman Cassie Ann had to have her call button taken away, because once she became aware of its function she just sat there pressing it over and over again. This meant that now the nurses had to go out of their way to check on her every half-hour or so, and sometimes she would just wail for no reason, causing whoever was on duty to drop whatever it was she was doing and rush down the hall to find the old doll propped comfortably up on her pillows, gazing around herself like a great lady. The situation offended Ramona. It was a situation where the patient was not even sick, merely old. So old, however, that she might as well be deathly ill, being more trouble in her senility and decrepitude than all of the other patients put together. The woman should have long ago been admitted to a reputable home where she would receive constant care from professionals. That the family had opted to make themselves slaves to her needs for so long was unfathomable to Ramona.

The sister, the old woman's daughter, she disapproved of profoundly — it turned out that she was a nurse! The one person in the entire family who could have provided real aid where it was needed instead had offered to "take care of the house" while they attended their wedding, and "visit Mumma every day." Ramona sized her up as one of those selfish women, not unlike Tamara, who put their own comfort and frivolous desires before everything that matters. Ramona recalled how fresh and lively the sister looked compared to the son's wife, and even the teenaged daughter. She was probably the kind of woman who went to spas and what-have-you on the weekends.

Because she was also a nurse, the sister seemed to feel that she could just call Ramona by her first name, and double-check with her about her mother's dosage and other things that were normally no one's business but the hospital staff. Sometimes when Ramona returned to empty out the bedpan, she found that the sister had already performed this duty, and although, God knows, Ramona didn't begrudge her, she thought it presumptuous, to say the least.

"I just thought I'd make things a little easier for you around here, Ramona," the sister would chirp in her smiley voice.

Ramona had all sorts of comebacks for this that she was too polite to air.

When the sister left, Cassie Ann would cry and ask Ramona, "Why doesn't she stay with me?"

Ramona would say, "Because she's selfish and ignorant." Ramona didn't know why she called the sister "ignorant." She didn't know why she replied to the old woman in that way at all.

"She's my daughter," said Cassie Ann. "She studies the nursing up at Mount Saint Vincent."

Ramona snorted. The Mount. They were all lesbians up there.

"She's getting married in the fall to a tall man. He's too tall. No one will dance with her daughters."

"Isn't she doing well for a woman her age!" muttered Ramona. Time had no meaning for the senile. She remembered her own grandmother describing what her day had been like in school, talking to Ramona like she was her mother. It used to make her feel insane, in that room with her grandmother calling her "Mumma" and asking for treats. A dark, airless room, thick curtains always shut tight because the light made her grandmother depressed. An enormous picture of Humphrey Bogart above her bed the way most old women Ramona knew would have pictures of Jesus or the Pope, but her grandmother had been obsessed with Humphrey Bogart because she had once caught a glimpse of him on the streets of New York City, where she had worked as a much-coveted Nova Scotia nanny. She said she liked Humphrey Bogart because he looked "normal." He didn't look abnormal like the other movie star men. She cited Clark Gable as an example of a movie star who didn't look "normal."

Ramona's grandmother was said to have always acted like a big shot her whole life because she had lived in New York and stood within a few feet of Humphrey Bogart. But didn't she come flying back home at the end of her work period just like everyone did, looking for a long-faced, black-eyed husband, and toting a suitcase full of miniature Statues of Liberty and Empire State buildings to be distributed to family and friends. Ramona now had the largest and best of her grandmother's Statues of Liberty — the one her grandmother had purchased just for herself — on the mantelpiece of her home. The old lady had left it to Ramona in her will along with the china and silverware.

Ramona's grandmother was named Ramona also. Day in and day out Ramona used to come home from school and toil away in Ramona senior's shrine to normal men and darkness.

They had kept Tamara's father at home as long as they could, but later in the week he had to be checked in. Ramona wondered if Tamara would stay until he died. This hadn't been Tamara's plan, as her father had always gone in and out of remission and had days when he was as strong as an ox and his wife would get up to find him pulling weeds in the garden. But now his condition had suddenly deteriorated, almost as if he was attempting to do the polite thing by dying while his daughter was home to see it. Ramona had seen terminal patients do this sort of thing before. It was really quite remarkable.

She was gratified to run into Tamara in the lobby, as they hadn't been in touch about coming to see the house.

"As you can see," explained Tamara, "things have been a little overwhelming at home."

"Well, come down for lunch, it's a five-minute walk!"

Tamara made much of Ramona's Statue of Liberty, which she hadn't seen before. Ramona thought it was foolish, the fuss she made over it.

"It's just so out of place with the rest of your stuff!" Tamara exclaimed. "This majestic, enormous piece of kitsch in the middle of such a tasteful little home. Everything else is so traditional."

Leave it to Tamara to exalt a thing so commonplace. Ramona was irritated at her friend for noticing something about the house that she never had — a paradox, an apparent contradiction in Ramona's well-ordered environment. She commanded Tamara to put the damn thing back on the mantelpiece and come into the kitchen for soup.

After, she served them tea in Ramona senior's delicately flowered china.

"God, I haven't had tea in ages," blurted Tamara.

Ramona put her cup down. "Are you crazy?"

"I mean," she corrected herself, "of course I've had tea ... just not caffeinated. I'll be wired all day."

"You drink *decaffeinated* tea?" Ramona demanded.

"No, no ... of course not...." Tamara's hand suddenly darted forward and she seized a teacake and shoved it in her mouth.

"Well, what in God's name are you drinking?

"Earl ... eee."

"Swallow your food, for Pete's sake, Tamara."

"Herbal tea," Tamara confessed, swallowing.

Ramona shook her head and smiled.

"There's all sorts of lovely teas...." began Tamara.

"I'm sure there are, dear," Ramona soothed. Tamara was two years older than Ramona, but Ramona called everyone "dear."

"I'll bring you some. I've got a wonderful blend from Indonesia —"

"No, no. You keep that for yourself," said Ramona. She changed her tone to indicate the subject closed. "So I imagine you'll be extending your visit for a while now," she began.

"Hm?"

"With your dad's condition."

"Oh." Tamara's honest face folded up into its little expression of pain, again. "Yeah, Dad's gotten worse. There's nothing I can do, though."

"Well, at least you're able to be with him throughout the ordeal."

"Oh — wouldn't I love to."

"Well, what's stopping you?"

Tamara glanced up with a bewildered, irritating smile. "I've got to go back to work."

"My God, Tamara, you're father's dying."

"There's nothing I can do about that, Ramona."

"You can stay with him. For God's sake, it's bad enough you've been gallivanting all these years, never paying your family a second thought —"

"I've been working, Ramona!"

"Working!" Ramona snorted.

Tamara cocked her head. "What do *you* think I've been doing?"

"I think you've been doing exactly what you've pleased your entire life."

The women had been smiling at each other and speaking in pleasant tones the entire time, so it did not sound particularly abrupt when Tamara suggested they tidy up the china and return to the hospital. Ramona told her not to be ridiculous, that she would take care of the dishes when she came home that evening.

While she was gone, Cassie Ann had demonstrated sudden and surprising vigour by throwing a half-filled bedpan at one of the student nurses. It hit her square in the chest and knocked her to the ground, and Ramona discovered the young woman, wet and weeping, in the staffroom cradling her right breast.

"What did you do to her?" Ramona demanded.

"I didn't do anything. She told me to stop singing."

"Why were you singing?"

"I *wasn't* singing!"

"Show me your tit," said Ramona.

With the entire bottom half of her face quivering, the student nurse exposed herself. An ugly bruise was forming. The student nurse saw it and cried harder, like a child who suddenly notices she's bleeding.

"It's nasty," admitted Ramona.

"I didn't expect people to hurt me," the student nurse sobbed. "Nobody told me people would be hurting me."

Ramona suggested the student nurse take the afternoon off, more to get rid of her than to be kind. Self-pity turned Ramona's stomach. She went to check on Cassie Ann, in whose room an orderly was mopping up pee.

"Well, my darling, you're turning this place upside down, now, aren't you?"

The orderly looked up to see if she was talking to him. He was an old, feeble-minded man who had worked there for as long as she could remember, perhaps even back when Ramona was born.

"I don't care for people singing. Everybody singing their songs all day long," responded Cassie Ann.

The orderly wrung out his mop and shuffled off down the hall.

Ramona fussed around the room, straightening. "What songs would those be now?"

"La, la, la. Hm, hm, hm," stated Cassie Ann in a monotone. "The same songs over and over again, day in and day out. No one gets tired of them but me."

"I get tired of them as well," said Ramona. "La, la, la, hm, hm, hm."

"Well, this is it," agreed Cassie Ann.

Ramona was tickled with herself for playing along. She didn't often indulge in such foolishness.

She saw Tamara in her father's room a couple of days later, singing to him quietly. Ramona deliberately went on to glance at a few patients down the hall before returning to see if Tamara was still there. She was, and to Ramona's disappointment, she was still singing. "Leaving on a Jet Plane." Ramona loitered in the hall, impatient, because it was time for her break and she wanted to ask Tamara to join her for a cup of tea. Then she realized that she was the nurse, and had every right to barge into people's rooms whenever she liked.

"Mr. Rutledge, dear, how are you today?" She picked up his chart and examined it busily. "Tamara."

"Ramona! Why haven't you been to visit me before now?" Tamara's father demanded in his kind, weakened voice.

"Oh, we're awfully busy around here, as you well know, now, Mr. Rutledge."

As soon as decorum allowed, she had disengaged Tamara from her father and brought her to the cafeteria for tea.

"How's he been?" Ramona asked to be polite.

"Well — you saw his chart."

The fact was that Ramona had only pretended to read it, and otherwise had no idea of Mr. Rutledge's condition, as he was not on her ward. She nodded sympathetically. "When do you leave?"

"Sunday."

"Oh, you'll have to come for dinner Saturday."

"I really should be spending time with my mother."

"Bring your mother," Ramona decreed magnanimously.

"I've only got two more days home, Ramona, and I don't know when I'll be back again."

The last part of what she said was a line from "Leaving on a Jet Plane." "It will do the two of you good to get out," said Ramona.

Tamara had been twiddling with her hair in her usual, childlike way, but abruptly she raised both hands to either side of her head, taking her hair into handfuls, and yanked. It looked as if she were trying to pull her head open.

"I can't do it," she said.

"Well, then, fine," replied Ramona. "I see," she added.

Ramona waited for Tamara to either change her mind or offer effusive apologies, but Tamara sat yanking at her hair, letting there be silence. "I see," Ramona repeated, to prompt her.

"I don't see the point to this," said Tamara, releasing the hair on one side of her head in order to pick up her teacup, peer into its depths as if to read the future, and put it down again.

"What?" said Ramona.

"I won't be a martyr."

"What?" Ramona almost hooted at the word.

"I can't be the big person any more. It does no good. It changes nothing. I suffer. I suffer along, pointlessly."

"What, in God's name, are you talking about, Tamara, and when have you suffered a day in your life?"

Tamara smiled suddenly, not happily, but she let go of her hair. She leaned over and spoke to Ramona as if the latter were deaf. "I'm very sorry," Tamara articulated, rising.

And she didn't even call her friend to say goodbye before leaving on the jet plane. Ramona felt angry on behalf of poor Mr. and Mrs. Rutledge, having raised a daughter who would not even stay to help them towards death. She went to visit her own mother on Sunday, and yelled at her for keeping the house in such a mess and having the heat turned up so high. She cleaned the house from top to bottom, complaining all the while, as her mother sat in the front room playing hymns on her wheezy old organ and wiping occasionally at her eyes. Then she made them a casserole out of the groceries Ramona had brought from town and they ate it together for supper. She told her mother all about Tamara and how shoddily she treated her family and how she flew all over the world and you never knew where she would end up next.

"Where is Tamara these days?" Ramona's mother asked, once they had eaten dinner and she could speak to her daughter again.

"Indonesia," Ramona spat.

"What is she doing in Indonesia?"

"Who knows," said Ramona. "Getting a tan." She washed the dishes, broke a cup, cleaned it up, and then went home.

"La, la, la. Hm, hm, hm," Ramona announced to Cassie Ann every time she entered the room. Sometimes Cassie Ann responded, and sometimes she did not. One time the daughter was there when she said it, and smiled at Ramona quizzically.

"It's our own private joke," said Ramona, flustered.

The daughter seemed to approve of her mother having a private joke with the nurses. Ramona told her about the bedpan incident with the student nurse, playing up the girl's injury and subsequent trauma. Rather than being alarmed or guilty, Cassie Ann's daughter merely shook her head and related an incident of her own, when she was in her twenties, and a man she was giving mouth-to-mouth resuscitation to threw up. Then and there, three months before graduation, she'd almost quit the nursing program and enrolled in secretarial college, she claimed.

"Now you behave yourself, Mumma." The daughter smoothed Cassie Ann's hair and kissed her tenderly goodbye, but Cassie Ann was gazing out the window and humming, oblivious. The daughter turned to Ramona and smiled again. "It's certainly an improvement over the screaming and crying! I think she's adjusting well. You girls are so good with her." With that, the daughter flounced away, free and pleased.

Of course, not five minutes later, Cassie Ann realized her daughter had gone and began screaming and crying. Ramona watched her for a few moments, considering a sedative, as the old thing raved.

"Why, why, why? I wish, I wish, I wish!" Cassie Ann shrieked. Instead of going to get the sedative, or doing anything at all about it, Ramona sat down on a nearby chair and continued to watch. Everything about Cassie Ann's demeanour screamed impotence. She bashed her crumpled-paper fists against the yielding white bed. She flopped her head back and forth across the soft pillows. She was absolutely like a child throwing a tantrum, but even a child would have been able to do some kind of damage, to produce a result, however mindless. A spilled drink. A broken lamp. A bruised body. Today there wasn't even a bedpan to throw.

After a little while Cassie Ann broke down into weak sobs, and Ramona sat marvelling at herself and all the rare and precious time she was wasting. Nurse's time. Critical to her job was the ongoing awareness of how people depended on her to parcel out these moments of her life in the most useful and efficient way possible.

And yet an hour had passed during which Cassie Ann sobbed herself into exhaustion, not a tear having worked its way down into the innumerable gullies of her face. At last, Ramona witnessed Cassie Ann returning to herself, seeming to take note of her steel and grey surroundings as if she had only just arrived. It was almost a comical contrast to the wild way she had looked around moments before, like the world was on fire — one vast, encircling threat.

Ramona shifted in her chair and felt her back pop, and Cassie Ann, somehow uncommonly alert in her exhaustion, looked right at her.

"The devil has my soul," she sighed, quite matter-of-fact.

Ramona got up from the chair and straightened her skirt, looking around for anything else that might need straightening.

◇

In Disguise
as the Sky

◇

I AM A SADIST FOR DOING IT, but they have to learn. I give them test after test after test every week. They almost weep at the thought. There's no rules. They just have to keep practising, memorizing, testing and re-testing themselves.

I understand how it insults them, how the English language in general is an insult to reason with its *there, their,* and *they're,* its *it's* and *its.* "*I* before *e* except after *c*" and all that pointlessness. *Though* and *through* and *trough.* It's infuriating. They get angry at me. They demand: Why? And I'm a teacher, but because I am a teacher of a very insane and arbitrary science, the only answer I can give them is this — it's a child's answer: *Just because.*

And spoken to like children, they respond like children: Who say? *Who says,* I correct. *I don't know. Whoever made it up. Just some guy.* I don't feel like much of a teacher, saying things like that. But it's true. And thus do they come to understand what an embarrassment to English speakers our language really is. All of them leave the class feeling a good degree more contempt for me and my countrymen than they started with. That means I am doing my job.

On the last day of class I usually ask them to tell me a little bit about their own language, not for their own benefit, but because it's fascinating to me how much more rational they all seem. A Japanese student showed me how the characters for things were basically just drawings of them. A Thai student showed me how the little round heads on all the lovely, looping characters where what made up vowel sounds. The one Russian I ever taught merely spat at me: "Russia language make sense."

Russian makes sense, I told him. *You don't have to say 'Russian language,' it's implied.*

He rolled his eyes, as he had been doing all along. Over the semester, it becomes harder and harder for them to believe that this is the language of the most prosperous nation on earth, of the Internet, of the global marketplace. This is the one out of all the others, for all their beauty and simplicity, that's won out.

One, won.

But prepositions makes them angriest. At least for some things you have the handy little rules of thumb. The *i* before *e* stuff. Subject and object. It's "my friend and I" if it's the object, but "my friend and me" if it's the subject. That's a tricky one but you can learn it. You can study it and you can learn it. All I can do with prepositions is give them long, endless lists. *A secret between us. A story about a man.* Is it always a story *about* something? *Yes, that's right.* So then they go and write something like, "This is a story about Ernest Hemingway." *No, it's a story* by *Ernest Hemingway* about *an old man dying with his hat off in the rain.* But you said it was *always* a story *about* something. About *something* but by *someone.* So a book can only be about something or by someone? they ask with so much hope. *A book is an object. It can be* on *something,* off *something,* by *something....* But you said it could only be by *someone!* I don't know how they keep from killing me.

But they don't. They come to feel sorry for me because I am only a dumb representative of my dumb language. A dumb citizen of a dumb English-speaking country that should be clamouring to join up with the wealthy and fearsome realm next door, they think, but remains stubbornly sovereign, middle-income, and weak. They don't get it, because to them we are all the same. It's not like we're a bunch of Latvians on this side of the border, with Ukrainians on the other side. That's precisely how my Russian student put it to me. "You are all mongrels," he said. "You have no culture, why do you care? It is not as if you are a bunch of Latvians or something."

"Not as if you *were*," I corrected. Eye-roll.

I had taught them the word *mongrel* the week before. They loved it. They used it all the time after that. They loved having a word to express what it was about North Americans that had baffled them for so long. This blandness. This striving towards homogeneity. This relative indifference to immigrants, for example, people of all races and creeds. This relative indifference to our own families and communities. That I had moved across the continent away from mine and not yet dried up from despair.

But I like my country, if not my language. I like that we're not all a bunch of Latvians. They may have simple languages, but their nations are complicated. Indonesia, for example, is complicated. Yugoslavia is complicated. I like simplicity. I like that slogan, "Keep It Simple, Stupid," and would have it posted up in my classroom, if it weren't such an outlandish contradiction to what I teach. *Obscurify, students. Clutter. Complicate.* So I have it pinned up in my kitchen at home instead. In my apartment, I forget about the Byzantine world of English grammar. I get take-out food, everything in medium-sized portions. I watch television shows that were not created to be enjoyed by people with imaginations. I sleep on a futon. I don't dream.

In the office, two male voices are talking about something called "day-cake." One of them is my student, Kunakorn, from Thailand, and the other is someone I don't know, hanging around the desk like he works here. He probably does work here. This is such an irritating place to work that people quit and get hired all the time, so I am always running into people I don't know who are supposedly my co-workers.

Kunakorn says, "My favourite is day-cake," and my new co-worker replies that he is partial to day-cake as well. Then I remember what day-cake is. Kunakorn has a habit of making up his own words for objects when I'm not around to tell him what they are. He has an even worse habit of deciding that the word he makes up is more appropriate and easier to remember than the actual English word, once he's learned what it is. So he'll go for months, for example, refusing to call a basketball net anything other than a "sky-hole."

One of Kunakorn's pet peeves about North America is how much bread we eat. He's had some bad experiences with bread. When he first arrived here, his host-family served him nothing but sandwiches and hamburgers. Finally he just went out and bought a bag of rice and sat down and ate an entire pot of it himself. He thinks almost all the food we eat is a variation on the loaf of bread. Cinnamon buns, meat loaf, cookies, cake. To him it is all just bread. One time he was rhyming off a litany of such food to me, pretend-bread, he called it, bread products we Westerners irrationally gussy up in order to disguise its fundamental bread-character.

"Biscuits, scones," he said, impressing me with his baked-goods vocabulary. "Cake," he added. "Day-cake," he finished.

I told him there was no such word as *day-cake*, and he got frustrated. Kunakorn always claimed that he preferred to use the words that he made up because they made more sense. This was undeniable, but I insisted on correcting him nonetheless, because that was my job. That's the job of language. To impose arbitrary rules.

"Day. Cake," he repeated impatiently. "You often have in day."

"That's just regular cake!" I said.

"No, no! You don't have day-cake at night, that is difference. You can have regular cake at night."

"It doesn't make sense," I emphasized to him. Usually when his own personal vocabulary made sense, I would acknowledge it. I even praised him for his ingenuity sometimes, because he could come up with some quite reasonable substitutions. He called pillows sleeping bags, and sleeping bags out-blankets. You could not deny the logic.

But day-cake was nonsense, I told him. He gestured and jumped around trying to describe it to me, and finally I asked him to draw a picture on the board, which he did.

"It's a muffin," I said.

"Muh — "

"Muffin."

"Muh-vin."

"Muffin."

"Muffin. What 'muffin' mean?"

"It means that," I said, pointing to the board.

"But what it *mean?*" he repeated. "Day-cake?"

"No," I said. "It doesn't mean anything. It just means that." I pointed again.

Eye-rolls all around. That was their problem with English in a nutshell. It is no wonder Kunakorn refused to give up his own thoughtful creations for something so ridiculous-sounding.

So I come stampeding out from behind the partition where I'm photocopying lists of prepositions, hollering, "Muffin! Muffin! Muffin!" Kunakorn gives me a look as if his suspicion that I just make up all the craziness I drill into him day after day has been vindicated. He points with triumph at the new co-worker.

"He say 'day-cake.'"

"Why are you standing there talking about day-cake?" I say to the new guy.

The new guy is shorter than me, and about ten pounds lighter. He is absurdly overdressed to be sitting at the front desk. He looks like a boy who's been polished up for his first communion and I try not to wince.

But I do wince when I realize I've scared him. It is awful to scare a short man in a communion suit.

"Day-cake," he repeats. "It sounds nice!" He tries to be bright, breezy, the way people he's seen who work in offices in sitcoms always interact. Chipper, sardonic. Not jumpy and horrified at the sudden appearance of a tall woman with large breasts screaming "muffin."

That I know all this about him already is making me depressed and I want to go out and buy a coffee and walk around the block. First I have to make him feel more at ease, and quickly, or I will feel sick to my stomach all day long. I hunch my back so that my breasts won't further unnerve him and wag a finger at Kunakorn.

"This guy thinks he can just make up his own language and get accepted into Harvard Business School saying 'day-cake' for *muffin* and 'out-bed' for *sleeping bag* and God knows what else. It's our job to break him of this terrible habit!"

I make a half-assed gesture as if to chuck the new guy on the shoulder like the buddy I am, and the new guy smiles and lets his breath out. But then something terrible happens. I watch his face as he attempts to make it a perfect imitation of mine — the easy, co-conspirator grin meant to put him at ease. The fakeness on my face when transferred to his own magnifies itself about ten times over and my stomach contracts at the sight. No, I think. This guy cannot be this uncomfortable. I want to give him liquor.

I'm just about to rush hunchbacked out the door like an office Quasimodo when he says something nice, something that relieves me. It's nice because it's honest. He has forgotten himself for a moment.

"It's just so refreshing," he says, "to hear a different version of things every once in a while."

I turn around then because I want to smile at him again and be encouraging of unguarded moments like this, but already he has gone green. He picks up a pen and tries to twiddle it and ends up writing on his face, like the open book that he is. Clearly it's precisely such moments that he's desperate to avoid.

Now I'm going to feel sick to my stomach all day long. I walk around the block and can't drink my coffee. Everything I see exacerbates the situation. There is a man who sits on the corner every day surrounded by pigeons, asking people for change. Usually he is able to put on a brave face, crack jokes, say please and thank you to the passersby so they won't be intimidated or offended by him, but today must not have been a good day. Today he can't quite hold up the façade that he is just a regular Joe, a good, decent guy down on his luck, bearing ill will towards no one. As I'm walking towards him, he's still doing the please-and-thank-you thing, the obligatory have-a-nice-day, but already my antennae is out, he's sort of weaving, chanting the pleaseandthankyous and haveanicedays like cynical prayers, and finally, just as I'm passing, he bashes the back of his head against the building and howls:

"For the love of God and Jesus, people! I'm in pain!"

I am more like one of the pigeons at his feet than a pedestrian. The pedestrians alter their courses slightly, scarcely looking up, but me and the pigeons — the pigeons and me — we fly off in every direction.

At my apartment I classify this day as having been a Bad Day in my journal, taking note of the events that made it so. I do this every day, examining why it was good or bad and taking note of the events so that in the future I can try to recreate the good events and avoid the bad ones.

But the good days aren't really characterized so much by good events as lack of bad ones. I write that down in my journal. That is a little bit of wisdom for later on. I walk around my apartment for a while and eat some of my medium portions and repeat to myself, *Go to sleep, go to sleep,* which is meant to settle my stomach and calm me enough to sit and watch sitcoms before it's time for bed.

The first step is to remove yourself. I have students who come from, literally, the other side of the planet. If you took a long spike and drove it into the ground here, and it went all the way down the middle of the earth and out the other end, it would come out practically in their own backyard. But these same students, who had all the power to wrench themselves out of their huge families and their tiny communities and sit on a plane for fourteen hours, are the same ones who will sit in class weeping for days on end, and it's usually the same reason: *Because I miss my mother.* They will call their mothers every night, asking for news about their grandparents, siblings, cousins. When they hear that so-and-so has lost a hand in the factory, they cry. When they hear that so-and-so's daughter has ran away again, they cry. They come to class crying about one thing or another happening on the other side of the planet on a regular basis. But mainly their mothers, or lack thereof. My point is, they haven't removed themselves at all.

It is that intimacy that is the problem, I have determined this long ago. The intimacy of little towns and families. You cry because of the intimacy. It may as well have happened to you. The less intimate you are, the less it bothers you. That's what cities are for. That's what I thought cities were supposed to be for. But the city is becoming a disappointment to me.

It is not so much hands being cut off and daughters running away, in the city. It is more like this:

I was sitting in the park reading a book on a beautiful day in the summertime. People walked by me in couples, groups, and families. There was a little canteen close to where I was sitting and all the people stopped to get ice cream and popsicles.

But then a man in a white cap who didn't seem to be enjoying the sun very much came and sat down on the other end of the bench. He was huffing and puffing from his walk and just sat there for a few moments, wiping his face with his cap. He wore a terry-cloth shirt the same colour blue as the sky, and white pants, like his cap. If he had, for whatever reason, started to levitate and float off into the horizon, he would have blended in perfectly with the sky, like Winnie-the-Pooh had hoped to do one time, but failed.

The man kept glancing at the canteen and all the people coming and going to get ice cream and popsicles. He'd stare at the beach for a while, and then glance back at the canteen, as if to see if it were still there. I couldn't read at all at this point. Finally he heaved himself up and tottered over to the canteen to buy himself an ice cream. It was obviously difficult for him to walk, not because he was so fat, but he also had some kind of limp.

So then he sits down beside me again with a rocky-road ice cream and eats it in about five minutes.

Then, the glancing-back started up again. Gazing at the beach, glancing towards the canteen, elaborately casual. After another five minutes of this, he stood up again and staggered back towards the canteen.

And this is what he said then:

"I'll have another rocky-road, please."

And then he came and sat down beside me again, with his second ice-cream cone.

He did this four more times in the space of an hour and a half — gazing and glancing, convincing himself that no one was paying attention, working up his courage — and I remained cemented to the other side of the bench like one of those bronze statues they sometimes install in parks to blend in with the real human beings, not having turned a page since he arrived. My tailbone had started to ache and sweat was trickling down my sides, but I couldn't budge until he left. I couldn't risk giving the slightest hint that I knew exactly what was going on. It was unthinkable. It was unspeakable.

That's the sort of thing I mean.

When I talk to my mother on the phone, we have a very pleasant chat. She tells me about neighbours and relatives I don't even remember any more, but even so it is never anything too lurid or horrifying. There are lots of operations, but most of them are successful. Daughters and sons are always getting married to other people's daughters and sons, and then having babies. It washes over me. Then my father is allowed to speak and asks me how I'm doing and I tell him fine. Then he asks me if I need any money and I make a joke about how if I needed money, I wouldn't say I was fine. We laugh. We hang up. It wasn't always so painless, but over the years we've managed to lay down some unspoken ground rules. It took a while. It used to be like a game where you scored or lost points despite yourself. Now it is more like a little play.

✧

He's dressing in casual wear. Like after the first day on the job he went to the Casual Wear section at Eaton's and announced "office casual" to a salesgirl who decked him out from shoes to shirt. And she made him buy two shirts, three pairs of pants, and a couple of sweaters, all in coordinating colours to be mixed and matched throughout the week. And everything is ironed. And the brown sweater still has the tag. I shadow him around the office making small talk with a pair of scissors behind my back until one of the advisers simply calls out, "Nice tag, Sandy-boy," on her way to the bathroom, turning him green again and making me wish to nestle the scissors into the socket of her eye.

Even his name, Sandy. It's a description, like a dog's name. Scruffy. Fluffy. Makes you want to pet him. Weeks go by, and after Andrea has referred to him as Sandy-boy for the eleventh hundred time, I slam the photocopier and demand to know if he doesn't have any other names.

"Leopold is my second name," he tells me, quivering, because I've frightened him again.

"Jesus! That's it? Isn't Sandy short for anything?"

"Alexander," he shrugs.

"Alexander! You have a name like Alexander and you go around letting people call you Sandy? People could be calling you Alex. 'Alex, what time is the meeting? Phone call, line one.... Oh, thanks, Alex.' Doesn't that sound nice?"

"But my parents call me Sandy," he pleads.

"Your parents named you Alexander Leopold. Clearly they had some big plans. They just started calling you Sandy when you were a baby and couldn't get out of the habit."

"But everybody calls me Sandy. It's on my driver's licence."

I start calling him Alex all the time so he'll get used to it. I even refer

176

to him as Alex when he's not around, and nobody knows who I am talking about. I make a special point of calling him Alex around Andrea.

"His name's Sandy."

"No," I correct. "His name's Alexander. Sandy is just a nickname."

"I asked him what his name was, he told me Sandy."

Andrea is a hard nut. She is one of those disquieting people who gives off an air of knowing how everything should be at all times. She has all the answers. She's an adviser, as I've said, and one of the few people in this place who is qualified for, and good at, her job. She was born to advise.

"Don't you think Alex is a better name?" I beg her.

"Yes. But I don't think it's *his* name. I think his name is Sandy."

Andrea calls things as she sees them. She has no vision.

I have come home from work some days and written in my journal about Andrea that she represents the way the world is. There are all sorts of holes dug into the world in certain shapes and sizes and people are born and shoved into those holes whether they care for them or not. Then they just grow into the shapes and sizes of the holes. And then everybody marvels about how those particular people are perfect for those holes, and isn't it great how perfectly things work out in this world of ours.

You can do the same thing with pumpkins. We had a pumpkin patch in our garden and my little brother used to grow them into whatever shapes he wanted. He'd put a band around the middle and make them grow into figure eights, for example. Later on, he saw in a farming magazine where you could buy little masks to put over the growing pumpkins, and when you took it off the pumpkins would have faces. He would line them up at Hallowe'en and everyone would wonder how he did it. And he'd tell them: *They just grew like that.*

And this being an Andrea kind of world, a lot of people believed him. They thought: If they exist, then that just must be how it is.

It seems a very passive way to live your life, and yet people like Andrea are the most stubborn I've met.

My brother was always doing things like that. How many boys do you know to whom it has occurred to direct the growth of pumpkins? He was a real original, my mother used to say. A genuine authentic, she used to say. She would desperately try to come up with all sorts of upbeat expressions to describe him. He was another one who liked to hear a different version of things every once in a while.

The Thai students have taken to Alex. They sense that he is like them — horrified by everything around him. Kunakorn often tells me of his first night in this country. He was bussed to the university after his sixteen-hour flight and deposited in a dorm room, given instructions in English, and left alone. He could speak not a word of English, of course, and was hungry. He took his key, screwed up his courage, and ventured out into the quad where young, drunken North Americans were celebrating frosh week. He bumped into a few staggering students and nobody was kind to him when they realized he was a foreigner as they were all intoxicated not so much by alcohol but by being together in a group with people exactly like themselves. So he was shoved by some guy in a backwards baseball cap who called him "loser." He remembers this word quite clearly, thinking it was maybe a pejorative North American term for *Asian*, and fell into a girl who shrieked and spilt her beer all down his back.

At long last Kunakorn arrived at some sort of all-night campus convenience store and purchased the largest bag of the most filling-looking food he could find. It was a bag of Wonderbread. He made his way back to his room and padded his stomach with it so he could sleep. He couldn't believe how utterly bland it was. His first taste of North America.

And then it was on to the sandwiches and hamburgers of his homestay family. Thus was an unhealthy fascination born. He'll come into class every week announcing yet another bread-product he's discovered.

"Cracker."

"Oh, come on, crackers?"

"Yes, cracker. Flour, water. Bake."

"But that's like saying chips are bread."

That gives him pause. "Maybe chip *are* bread!" At lunchtime, he scurries off to investigate.

"No," after he returns. "Potato." He crosses his arms triumphantly. Don't even get Kunakorn started on potatoes. The potato is the second bizarre thing we eat in far too many forms, according to him. I have promised to bring in mashed potatoes at the end of the semester to show them all how lovely these grey lumps from underneath the earth can be when properly prepared.

"Comfort food," I teach them. "Food that makes you feel warm and safe. Perhaps your mother gave it to you when you were a child." I make a list on the board of all the foods that do it for me. Mashed potatoes, number one. With cream and butter and garlic, oh my God. The garlic was my brother's idea when he was fourteen and getting more creative with every passing minute. We all thought he was crazy. My father wanted to know if he was turning into some kind of Eye-talian. *Trust me*, he said. *Trust my palate*. My father couldn't stand him using words like *palate*. But no one could deny the potatoes were great that way.

Peanut butter and jelly sandwiches, I write. Kunakorn exhales with disgust. Boiled eggs. They all nod at that one. Pumpkin pie. Blank stares.

Then they all have to make their own lists. Kunakorn writes:

rice
rice
rice
rice!

"Rice is every bit as bland as bread!" I protest, a patriot.

Kunakorn looks at me like my father at my brother saying *palate*. "Noooo! Rice *heaven!*" he croons.

So the Thai students take Alex out for Chinese food all the time. They pay for him, they sort of make a pet of him. There is a syndrome among English as a Second Language teachers that it reminds me of. Some ESL teachers have no life and no friends, just like lots of people in lots of other jobs. And when they start teaching foreign students, they are given the kind of attention and regard that no self-respecting North American would ever deign to lavish upon someone so low on the social scale as a teacher. So their students become their social circle. Suddenly, the teacher finds him or herself popular and beloved in a way he or she has never known. It gets messy, obviously. Students start expecting their marks to reflect the goodwill they've shown. Everyone's around the same age, so teachers start sleeping with students. Lines are crossed.

That's kind of what's happening with the students and Alex except there is no power imbalance at play, so I suppose it is benign. Alex has some friends, friends who aren't instinctively aware of things like his trip to Casual Wear. Friends who don't tack "boy" to the end of his name. Friends who have their own dangling metaphorical price tags. I am happy for him. But I cannot convince them to stop calling him Sandy.

❖

I still have to keep careful watch. His collar is always flipping up and I have to put it down for him. Once when he returned from the bathroom with his fly open, I had to stop myself from going over and doing it up. He's getting used to working around breasts, but the office is still riddled with female landmines, full of grown women who aren't as protective as I am. Andrea came raging towards me one time, demanding to know if I could give her a spare tampon "before I start gushing into my shoes." I tried to cover his ears, but it was too late.

"You're always fussing over that boy," says Andrea to me.

"He's not a boy," I say. "Don't call him 'boy.'"

"People will think you're in love with him." I look up at her and see that she's grinning. Of course she knows that nobody is ever going to think that.

"You need a man," Andrea says. "Why isn't there a man in the picture?"

A man in the picture. She puts it this way every time she asks me about it. Apparently there is a picture, and there is supposed to be a man in it. The hole in the ground that was dug out for me is of such a shape that there is supposed to be a man there as well.

"What would be your perfect man?" Andrea persists.

Well, let's see. I write a pointed response to Andrea in my journal since I'm incapable of doing it in person. My perfect man, Andrea, the man I want, is a character in a story I have been told ever since I was capable of understanding stories. He is big and strong. He is kind and compassionate. He is everywhere and all-powerful. He does not let bad things happen to good people. He is merciful. He is perfect. He can do it all. He takes you in his arms and wipes the tears from your eyes. You forget about everything. It's just a story I was told, and it wasn't fair to me, and it sure isn't fair to men, but this is the man I've been told about my whole life, so this is the man I'm waiting for. In the meantime, someone has to take care of Alexander.

At the end of the semester, everybody brings their favourite food, and we always invite the office staff to come and have some. All the women come trundling in, sampling and exclaiming over the exotic dishes, and I stand there looking around for Alex until I realize they've left him to answer the phones.

"Where's Alex? Where's Alex?" I keep saying. They pretend not to know who I'm talking about.

Another Thai student, Maliwan, comes up to me, taps me on the shoulder, and then takes a huge step back. That is how she asks for my attention, like I'm carrying a two-by-four and could whirl around and catch her on the side of the head. She's one of the most timid people I've ever met. I poke her on her own shoulder a few times to demonstrate how annoying it is.

"Just say my name. Don't poke."

"Sorry. Sorry. You are stress out."

I taught them "stressed out" last week. They liked it. *Stressed out* and *mongrel.*

"No, I'm not. Why don't you go get Alex?"

"Why you call Sandy Alex?"

"Why *do* you —"

"Why *do* you call Sandy Alex?"

"Sandy is his nickname."

Maliwan knows what *nickname* means, because she used to have one too. When she first arrived in Canada, she tried to convince me her nickname was Sharon Stone.

"Ah," says Maliwan, remembering how I refused to call her Sharon Stone. "You don't like nicknames."

I decide to just let her believe I don't like nicknames.

After much prodding, Andrea finally agrees to pile up a plate for herself and go back to the office so that Alex could come and get some food. The greeting that rises up from the Thai students takes me aback. They swarm him. Maliwan takes him from dish to dish, explaining what everything is and what it has in it.

"I usually can only eat shrimp if it's battered," I hear him tell her.

I glower at the office staff before they can react.

"You are allergic," Maliwan prompts.

"That's right!" Alexander replies, beaming.

I'm exhausted after the party, but can't keep myself from following him around trying to make him take the leftovers home. He won't take it. He keeps telling me that he's a meat-and-potatoes man.

"I'm a meat-and-potatoes man," he tells me. "I don't like my meals fancy,"

"Listen," I step in close, fed up. "I know things about you. You are not a meat-and-potatoes man. You eat your mother's cooking, or else you eat an exact replica of your mother's cooking in fast-food form. You're afraid of anything else. You're not some rugged food-individualist. You leave here at night and you go to Burger King. You are destroying yourself."

It's too much. His face like a landslide. I regret it the moment it's out.

"I'm allergic —" he starts to protest, but I smother it with a hug. I long to suffocate us both.

◇

Now I have three weeks off before the semester starts again, the second week of which my mother is coming to visit. In the meantime, the only thing to do is update my journal and go visit the doctor to complain about the awful, hideous, monstrous nightmares I have been having. In fact, I haven't been having nightmares at all, but I have started dreaming from time to time, and that is enough. A pumpkin patch with faces. All sorts of different expressions. She gives me a powerful drug that will blast it from my head.

Usually this time of year I would go to the park with a book but I haven't been able to do that since seeing the man in disguise as the sky.

The school is late with my pay as usual, so it gives me an excuse to drop by the office from time to time and pretend to kick up a fuss about it while making sure everyone is being nice to Alex. Maliwan and Kunakorn are always hanging around, waiting to take him to lunch.

"Is Maliwan your girlfriend?" I ask Kunakorn one day when we're kidding around and feeling chummy. These are the sort of questions I put to students point-blank, as they don't tend to understand our inane North American euphemisms. *Do you two have a thing? Are you guys going out? Are you seeing one another?* But Kunakorn looks at me like I've uttered the most obscure one of all.

"No! I...." he stumbles.

"Boyfriend?"

"No! Not boyfriend! I go ... with Maliwan...."

"You go out?"

"To lunch! I just go with Maliwan and Sandy...."

"You're just friends," I help, thinking I shouldn't have put him on the spot.

"Yes! But what word? Thai friend. There is word...."

"'Friend' is good enough." I try to calm him down, but Kunakorn is not the sort of person who can tolerate knowing he doesn't know something.

"I will find the word and tell you," he promises me.

He calls me at home at three in the afternoon. They know they are not supposed to call me at home unless they are having some sort of grammar crises, but they always do anyway, usually at night, in the middle of their parties, in order to settle bets about the meaning of words and idioms.

It so happens I am still in bed at three in the afternoon, unused to not having to go to work, and unable to muster up enough imagination, thanks to the anti-nightmare pills, to think of anything else worth doing. When the phone rings, it's as if my brains are lightly spread out across the pillow, and I have to mentally gather them up together in my head before I can figure out what the sound means and how I am supposed to respond to it. I pick it up on the seventh or so ring.

"Hello?"

"*Chaperone*," says Kunakorn.

I'm distracted when my mother comes, wanting to check on him. I had taken him to dinner at a steakhouse after talking to Kunakorn and encouraged him to eat as much meat and potatoes as he wanted. I'd talked to him like he was one of my students: *Is Maliwan your girlfriend?* He didn't turn green this time, but baby-girl pink. And he smiled. *Is she your first girlfriend?* A pointless question, as obviously she was. And of course he told me she wasn't and I was so happy I pretended to believe him and apologized for saying he went to Burger King all the time.

"It's true though," he admitted. "That's the kind of food I like, I can't help it."

"No, you can't," I agreed. "You should eat whatever makes you happy." I gave him my home phone number in case he ever needed anything.

It only occurred to me afterwards how painful and nasty and miserable first girlfriends and boyfriends could be and that was why I kept wanting to get rid of my mother and head down to the office with some kind of picnic basket loaded down with pre-emptive comfort.

I had spent a week doing a sort of tailor-made meditation in preparation for my mother's visit. Writing lists in my journal of everything I could think of. Cloud formations, for example. Cumulus, stratus. Berries. That was a good one, I could think of so many different kinds. I got down to Saskatoon berries and salmon berries and then huckleberries, which I wasn't even sure existed, and chokecherries, which I wasn't sure qualified. The berries list was a couple of pages long. Then I tried doing a list about the names of famous dogs, which at first I thought was a great idea — Lassie, Old Yeller, the Littlest Hobo — but of course I inevitably found myself writing the word *Sandy* and realized my brain had ambushed me again.

◇

My mother is concerned that I no longer go to church and feels we should go together, but I tell her I don't know where any churches are, which is a lie. I walk past a Catholic church every day on my way to work, situated right alongside of a Catholic elementary school called Our Lady of Perpetual Help. A big white Mary perches upon the school's rooftop like a slender owl, looking down at all the little children in their uniforms, running back and forth behind the chain-link fence.

My mother says that's fine, she will find a church for us to go to together. I tell her we won't have time. I spread out before my mother catalogues, pamphlets, brochures, and outline for her all the activities I have planned for the week. Walking tours. Suspension bridges. Native art exhibits. High tea. Ferry rides.

Oh, my darling, she says. I just want us to spend some time together.

Very sincere, my mother. Warm, melting eyes. She's not lying, that's really what she wants. She want to get inside my apartment and see me in it. Open up my cutlery drawers, poke around in the cupboards. Cook meals with my pots and pans. Buy me things, to go in the apartment, so she'll always feel she's there, inside my life.

There is no alcohol in my apartment, so she takes it upon herself to empty out a cupboard and stock me a little bar — wine and gin. I don't play along.

"But, Mother. I don't drink."

"Everybody should have a little wine and gin on hand, my darling!" Festive. Trying to get that festive feeling in the air. Get things uncorked.

This is her plan: To get inside my apartment and get me drunk. To get me talking.

I wake every morning at six and drag her off my futon and out into the city. We ride the trolley around the park and go on a bird tour and listen to a lecture about soapstone carving. Lunches and dinners are tricky. She'll go for the wine every time. After she finishes the first glass, it's: "Oh, may as well get a half-litre. What do you say, my darling?"

"None for me, thanks, Mother."

"But it's your holiday! Live a little!"

"We've got the suspension bridge next. You don't want to be falling off."

Next tactic: melting eyes, trembling lips. "Let me do something nice for you, you work so hard, I see you so rarely."

"I'm having a wonderful time, Mother." Thoughtful pause. "Aren't you?" Searching look, borderline hurt. Two can play at this game.

The day is mine. By nightfall, she is so wiped out her bedtime belt of gin knocks her off her feet. I open up my journal to gloat over the victory and strategize for tomorrow. Walk on the beach in the morning followed by a lunchtime concert at the university. Then a sudden wave comes over me, my eyes glaze. Exhaustion, from keeping my guard up all day. I'll use the concert time to think about how to spend the afternoon and evening.

I dream about scooping the guts out of a jack-o'-lantern with my hands and wake up and vomit all over the couch. My mother comes rapidly tip-toeing out of the bedroom, face slick with Mary Kay night cream. It shimmers in the grey, pre-dawn light. She says, "Oh! My darling!"

I'm lying on my back shuddering and start to say, "Isn't it supposed to absorb into your skin?" before turning my head and vomiting again. My mother goes to wipe off her face and put on some clothes and take care of me.

Stomach flu, like when I was a child. I vomit throughout the day. My mother goes out and buys consommé, crackers, and rum and honey. To make me hot toddies, she says, when I'm better.

"I knew we were pushing ourselves too hard," she mutters loudly to herself in the kitchen. "I'm an old homebody anyway. I'm happy to just hang around the house and spend time together!"

She is in heaven. Myself, on the couch with ginger ale and Mr. Dress-up on television, appalled by what my body has done to me. It was on her side all along. Nausea keeps me prone. My mother can sit and talk to me, her hand around a cool glass of gin, for hours on end.

It is so good, to have this time with me. How lucky for this to have happened while she was here! What would I have done if she hadn't been? No, really, what would I have done? Did I have someone to call? Didn't I get nervous, living all by myself? A young women in the city? It would make her nervous. Oh yes, it seems like a very secure building. I don't go out by myself at night, do I? Oh, my darling, I really shouldn't. Of course, I must have friends I can always call. Not that I've introduced her to any of them. Haven't I met any men? Great big city like this? Still no man in the picture?

Glass of gin number two: It is hard, having me so far away, for both her and my father. They feel so removed from my life. They want to be of support to me, but how is it possible, my being so far away? If I moved back home, they could be of so much more help. There is lots of work back home these days, the economy has picked up quite a bit, had I heard? She could help me find an apartment, we could shop together for things. It would mean so much to them, now that they are getting on. The years just seem to fly by. The house so big and empty. Nothing left but memories. Not all good. And after all, I am all they have left in the world now that....

"This isn't fair," I manage to gasp, gripping the empty ice-cream bucket she's given me in case I can't make it to the toilet. "This isn't fair, Mother."

"I'm sorry, my darling," she murmurs, adjusting the cloth on my head. "You're sick. We can talk about these things later." And she wobbles off into the kitchen for gin number three, having granted me a temporary reprieve.

By evening, I'm finally able to sip some consommé and sit up to watch a weepy women's movie with Bette Midler that she's rented for us. We've both lost count of the glasses of gin and my mother sits with a roll of toilet paper on her lap, snuffling. Every now and then she pats a spot beside the toilet paper, inviting me to put my head there like when I was a girl. I ignore her. I have spent the entire day at her mercy and have dropped all pretence of civility.

Weirdly, the phone rings, the first time since she's been here. She jumps up and runs all around the apartment trying to find it, which I allow. Finally she discovers it in the bedroom, alongside of the futon she's been sleeping on, and drags it out to me on the couch.

"It's a boy!" she declares, like someone has just given birth. "He says his name is Sandy! What a nice name!"

"Hi, Alex," I say into the phone, glaring at her. She pretends to have gone back to Bette Midler, a huge mound of tissue pressed against her nose.

He is confused about Maliwan, and keeps telling me he doesn't understand her culture. It is such a different culture, he says, I don't know what's going on half the time. I don't understand her way ... the ways of her culture. After listening to him ramble for a few minutes, I figure out what he means by culture and take over.

"First of all, Alexander, calm down."

"I'm calm!" he protests.

"Calm down!"

"What's wrong? I'm very calm." I can picture his face arranging itself into a look of sitcom tranquillity. Convincing himself.

"I'm sick," I fret.

"Oh, I'm sorry ...."

"No, I just mean ... I want to help. I'm just really sick."

"I should go." He sounds as if he's getting farther and farther away. He sounds as if he's standing in front of a well into which he plans on doing a forward roll as soon as he gets off the phone.

"Alex, Alex? Come and see me tomorrow, okay?"

"You're sick," he despairs.

"I'll be better tomorrow. Come and see me at around eleven."

"I'm sorry to —"

"Shut up! Come!" I give him my address. I hang up the phone and close my eyes. My stomach gurgles a warning.

My mother shifts on her side of the couch. "Visitors at last?"

"Tomorrow's Sunday," I inform her, eyes closed, seeking strength. "You won't want to miss church."

On the Lord's own day the nausea has subsided somewhat, but I'm weak like I've never been. I'm able to put on clothes for Alex's visit, but can't abide the thought of a bath or shower. My mother offers to help with a sponge bath, going as far as to try and ease me off the couch, and I flail my arms at her, grunting.

"You're a regular bear," she observes, snapping open a pink Mary Kay compact to touch up her eyes. "I'll say a prayer for you." I've scarcely spoken to her all morning. Conserving energy.

Alex shows up at eleven on the dot, toting a box of Dunkin' Donuts that I can't even look at. Oblivious, he starts shoving a Boston cream into his mouth, explaining that he hasn't had breakfast yet. I try to be indulgent. He is a man in pain. I avert my head while he finishes the doughnut, but as soon as the last blob of cream disappears, he goes to work on another one. I look up at the ceiling while he talks and chews and swallows. He has a large cup of coffee as well. He keeps forgetting it is too hot to drink and takes one searing, painful sip after another. I envision clouds and berries as he talks.

Maliwan is seeing an *old man*, he says. Some disgusting, probably married, businessman who saw her looking at sunglasses in the mall and bought her a pair. She goes with him to clubs and restaurants. He buys her dresses. She just told Alex this, one day. They were sitting on the beach with Kunakorn and she looked at her watch and said: Now I must visit Andrew.

"Now I must visit Andrew!" he repeats. "And Kunakorn just sits there with me! Why does she need a chaperone with me and not with Andrew?"

"Did you ask?"

"Yes. That's how I found out he was *old*. Kunakorn just waves his hand and goes, 'He old man.'"

"He didn't use a verb?"

"What?"

"Kunakorn. He's always dropping his to-be verbs. He told me he'd practise. Did you ask Maliwan about it?"

"She says she doesn't need a chaperone with Andrew because he doesn't count. He's too old to count as a boyfriend. She says he's more like an uncle."

"But you count as a boyfriend?"

"Yeah."

"Well, that's good."

"Yeah, but it's crazy!"

"Have you told Maliwan how you feel?"

"I don't know what to say! Maybe it's a Thai thing."

"I don't think it's exactly a Thai thing." I don't really know what kind of thing it is. I decide that it's beside the point.

"How do you feel about Maliwan?" I ask. He looks up at me in sudden fear. It's as if I've inquired: How would you like a punch in the face? Then the ersatz, sitcom casualness settles over his pasty features and he leans back and takes a wincing sip of coffee.

"You know," he says, draping his arms across the back of the couch, pretending like his mouth isn't full of blisters, "she's nice. I like her."

I know all right.

In the twenty-five minutes before my mother gets back, I develop and outline a plan. First, he has to find out how Maliwan feels about him. Is she just playing around or what?

"Because, if you're serious, Alex — *if*— then you have to let her know. Are you serious?"

"I don't know."

"Well, if you don't know, then you can't expect her to know. And there's no reason for her not to go out with as many old men as she likes."

"But —"

"There's this thing called commitment, Alex, and it sounds to me like that's what you're looking for."

"I don't know! It's all so serious!"

"This is grown-up stuff. You can't just ask a woman to stop seeing whoever she wants to see and not give her a good reason."

"But I don't know if I have a good reason. I just don't want her to."

"Then you have to think up a better reason than that."

"Like what?"

"Tell her you want to *explore* a commitment."

"Explore —"

"A commitment."

"You mean, go steady?"

From what era is this child? "Yes, yes, for God's sake, just tell her you want to go steady and see what she says."

"But what if she says no?"

"It's better to know that now before you get too involved." Listen to me. The endless thumbings-through of waiting-room women's magazines over the years has really paid off. I am some kind of relationship-savant.

"But I don't want her to say no," he sulks.

The front door rattles. My mother is home. My instinct is to leap off the couch and hurl my body against the door to keep her from Alex, but the attempt amounts merely to my standing up, experiencing a whirling head-rush, and collapsing back down onto the couch.

"You have to go now, Alex," I hiss.

Alex looks around. It's like a bedroom farce all of a sudden, my burly husband about to burst in and catch us.

"Oh, hello!" chirps my mother.

"Alex has to go now," I say, shoving him off the couch with my foot.

"I'm the mother!" says my mother, holding out her hand. Alex wipes the icing sugar off one of his and shakes it for her.

Beads of sweat bloom across my back and between my shoulder blades at the sight of them touching. "Leave him alone!" I bark, enraged and panicked.

"She hasn't been well," confides my mother, lightly placing her hand on his shoulder to torment me further. I can see Alex responding already to her sweetness, her innocent dusting of Mary Kay, her prim, motherly scarf tucked into her collar. Red Riding Hood and the Wolf, decked out like Grandma. I breathe through the knot in my chest.

"Alex," I say. "I'm going to throw up all over the place in a minute. Give me a call in a few days, okay?"

"I'll leave you the doughnuts," he says generously, bidding a hasty retreat.

My mother picks up the box after he's gone. "There aren't any doughnuts left," she sniffs.

One more day until she goes home. I am still very weak. The hour with Alex and the handful of horrific moments he spent in the company of my mother have sent me into a relapse. The fever returns and my mother has to wrap me in towels to keep the couch from wringing with sweat. I sleep until dinnertime and dream of the fat man floating up into the sky with his ice-cream cone, blending right in. I wake to the deceptively comforting smell of consommé. My mother sashays into the living room, working on a glass of wine, one in a series of who knows how many. My suspicion is a few, because she starts in immediately.

"What a nice boy, that Sandy boy was."

"His name is Alex. Didn't you hear me calling him Alex the whole time he was here?"

"He's very young."

"Yeah, he's like twenty." I speak rapidly, trying to put the topic to rest. "I work with him. He's going through everything at once. First job, first girlfriend. I'm trying to help him manoeuvre his way through."

"He's the sort of boy you want to help," she agrees. "I just took one look at him and I wanted to take him in my arms." The sheen of her eyes starts to wobble a bit. Brimming. She must be close to polishing off the bottle. "You know who he reminds me of —"

"Stop," I say.

"Well, you do, though. Don't tell me you haven't noticed."

"Stop. Off limits."

"But then, I get so lonesome for him — I think I see him everywhere —"

"Stop! Out of bounds!"

She keeps talking and I keep hollering sports expressions at her: "Foul! Penalty! You're out!" But she keeps on and I run out of sports words. The next thing I know, I'm hollering my lists.

"It's been five years and you never want to — "

"Cumulus!"

"The priest says that after a loss families need to —"

"Boisenberry! Saskatoon!"

"I know that you blame —"

"Pineapple! I bet you didn't know that was a berry, did you? Famous dogs! Benji! The one on 'The Little Rascals'! Sandy!"

"I haven't seen you in over a—"

"Sandy!"

"Why don't you ever let me *talk?*" she shrieks, and throws down her drink. I cross my arms. She jumps up to get a towel, ashamed of herself. She's been both wasteful and sloppy. Failing to live up to her own standards of motherhood. Shamed into silence. Victory.

◇

The next week is spent recovering from my holiday. It's slow going. I remain on the couch, absorbing televised reality, where nothing too evil happens to anybody and everyone is both cool and lovable. Alex calls to give me updates. Maliwan was pleased with the idea of going steady. At first she didn't believe him, that he would want to explore a commitment "with Thai girl," but somehow he convinced her of his sincerity. The old man with the money is now out of the picture. I tell him I am happy for him. I have dreams of Alex wafting slowly, safely up into the sky, waving bye-bye to me as he disappears into the blue. I sleep and sleep. The whole ordeal has left me spent.

My mother leaves without trying to make me talk any more, but she isn't quite able to keep herself in check at all times. So I have to show her something, to make her stop. I have to give her a small taste of what it would be like if I did start talking. She strides about the apartment, gathering up her belongings, mumbling, clucking, shaking her head from time to time.

"What are you saying, Mother? Say it out loud and strong, belt it out, Mother."

"I'm just sorry to have to tell your father we haven't made any progress," she clucks, sad-chicken-like.

"What makes you think I want to make any progress?"

She stops to shoot me a pious look that outrages me so much I sit up. "It's a terrible thing to hold a grudge," she intones.

"A beautiful boy," I say.

"What?"

"A beautiful, blue-eyed boy who liked pumpkins."

Her mouth falls open, thinking the walls are coming down at last.

"A beautiful boy who liked to hear a different version of things once in a while."

"Yes?"

"A genuine authentic."

Her bottom lip starts to work.

"A real original."

"Stop, now."

"Only one thing to do with a boy like that."

"All right."

"Pull his wings off." I make a gesture like I am plucking the petals from a flower. With each pluck I enunciate one word. "Tear. Him. Limb. From. Limb."

"That's enough," she says behind her hands.

"I agree," I agree.

With that, the last of my energy is spent. Pushing my mother all the way back to the other side of the continent. She kisses my cheek when the taxi comes.

"I hope you feel better, my darling. It was a lovely visit."

I've won. I'm beat.

That's an expression it took a long time for my students to understand. *I'm beat.* You're what? *Beat. Like when someone beats you at a game.* Beat by who? *Beat by whom.*

Beat by whom? *Nobody. Just beat. Whipped. Tired.* Shouldn't it be beaten? *The expression is "I'm beat."* But nobody has beaten you? *Not necessarily.*

Back at work, the beat feeling doesn't go away. I tell everyone I've been sick. The students bring me a variety of home remedies. Andrea prescribes a man. Put some colour in your cheeks. Good for what ails ya, she says, yukking it up, embarrassing Alex. Maliwan comes for Alex every day at lunch, Kunakorn not always in tow. Apparently Alex has proven himself a gentleman. They stand at the elevator holding hands. They are like kittens. Andrea extends a long finger down towards the back of her throat whenever they leave the room.

"Don't you think they're sweet?" I demand. Andrea has two of those "Love Is ..." posters hanging in her office, for God's sake. You'd think she'd eat it up. Instead she pronounces, "Too sweet." Grimly, a hard-nosed realist.

"They're happy!" I argue.

"They're not happy," Andrea contends. "They're blissed-out."

"Well, so *what?*"

"Icarus," she answers to my surprise, tossing her head towards the sky like he's actually up there waving a red flag.

Things get back to normal and I'm grateful. I work, come home, eat medium portions, watch television. Take notes in my journal about what is easy and what is hard. Take care the next day to avoid whatever was hard. The bus was hard one day because I saw the fat man from the park in his white cap struggling to climb the steps and making everybody wait and feel resentful of him. He was sweaty, too, and you could see the loathing on people's faces. So I leave the apartment an hour early and walk to work for the rest of the week.

I have to be easy on myself. I exchange pleasantries with Alex and avoid Andrea. I get engrossed in genuinely fascinating conversations about the future-possible with Kunakorn. He is in the highest level now and prides himself on his knowledge. Kunakorn is like a grammar textbook — he can rhyme off all the rules, do all the exercises flawlessly, but he still walks around dropping his to-be verbs all over the place and using "in" for "on" and "beside" for "under." He brings muffins in the morning, for a joke, knowing I will get agitated by his conversational sloppiness at some point. Then he'll hold out a muffin to me.

"Comfort food," he'll say.

Maliwan is in the same class and would be failing dramatically if it wasn't for Kunakorn's ongoing tutelage, and perhaps a bit of cheating, which I overlook. Maliwan is basically on holiday, sent over by her family to obtain the fastest, cheapest ESL certificate going before returning to Thailand to help run their factory. It is odd to think of how much more money than I — the privileged North American — Maliwan must have. She lives with two other girls in a $15,000 apartment and goes shopping for clothes every day at lunchtime and skiing on the weekend. But she shows up dutifully for class every day because she knows if she misses more than two she's out of the program and her parents will yank her back home to the other side of the world.

So it's odd when she misses one class in the middle of the semester, but downright troublesome when she misses a second. Kunakorn promises me he'll check in with her after class.

"Tell her, if she's sick, it's no big deal — she just needs a doctor's certificate," I say.

The next day Alex calls in sick and Kunakorn shows up with extra muffins.

"How is Maliwan?" I ask.

"Thai," he says, picking walnuts off the tops.

"What?"

"Thailand," he corrects himself, using the English term. He hadn't heard me properly. He thought I said "where," not "how."

The way Kunakorn tells it, one of Maliwan's roommates, a friend of the family's, called them up and told them Maliwan was planning to marry a Canadian. Apparently, the roommate had the idea that "going steady," which Maliwan constantly bragged about, meant the same thing as being engaged, or else she just decided one thing would lead to the next. To make matters worse, she got Alex mixed up somehow with Andrew, the rich old man, and told them Maliwan's paramour was in his sixties. The parents believed the roommate and told Maliwan to come home. It sounded to me like the roommate, who worked for her visa as a hostess in a restaurant, had merely tired of watching wealthy, twenty-year-old Maliwan having the time of her life.

"So she's just gone?"

Kunakorn looks at his watch. "Bangkok, now." He leans on his hands and puffs out his cheeks. "Sandy," he remarks, not bothering to try and find the words.

◇

Sandy takes the whole week off. I am grateful. So grateful I actually find myself talking to God again from time to time, muttering quiet words of appreciation in the bathroom or waiting in line for a coffee. It is such a peaceful week as we prepare for mid-terms and I walk to work with my eyes straight ahead, focused on large, blank buildings in the distance with windows like mirrors. Even the bum who cried out on the corner last semester is nowhere in sight these days. It's quiet and warm, the weather patchy, a little bit cloudy, a little bit sunny, not too much of either. Even. It is a good week. One of the best weeks I've had.

Another week goes by. Sandy, I tell myself, is licking his wounds. Taking some time off. Coming to terms with his emotions. All these inane, comforting euphemisms I come up with. I realize I don't brace myself when I push open the door to the office any more, expecting to see him doing battle with the photocopier or barely defending himself from Andrea or turning green at the sight of someone's exposed bra strap. The ease of knowing I won't be called upon to extinguish any flare-ups of mortification.

My parents haven't called since my mother's visit so I call them. "I'm so glad you called!" says my mother. "I meant to tell you. Your grade three teacher died last week. Remember? She had cancer for years. It was just a matter of time. Everybody was expecting it. She went peacefully. It was a relief."

"It was so nice having you here, Mother," I tell her.

"Oh, my darling," she says, voice a-tremble. "I had a lovely time."

I eat well. One day when the weather is mild, I return to the park with a book. The sky is clear. There is no one else in sight. The ice-cream stand hasn't even been set up yet because it's too early in the season.

◆

Run
Every Day

◆

ONE OF THE THINGS ABOUT CHILDREN that not too many people talk about is their instinctive fascination with power and pain almost as soon as they become aware such a thing exists. It comes before they can walk properly, before speech, before "mama," practically. I once witnessed a two-and-a-half-year-old pick up a block, look at it, look at her little friend sitting nearby, look at the block once more, and then hit. Apropos of nothing, as they say. Just a block, a fellow human being nearby, and a vague germination taking place in the brain.

Another one of the things not too many people talk about is the terror of childhood, and it is a terror that starts when you develop a peer group, once you are permitted to roam. You aren't allowed to roam far, but you're allowed to roam as long as you're with them. It's as if parents believe that children are going to take care of one another, like it's instinctual or something. In my town, kids ganged together and hid in the woods and waited for other kids, alone or in pairs, to ramble into pouncing distance. That sounds more like an instinct to me. I did it. I threw crab apples at a boy one time until he threw up. I felt horrible afterwards. But I didn't feel horrible when I was doing it.

For a while, the worst possible thing that could happen to you if you were a kid in my town would be to run into Gerald in the woods. He was around twelve then, and no friend of mine, although we were almost inseparable when we were little. But when we were twelve, it was like we had never met. He was a legend and I was a nobody. I was one of the endless gaggle of kids who scurried to get out of his way, but also drank up the tales of his horrific doings like he was a character in a comic book — the kind your parents never let you read. Gerald and his disciples would stomp off into the woods after school and on weekends, take off their shirts and booby-trap every inch of the area surrounding their fort. The whole woods, really. Often they would just lie in wait. People in school whispered to each other about the wild and obscene things Gerald would do to you if he caught you in the woods. I never went in. I used to spend my whole life there, but I never went in once Gerald took over. I knew boys who went in armed with sticks and crab apples, hoping to siege the fort, and I knew girls who went in on dares, just to be brave, or because deep down inside they just wanted to see what he would do. I understood that. But I never went in.

There was a time, not long after we stopped being friends, when myself and a bunch of stupid girls were coming back after a birthday party. It had been stupid because Sharon Crisp had gotten in a fight with Madonna MacLeod's older sister. Madonna was the birthday girl, and friends with Sharon, but Sharon and Madonna's sister had never gotten along. We were playing kick the can and Madonna's sister kicked the can directly at Sharon's head. There was a huge fight and everybody started taking sides and I got depressed and ran into the woods. This was back before Gerald had made it the incontestable property of himself and his gang, and it was still the most peaceful place I knew to be. I was a morose kid and hated conflict ever since I had made the boy throw up with the crab apples during a war over some-body's tree fort. Also I think I must have known that once everybody realized I was gone they would get worried and come looking for me.

That's what happened. They split up into two groups and went in at either end of the woods, playing search party. I could see what they were doing because I was sitting up in a tree on a plank someone had nailed across the highest branches, so I climbed down and found a clearing and pretended to be dead. Then Sharon's search party found me and gave me mouth-to-mouth resuscitation and CPR and electric shock therapy and everything they could think to revive me and finally I leapt to my feet and said I was cured. Then we all went looking for Madonna's search party, which took forever because it turned out they were hiding on us, watching and laughing behind a tuft of bushes the whole time. By that time it was getting late and we were all friends again, and just as we were heading home, Gerald and his disciples came out of nowhere. Gerald was holding a rusty coat-hanger out in front of him like a divining rod.

"If anyone moves," he said, "I'll electrocute you."

I just bolted. I think all the other girls took their cues from me and ran away too, squealing, like it was another game. If I hadn't gone first, though, they might have stayed. Madonna's sister, who was big, might have tried to out-tough Gerald or something. But they saw me fly, and thought that I had named the game: Chase Through the Woods. That's not what I was doing at all, though. I was just going the hell home as fast as I could.

Somebody chased me partway. It might have been Gerald, but it could have been any of them. It seems characteristic that he would launch himself after the first person to bolt, sort of to teach them a lesson, but I don't know. The person behind me didn't say anything, but I could hear him panting and breaking twigs beneath his feet and slender branches with his face. There was a moment when I'm sure I felt fingertips brush my back. I kept my eyes straight ahead. The edge of the woods, down Cosgrove Street, past the playground, down the steep hill practically head over heels, across the church parking lot and, by the time I hit Harbour Street, I was alone. Maybe even well before then, I don't know. I didn't care. I kept running anyway, all the way to my house.

And this was before he had even really established himself as the genuine holy terror he eventually became. A year or so later, Madonna MacLeod was telling me a story I had already heard twice that day about how Gerald's gang nabbed a girl called Kerrie Retard (she wasn't really retarded, just despised) and her brother, tied them to trees for a while, and then made them kiss each other on the mouth. And that was just for starters. Right in the middle of the story, though, Madonna thought of something and her eyes went wide and glittery. "Holy cats!" she whispered. "It's a good thing we ran that day!"

He was kind of like a god, but a bad god. Since the only theology I knew back then was Catholic, the only god I could compare him to at the time was Jesus. I thought about how all Jesus' friends must've felt when they realized he was actually kind of a superhero. When my mother started referring to Gerald as that Antichrist, it struck me as being the most perfectly apt thing I had heard in my life.

But now I realize Gerald fit in better with the pagans. The original gods were all bullies, too.

That's how he was for a couple of years, and then something happened. To tie other kids to trees and menace them is one thing when you're twelve, something else entirely when you are suddenly well over five feet and can palm a basketball. All that stuff stopped. Maybe because there were one too many phone calls from parents, but probably he just decided it was stupid after a while. He was still bad but somehow not as powerful — because he had grown up. Here's what I think: Everybody loves a bad little boy. The very phrase is adorable. But how about a bad, big fifteen-year-old. Not much encouragement there. The word that people started using was as follows. *Thug*. Gerald sort of went underground for a while and then he emerged, a fledgling thug. He skulked, he smoked. He wore a jean jacket with the names of bands written on it in magic marker. He talked back to adults. He was nowhere near as popular as he used to be.

This, the memory-flotsam that comes bobbing to the surface at the prospect of going home to help my mother pack. Nobody wants to buy the house but she doesn't care, she is moving. Somehow, in the past five years, it has become her dream to sell the quaint little two-storey structure built by shippers at the turn of the century, and move into a mature person's apartment complex on the outskirts of Halifax. Over the past five years she has started talking about the house like it is her own personal nemesis, like it's out to get her. Like the house harangues her to clean it day in and day out. It points a gun to her head and tells her to shake out the rugs. It holds its breath until she Windexes the smudges from every single window. It's too big and empty, she says, even though it's small and crammed full of her and my father's stuff. All my stuff, too, from day one of my being. She never used to like to get rid of anything. Not like now.

You can hear the excitement in her voice over the phone. She says, *One big purge.* The idea of getting rid of practically everything in one fell swoop seems downright sensual to her. She enumerates to me in shameless detail all the stuff she's going to give away. For example, she doesn't say, *All the furniture,* she says, *Your dad's old chair with the rip. The blue loveseat the dog used to climb up on. Those two end tables my grandmother gave me — they're history. I don't care, dear, I'm sick of the sight of them. If you want them, you come and get them, because they're going to Goodwill or on the junk heap, either one.*

Normally, I wouldn't go. My mother threatened to kill herself one time, and I didn't go. She threatened to set the house on fire and jump in the strait, and I didn't go. But that was because I knew she was full of shit. She was angry and sad and at the end of her rope, but ultimately she was full of shit and I could hear it in her voice. She had always felt that way, and she always tried to get me to do something about it instead of doing something about it herself. So I didn't go and I never went. But what's happening now is something else. She sounds neither sad, angry, nor at the end of her rope. She sounds, in fact, ecstatic, and because I've never had occasion to detect that particular note in her voice, I'm assuming my mother is going crazy. So I go.

It is not that I walk around thinking about Gerald all the time at the age of thirty living hundreds of miles away; that would be ridiculous. It is that every time I talk to my mother, she pictures a girl of seventeen. Everything she knows about me beginning from my birth and ending there is all that she knows about me, so she pretends there isn't anything else. Gerald is the biggest, most dramatic presence from this period. He had the starring role in my youth, and since my mother doesn't acknowledge any other aspect of my existence, Gerald is still her number-one reference point.

So rather than asking me about Dave, the man I've lived with for the past three years, she'll say, "I saw your honey-pie at the Sobey's the other day buying a can of poutine sauce," and I'll know exactly who she means. "He has a shaved head and two earrings in both ears. Just imagine! One week it's the hair down to his arse and the next it's no hair at all. I certainly don't know what the attraction is, my dear, but I can't say I share your taste in men."

At which point I will remind her that it has been thirteen years since I professed myself attracted to Gerald. One decade plus three years, during which time I've acquired two university degrees and held exactly eight different jobs. I've lived in six different cities and towns and had four serious relationships with men. If she pushes it, I will go on to reveal to my mother how many different people I've had sex with since then.

And then she'll sigh and say something like, "Well, I guess love is blind."

Because Gerald was such an enormous mistake, maybe she assumes that the rest of my life all just went irrevocably wrong as a result. Maybe she thinks that anyone who could be so catastrophically dumb as to get involved with Gerald Newhook can't be doing so well in the real world. Maybe she thinks she is being kind by not inquiring into what kind of sad semblance of a life I've managed to piece together since then. Maybe she gave up on me at that very moment.

We always pretended like we had just met when we were sixteen. Like we'd never been best friends in our lives. It was embarrassing to have been children together, and we were such complete strangers by that time that it was easy to get romantic about one another all of a sudden. Of course our parents would never let us forget, so we stayed far away from them. My mother figured things out pretty quickly, though. In fact, she had never forgotten Gerald since the first time he and I met, walking our dogs in the woods, not much more than five years of age. His dog attacked my dog and killed her, and somehow after that we were always together. My mother considered this the first incontrovertible evidence of my self-destructive streak. Even when he was twelve, and bad, and thoughts of meeting up with him in the woods gave me nightmares, my mother would report to me on his doings as if I were always some kind of silent partner, an accessory after the fact. She'd always say it like this: "See what your *boyfriend's* done now? You're to stop wasting your time with that christer." But neither of us had spoken in years.

She was psychic, really. When we started sneaking around together in high school, it was as if nothing had changed for my mother. In her mind, things kept on as they always had: me making the same old screw-up.

She's changed in almost every respect except that. Otherwise, I'd be talking to a stranger. The house is stripped except for a few functional items of furniture. Afghans that have languished on couches and armchairs for so long I had thought them indistinguishable from the upholstery have been snatched up, shaken out, and, in my mother's word, "tossed." The set of encyclopedias purchased in 1978 for my betterment "tossed." My father's collection of *National Geographic* and *Horizon* "tossed." The interior of the house looks freakishly modern because already my mother has "tossed" all the old furniture, heirlooms and all, and replaced it with Swedish-style "apartment furniture," in anticipation of her move. We sit at the stark, square wooden table that has replaced the seventies' pedestal and I sit there expecting to be given a cup of boiled black tea in my grandmother's china. Instead, she takes down a sleek, white ceramic pot from K-Mart which she says she got for five bucks. She liked how it matched the table in its complete lack of interesting detail. She shows me a sugar bowl that also matches. Plain and white. "Two-fifty," she tells me. "Cheap, cheap, cheap!" she chirps.

"You never used to care about cheap," I say.

"I know," she agrees. "For some reason, I always wanted everything to last."

She drinks only green tea now and offers me some because she says it's good for the blood. I am too disoriented to make conversation. After some silence, she remembers our only common ground and actually relieves me by starting in on Gerald. For a moment, things come into focus.

"You two were an awful pair of tea grannies, weren't you?" she remarks.

"Who?" But I know immediately.

"You and that boy. I remember the two of you, three bags a pot, boiling the piss out of it."

If the script had been playing itself out normally, this would be the point when I would launch into my elaborate reminder that the incident, or incidents, she was describing took place more than thirteen years ago, that I am now thirty, with two degrees, eight jobs, and so on and et cetera. But at present I am so unnerved that I find myself actually playing up to the old script, the one I always despised. Come back, Mother. Walk towards the light.

"Yes, we were, weren't we?" I agree.

"So you could walk on it," she mutters, her old self.

"What?"

"The tea. So strong you could walk on it. Foolishness."

"Yes, it was foolishness, wasn't it?" I encourage. "I guess we didn't have anything better to do."

She shakes her head, the old look settling into the spot between her eyebrows. Contempt, and disdain and disbelief. Ah. I sit back and wait for the "What in God's name did you ever see in that little christer" tirade. But then she shakes her head again, shakes the lines right off her brow. "Oh, well!" she chirps.

She tells me about the mature person's apartment complex. It has a big elevator so she won't have to climb a lot of stairs. It has a courtyard with a fountain that all the rooms look out over, and a gas fireplace. She starts referring to it as her "bachelor pad" as I chew on my the nail of my right thumb. She says she has already met some of the women who live there, and they can't speak highly enough of the place. She and the women are going to have "wild parties," she says. In her bachelor pad.

I stand up and start poking at the buttons on the dishwasher. "Where did you meet these women?"

To my surprise, the dishwasher starts up. It hasn't worked since I was thirteen. The lines come back to my mother's forehead and she hurries over, batting me out of the way.

"For Christ's sake, dear, don't go fiddling with that, I just got that fixed, now."

"You got it fixed?" I repeat. She always used to store my grandmother's dishes in there because it seemed like the safest place and because we never owned a china cabinet.

"Yes, I got it fixed." A hint of the old tone returns. Dolt, the tone says.

"What about the good china?"

She straightens up and smiles. Gone again are the peekaboo lines, gone is the tone.

We say it together: "Tossed."

I stop asking questions by dinnertime. It ends when she tells me about having met the apartment building ladies at her craft co-op. I ask her what a craft co-op is, and she says all these ladies get together and make quilts, hook rugs, weave baskets, crochet pillowcases, and then peddle their wares to some of the tourist shops around town. "It's more of a social thing than a business endeavour," she assures me. "But we make a little here, a little there. Sometimes somebody will bring in a new pattern we've never tried before."

It's all so outlandish I lean over and stare into her face. "You hate crafts," I say, holding up one finger. "You hate ladies." That's another finger. Then I just give up and spread my hands wide. "A social thing?" My mother's hobby used to be writing letters. She would simply write letters about how stupid everybody was and send them to magazines and newspapers to make herself feel better. The provincial paper used to be her own personal Wailing Wall. She sent them a letter a month, usually having nothing to do with what was in the news, but personal slights that she had suffered throughout the course of her days. But she was clever about it, she couched her complaints in terms of society's widespread moral malaise. If somebody cut her off in traffic, it would be "What has happened to common courtesy?" When I started talking back, it was "Why are today's teenagers so disrespectful?" When the bank teller closed his wicket after she called him a tit-head, she lamented "the shameful decline in standards of service." The newspaper printed every letter faithfully. They thought my mother was the Common Man. Sometimes her heartfelt moral concerns even sparked the occasional editorial response. That was my mother's social life. For years.

I'm reliving all this when she blows at her hair and sort of slouches backward like an impatient teenager. "My dear, my dear," she sighs. "You don't know what I hate. You don't know what I like. You don't know a darn thing about your old mother."

Your old mother. And then she tops herself.

"Tell me about your friend, Dave."

Dave thought it was funny I was taking my running shoes because I'm an awful runner. I'm sporadic, I have no discipline. I can go maybe fifteen minutes without stopping, but that's all I've been able to do for years. I haven't improved at all. I can't force myself to go every day. My back gets sore and I feel sorry for myself. But I take the shoes wherever I go with the best of intentions. I want to be the kind of person who just goes out and flies.

"What are you planning on doing with those?" he asked me. Dave is the kind of person who goes out and flies, for hours sometimes. Through parks, along the beach, into the woods, and all the way back. Everyone in the neighbourhood knows him.

"These will be my sanity-makers while I am home," I told him.

"I think you have to put them on your feet and run around for them to work," he said. "To derive the specific sanity-making benefits, that is."

Ha ha. Twenty km weekend marathon fun-run freak.

"Every day," I vowed.

"Don't go every day," he said seriously. "You'll kill your back and your knees."

"All day, every day," I prayed into the suitcase. He left me alone to pack after that.

My mother asking me about Dave reminds me of my shoes, once the shock has worn off. This being the first time ever. There have been days when I've deliberately spoken about him to her on the phone for over ten minutes — how he was feeling, his job, how somebody gave him this video game and he stayed up until four in the morning playing it three nights in a row. And she would wait for me to finish, sighing and huffing into the phone the entire time, and then she would say something like, "Well, that arse of a doctor up the street still doesn't know what he's talking about. First he says it's my thyroid, then he says it's my diet." She'd say something like that or she'd say something about Gerald. That's as close as she ever got to acknowledging what I was talking about. "Well — you and men, that's something I've never been able to figure out, going around with that lovely fellow you managed to hook up with." She never called him by name. "The Antichrist" or "that young bastard," "that christer," "the little creep," or when she was being sarcastic it was "that lovely fellow." "The beautiful young specimen that he is."

I go over to my suitcase, still on the porch where I dropped it upon arrival, and dig around for my shoes.

"I'm going for a run," I tell my mother.

"Are you running these days?"

"I've been running for years," I say. She has no way of knowing otherwise.

"Your Dave is a big runner, isn't he?"

Another shockwave. "Yes. Yes, he is. He's the one who got me into it. When we first moved in together. Three years ago, that is."

She just gazes out the window, seeing nothing, because it's dark outside and it's basically a mirror. "I think that's great," she murmurs.

God almighty, my mother thinks something is great. "What?" I demand. "What's great?" I'm just waiting, waiting for the jab, the barb, the dripping, festering, fetid spew of sarcasm.

"That you're taking such good care of yourself. I've been getting more exercise these days too. Some nights the ladies come by after dinner and we'll all go for a walk along the water."

It doesn't seem fair that my mother is just allowed to turn herself into a nice person all of a sudden. It seems like the kind of thing that should only have come about after a period of prolonged suffering. Like Saint Paul on the road to Damascus, she should have been struck blind and given a good greasing out by God first, it seems to me. She could be as kind and decent and laid-back as she liked, after that. It shouldn't have all been on my part. The suffering, I mean. I suffer for my mother's sins, and now she is redeemed. She goes tottering off to her ladies and her bachelor pad and her embroidered pillowcases while I pack up thirty years of shit.

On the other hand, of course, I should be happy.

The running is terrible, painful from the first step. I haven't been out in a while. My lungs burn. I have to stop three times, and every time I stop, I think I might die because I can feel my heart and my blood speed up in a really alarming way. When I was a kid there was a rumour about this woman on TV, that her heart exploded from doing aerobics all the time. It feels like that, like it's a possibility.

At one point I find that I am standing at the bottom of the steep hill beside the church parking lot, the same place I almost broke my neck running from Gerald, or somebody. Blood like a washing machine inside my head. I stand there with my hands on my hips for a moment and a perverse, masochistic part of me wants to try and run up that hill. When we were kids, even, we couldn't. We had to claw with our hands, because it's practically vertical. I just remember hurtling down it, scarcely able to keep my feet beneath me, and something in me wants to try and run back up again. One of those strange impulses you get when your pulse is going a hundred miles an hour. A car pulls into the parking lot, high beams hitting me like a prison searchlight. The person in the car honks and waves and I am about to bolt away from this friendly weirdo when I remember that this is a small town, where everyone assumes they know everybody else, even women standing alone in parking lots at night. I wave to be polite but the person doesn't acknowledge me further. He or she has recognized that I am a stranger. He or she pulls into the church, maybe it's the priest or the janitor or a member of the Ladies Auxiliary. He or she turns off the engine and headlights but doesn't get out of the car. I do a token stretch and then jog casually away, a fraud in every respect. Not only am I stranger, but I'm not even a real runner.

And even my identity as a stranger isn't quite the truth. "Well, the town is abuzz," says my mother the next day. She is returning home from the craft store and I am going through boxes that have already been packed on my mother's instruction, seeing if there's anything I might want. I've spent the morning sitting in the same position on the floor, transfixed by the contents of the boxes. In one I discovered piles and piles of those Mad-lib books I used to buy when I was a kid. Books full of stories with all the nouns and verbs and exclamations taken out. You were supposed to do them with friends, ask your friends to supply vowels and nouns and exclamations and fill in the blanks. Then you would read the stories to each other and get a big laugh out of them. For some reason, though, I preferred doing the stories by myself. There was no element of surprise involved or even comedy, I would just read the stories and fill in the blanks with whatever words seemed most appropriate. I filled pages and pages with this sort of banality.

"Why is the town abuzz?" I ask. The page in front of me says: *When I grow up I would like to be a* <u>dog</u>. *Then I could* <u>bark</u> *all the time. People would* <u>hear</u> *me and exclaim,* "<u>Be quiet</u>!" *I would also* <u>sniff</u> *and* <u>dig.</u> Just mind-numbingly boring.

"Well, the craft store is abuzz, anyway," my mother amends. "That's the only place I've been so far today."

"Abuzz with what?"

"Everybody has heard that you're home. Someone saw you out running around last night."

I am aghast. And the phone rings then and it's Madonna MacLeod. "Weren't even gonna call me," she says.

Of course I wasn't going to call you.

"My God," I say. "How the hell have you been?" I exaggerate the amazement in my voice in order to counteract the familiarity in hers.

"The same," she says. "So are you coming over for a drunk?"

"I could come over for a drink," I reply slowly. She snorts.

"Guess what?"

"What?"

"You know how Peter Pecker Jessop was living with Therese" — she pronounces it "Traz" — "Cormier?"

"No."

"Wanda Cormier's sister?"

"Okay."

"They split up because she spit on his dad the one time."

"Huh."

"Ten years!"

"Tch."

"Oh, fuck off!" She barks impatiently. "I know you weren't gonna call me."

"I was so. How is your mum?"

I promise Madonna I'll drop by later on, although probably I won't, and she should know that. She should know there's no reason why I would drop by. Madonna calls me, no matter where I am in the world, a couple of times a year, with all "the news." I never call her and ask for the news. And she never asks me for any of my own news, either. It's like I'm an astronaut, floating around all by myself up in space, and Madonna's down on the ground in Houston, my only link to the rest of the world.

"I got all the news for ya," she'll say. And it's always a different version of Traz Cormier and Peter Pecker Jessop. A litany of names, all familiar and meaningless, one name doing something to another name. Oh, you don't remember that name? You know, the name who's related to this other name. Her name's cousin was my dad's friend's brother's name.

Worse are the times when I'll know the names. I'll know every other one. It will leap out at me like a fish from an otherwise undifferentiated stream and land in my lap. It will feel like a pinch on an unexpected part of my body. Shane, who I kissed at the dance, even though I was supposed to be going out with Gerald at the time. Vesta, with whom I shoplifted condoms and nail polish at Shoppers

— because if you get caught, you don't want them thinking you were shoplifting *exclusively* for condoms — and who is Gerald's second cousin. Sharon, who got along all right with Madonna but hated Madonna's sister. All three of whom I left behind me in a cloud of dust the day Gerald came upon us in the woods.

Like Kafka, Madonna is a memory come alive. She'll talk about that birthday party like it was a day ago. She'll talk about how much she enjoyed the cake. Not just how it tasted, but the way it was decorated. She is in league with my mother, or how my mother used to be, in that she doesn't particularly bother to acknowledge the passage of time or, at least, the occurrence of change. There is no change. There's only "news." In Madonna's world, it is everybody's desire and responsibility to make sure they are as caught up on "all the news" as they can possibly be at all times. I can only assume that's why she always sounds so disappointed in me.

But with the next run, I can feel the change already. My thighs have braced themselves, and my lung capacity seems to have expanded. I do about ten minutes, stop, and immediately realize I don't need to, so I keep going for another five. I stop again, look around for the ghostly fireflies that appeared in front of my eyes last time, but they are nowhere to be seen. I'm getting better. I walk for a couple of minutes, deeply impressed with myself. A car heading in the opposite direction slows down to get a good look at me. An old person with a helmet of close, white curls peeps over the steering wheel, and I wave. The old person raises an index finger carefully. I can't tell if it's a man or a woman. I can't see if he or she is smiling or frowning, because the bottom half of its face is hidden by the steering wheel.

This time I'm running in broad daylight, and all sorts of people can see me. Cars honk, people nod from their porches, kids follow me a couple of blocks on their tricycles. I'm considering heading off towards the highway for less conspicuousness, but it's quite a few blocks away. It would be easy to run into Madonna, Shane, Sharon, Vesta, Madonna's sister, the kid I made throw up with the crab apples, whose name was either Earl or Wayne. Or Gerald, anyone, on these bustling streets. My mother runs into Gerald all the time, the way she tells it. In the store, at the crosswalk. He never says anything to her, she brags. He wouldn't dare. He knows her feelings all too well. I used to imagine my mother giving him the evil eye and scuttling away, cackling to herself like some kind of medieval crone. Gerald actually used to do some pretty funny impressions of the look that would settle over my mother's face whenever he caught her eye. Like she had just been getting ready to sit down to dinner with the Queen at one end of the table and the Pope on the other, he used to say. When what do they set down before her, but a silver-gilded tray laden with the finest Parisian turds.

I'm at the highway, I must have been running for thirty minutes now, and it is probably too much. Dave always warns against pushing myself too far early on, but I'm feeling great. I congratulate myself on having thoughts about Gerald that are grown-up and very nearly fond. Untainted by cringing memories of the past. I could run into Gerald, I think. And that would be fine. He would see that I am a runner, that I live a healthy, productive lifestyle. You see, Gerald, I had to take some time off from my fulfilling job as a cataloguer at a museum where I work while I'm finishing up my Master's thesis. Yes, that's right, another Master's. I had to come back and help my mother pack up thirty years, something I did not dread doing in the least, seeing as how she and I have such a close, caring relationship based upon mutual respect. Now that I have come to terms with all my past issues and what have you. Oh, yes, completely to terms. Yes, Gerald, I really can't tell you how gratifying it is. To bestride the earth, fully in command of yourself, utterly at ease. Healthy, of sound mind and body. Secure with your place in the world.

A pulp truck comes up from behind and *blats* me awake, passing within inches. I'm enveloped in a harrowingly warm cloud, the truck's own breath. Splinters and the smell of bleeding lumber, but also sheer nearness and speed. I turn around and teeter home, fireflies dancing in front of my eyes, legs of brine.

✧

There is truth in the observation that we always seemed to come together whenever nobody else was interested in hanging around with him. Who do you think had the kindness to point that out to me if not my own dear mother? When we were children, he had just moved into town and was regarded with the suspicion of anyone with a weird last name and no identifiable relatives in the community. That's one of the reasons I liked him so much. To me, he was exotic. Like in kindergarten, there was a boy named Simon from Quebec who could scarcely speak a word of English, and he fascinated me. He was bad-tempered and potato-faced and boys and girls alike would torment him quite successfully, but I alone would fight them off and follow him from place to place like my old dead dog used to follow me. I always wanted to kiss him and take hold of his bulging cheeks and after a while he would run if he saw me coming, so that was that. But then there was Gerald, who was more fun than pudgy Simon had ever been.

And then we were older, and his popularity waned again and he seemed angry and disturbed about everything, going around with this slouching demeanour as if he wanted to pull in his lanky limbs and regenerate into a fetus and disappear. His blond head dulled to mousy brown and black sporadic hairs began sprouting on the most unlikely parts of his face and his eyebrows grew rapidly together and sometimes he'd just be walking along and he'd trip for no apparent reason. When we were little, I had always thought he looked like a Viking. He didn't look like a Viking any more.

And so I loved him.

It seemed to help. Sometimes we'd be watching videos in his basement after his parents had gone to bed and he'd jump up and point

218

at the television and yell, "That's just like me!" even though it was usually nothing like him. But I understood what he meant. It was just like the way that he was in his head. I understood how difficult it was to show people how you really were in your head. Sometimes, even, he'd yell that the TV was just like "us," and I'd be thrilled.

◇

My mother steps into the dining room and freaks, a good old-fashioned mother-freak-out, fond memories rushing back. She storms from one pile of mildewed history to the next, ranting about the boxes.

"My nice boxes!" she keeps shrieking. "My nice, good boxes!"

The nostalgia wears off and I hear myself snap: "What?" A good old-fashioned, sullen, teenage-me snap. I am a memory come alive.

"What are you yelling about?"

"My nice neat boxes!"

I look at the boxes to determine what's so special about them. They are brown, cardboard, mainly from the liquor store. This End Up.

"What about the goddamn boxes?"

She kicks over one of the piles I've made, causing me to stand up and my hands to jerk in an involuntary anticipation of throttling.

"Do you know how long it took me to *pack* all this stuff?" she shrieks.

I look around at my piles. It's true, all the nice, good, neat boxes have been laid bare.

"But," I say, "you told me to go through them."

"I didn't tell you to unpack every goddamn one!"

Okay, she didn't. And I, being the grown-up, I, the evolved one, will deign to admit my part in the disagreement. I have practised this sort of thing innumerable times, writing out imaginary dialogues on the backs of envelopes and napkins. *Mother, I apologize for having upset you. Clearly there was a miscommunication between us, and I'm sorry for that. On the other hand, I want you to be aware that when you use that kind of tone with me, when you come in here kicking and screaming and accusing, it just isn't helpful to either one of us. I become defensive and resentful and lash back at you, and then we have a big blow-up that serves only to alienate the both of us.*

I take a deep breath and get my bearings. This is good, I'm thinking, this is the first time I've kept my temper enough to really lay it on her. Won't she be ashamed when she hears how rational I can be in the face of her own childish rantings.

"Mother," I begin. "I apologize —"

She plops down in a chair and starts laughing.

"Just *listen* to me," she says. "Getting myself all worked up like that." She blows at her hair in that new, strange young way she has while I stand there tingling with self-righteousness.

"Clearly there was a miscommunication —"

"I guess to God there was." She stands up again and looks around, hands on hips. "Don't tell me you want all this crap?"

I look around with her. "No...." I try to remember what I was thinking when I emptied the boxes. I don't recall thinking anything.

"Well, you'll put it all back nice and neat, won't you, dear?"

"Of course!" I snap. Defensive, teenage snap. It's a new dance craze. Everybody do the Teenage Snap. I collect myself and resume. "When you use that tone —"

She starts laughing again. "You mean this tone?" Then she does an imitation of herself, high-pitched and incoherent. "*Rar rar rar rar rar!* You mean that tone?"

Speechless.

"I know, dear, it's sickening, a woman my age. I just need to take my pill." She pats me on the bum and hops away up the stairs. I crouch among the piles.

That's gotta be some pill.

Later, when she's out with her ladies crocheting "God Bless Our Happy Home" onto various objects, it occurs to me. It's so obvious I practically slap my forehead and take the stairs two at a time to see if I'm right. There sits the box in her medicine cabinet alongside of all the medicinal artifacts of my family. This seems to be the one corner of the house she has yet to purge. My dad's ear medicine is still in there. My Kermit the Frog toothbrush. False eyelashes from the seventies that she only wore once, and then I wore at Hallowe'en. In the middle of it all, the box. The ultra-modern box with its sleek, proud lettering, cradling its ultra-modern cure within. The miracle cure of the twentieth century. Of course. My mother's harassed doctor must have wept with relief the moment it hit the market. I open the box and shake out its contents — there's still quite a few left. She must have just got her prescription filled. I carry the pills into my room and tuck them away underneath the balls of clothing that sit unpacked in my suitcase. Then I return the empty box to its place of honour beside the eyelashes. There is approximately nothing going on in my head as I perform these actions, and yet for some reason I bounce down the stairs giggling like a teeny-bopper on her way to the formal.

Seeing as how she won't be home for a couple of hours at least, there doesn't seem to be much else to do except wander into the living room and start emptying out a few *other* boxes.

Madonna happens to be standing outside the bank when I run by, lighting a smoke and retrieving a ratty little dog that she must have tied to a nearby hydro pole while she went in. It is not necessarily the case that I spotted and then ignored her. I am at the height of my run, blood churning in my head, and to see Madonna leaning against a pole inhaling smoke seems at once unreal and at the same time utterly expected. It's as if everything around me is wallpaper — the bank, the trees, the water, the crumbling street, Madonna, and the dog. To acknowledge her seems to make as much sense as saying hello to a picture on the wall.

Of course there's no way Madonna's going to let me get away with it. She barks, "Hey!" and the dog barks also, as if agreeing. I turn around but don't feel like I can just stop. Madonna pushes up her sleeves, holds the cigarette more securely, and runs to catch up with me, dragging the rat along behind her.

"Will you slow the frig down a minute?"

"I'm sorry!" I jog in place, pumping my knees, aware of how I look.

"What's the matter with ya?" To her I appear to be having some kind of fit.

"It's just ... my heart rate ... it's way up there. I shouldn't stop."

"You don't have to stop, I'll keep up."

I take her at her word, but adjust my pace. Madonna trundles along beside me, smoking.

"Looked right at me, didn't stop. I thought you must be going retarded."

"I was —" The only thing I can think to say is that I was "in the zone." Madonna will laugh to puke if I tell her I was "in the zone."

"I was spaced out," I say.

"I guess you were."

The dog whines, its tiny toenails clicking rapidly along the pavement. Madonna glances down. "Dora doesn't care too much for this."

"That's not the same dog," I say, squinting down at the thing. It's one of those infinitesimal terriers exactly like Madonna's mother had when we were teenagers.

"That's Dora," Madonna confirms.

"Jesus Christ, we better stop!" I am rapidly doing calculations in my head, trying to recall Dora's puppyhood. The dog stands trembling, a pink tongue the size of my baby fingernail protruding from her scraggily muzzle. Madonna picks her up with one hand and gives her a kiss on the face. I get a violent head rush from the sudden inertia and have to lean over.

"You're killing yourself with that there," my childhood friend observes. She drops her cigarette on the ground directly in front of my eyes without even bothering to step on it and make sure it goes out.

"I'm still getting used to it," I explain.

I straighten up and witness Madonna sort of adjusting herself mentally. She considers the sky and pushes down her sleeves again. "So Gerald Newhook's getting married," she says.

"I thought he already was married."

"No, no, he was just living with somebody for a few years, someone Beaton."

"What happened to her?"

"Oh, you know. He was always screwing around. But so was she."

"So who's this new one?"

"From out Mabou way."

"What's her story?" I hear myself saying. But there's no other way to talk.

"Oh, you know."

"Is he working?"

"On and off at the mill. Laid off last year, sold hash for a while. Plays with the band at the tavern."

"Well, I think that's wonderful," I say, finding my breath and trying to shake off the whole girls'-bathroom feel of the conversation. Madonna smiles.

"Well," she says, "you know Gerald."

"Actually, I *don't*," I point out. "It's been ... what?" I pretend to be casually racking my brain. "Thirteen years?"

Madonna shrugs and the dog pants and trembles against her chest. She holds it up to her face, puckering her lips and talking baby talk. "Is that how long it's been?" she asks it. "Is dat how wong it's been, Dora-Dora?" The dog wriggles and flicks its tongue towards her in adoration. I start pumping my knees again while Madonna looks me up and down.

"I gotta keep going, I'm right in the middle," I plead.

"You're heart's gonna explode like that one on television."

"That was an urban myth."

"No, I heard it from someone," she murmurs, bored already with the subject, casting her mind into the past like a fisherman's net. Then her eyes light up. I get a seasick conviction she's about to exclaim "Holy cats!"

Instead she says, "Remember that time in the woods? We were running then, boy. Scary."

What infuriates me is that I know precisely what she is talking about, the very day, the very occasion, eighteen years ago on her twelfth birthday. Because any normal human being with a normal memory span wouldn't, I pretend that I don't and fly away.

❖

Only one time, I remember, did we ever talk about being kids together, he and I. It was when we were having a fight. The beginning of the end. I got pissed off finally, and yanked myself away from him, and he followed me down the street. Hey! he kept yelling. Hey you!

Remember when our dogs killed each other? Remember that?

I thought he was trying to be gross and cruel, and I stopped.

You mean your dog killed my dog.

And then mine had to be put to sleep, he said.

So what? I said.

So your dog killed my dog indirectly.

I remember I stared at him with my mouth open. By being killed, by *your* dog?

That's right! he said.

So?

So, he said, everything is your fault.

❖

"Don't go into the woods!" Madonna calls after me, laughing.

So despite her, I do, I head straight there, ploughing through twigs. Bushes I remember barely being able to conceal myself behind have eaten up entire clearings. It's no place to run. All the old paths are so overgrown I can hardly make my way through, a gauntlet of thorns and whiplash branches. The kids must not even bother coming down here any more. On the street, someone in a car sees me stagger out from behind the wall of trees, legs and face ruddy with welts, and stops to ask if I need any help.

◈

Nice Place
to Visit

◈

MOUNT BAKER ROSE LIKE AN ICEBERG up from the centre of the August haze, and Bess was feeling guilt again, because it was all so beautiful. Below her, green islands dotted the blue sea and Meghan was pointing out whales and screaming to be heard over the engine. In the seats ahead of them were three fat rich people, packed together like marshmallows while she and Meg luxuriated in all their space at the back. On Saturna, when the three fat rich people were boarding, Bess's instinct had been that she and Meg should offer up their seats, but she glanced over at Meg and saw she was pretending to be asleep. As the three fat rich people crammed in, she heard graceful, subtle mutterings about the thin young girls in the back. "Perhaps those lovely, thin young girls ..." and so on. Certainly unassertive, but insistent all the same. Bess felt guilt the entire half-hour flight. It was that, and having left her son at home, who had begged and screamed to come.

The plane lowered itself towards the island and skipped across the harbour like a pebble and Bess was reminded of the opening credits of "The Beachcombers."

"They were fat, they were rich," Meg rationalized on the dock. "Here's what would have happened. You and I would have been uncomfortable the whole trip because *they* can't get off their big arses and lose a few pounds! So *we're* supposed to be inconvenienced."

The pilot heard their accents and asked where they were from. When Meg said, "East Coast," he thought they meant Toronto, so Meg stood there and explained that Toronto was not on a coast, and then went on to detail every pertinent aspect of Atlantic Canadian geography so that he would know in the future. She was very sweet about it, and the pilot unloaded their knapsacks, listening patiently.

Bess thought the West Coast had done wonders for Meg — she had somehow wriggled out from underneath a houseful of backwoods brothers and made her way here, where she had blossomed, apparently. She wore the kind of bright clothing that would never be seen in a tavern back home because people would think you were showing off, she wore hiking boots with dresses, and she didn't wear make-up. She was strong and assertive in a way that was still quite alien to Bess, and her boyfriend lived on a houseboat. Bess used to think that they had nothing in common, and she still thought she and her cousin had nothing in common, but somehow, out here in the alien beauty, she was finding she liked Meg better than she had at home.

But it was awkward. Bess had never been anywhere and felt as if she didn't know how to talk to people. She knew that Meg had stopped drinking as of two years ago, and couldn't imagine how they were going to have a conversation. Did it mean that Bess wouldn't be allowed to drink? Would it be insensitive? Was Bess expected to adopt the lifestyle while she was here and have to hike and swim and cycle all the time? She especially hoped no one would ask her to ski as she knew that she would break her own neck. Then Bess felt disgust for herself. The big adventurer, whining for a beer, needing to sit down and smoke every half-hour.

The boyfriend handed her a beer the moment she walked in the door, as he had just finished opening it for himself, and a few moments later he offered Bess a cigarette as well. At first she declined, because she was trying to train herself to smoke only in the evenings, but once finding herself with a beer in her hand, she realized how unnatural it was not to have a smoke in the other. Glancing at Meg, who was standing in the open doorway, but not complaining, Bess asked if she might have one after all. The boyfriend, whose name was Lyle, grinned and bobbed his head. "It was a valiant effort," he told her.

Lyle looked like what her father would describe, with his ancient frame of reference, as a beatnik. Bess had learned to understand that by this he meant people who did not iron their clothes or cut their hair when it needed to be cut, so almost anyone young, who wasn't in the military, was a beatnik by her father's standards. Still, Bess was surprised, because Meg had described him as a businessman. Standing out on deck, surrounded by water and mountains and sailboats, Lyle explained that he was an independent consultant.

"Oh!" went Bess.

"Well, it's great because I get to work out of my home and, you know, home is here." He swept his arm at the mountains and water possessively.

"You never have to *go* anywhere?" marvelled Bess. Her father's voice: *What in Christ's name kind of job is that?* The longer she had lived away from him, the more she came to realize that this voice had, at some point, usurped the position of her conscience. She was constantly beating it back. Her son running about the apartment in a makeshift Peter Pan costume — she had plastered her hands to her mouth, scarcely before hollering at him to stop flouncing around the place like a big fruit.

After the single beer, the jet lag caught up to Bess and made her wobbly, so Meg suggested they go into town for coffee and groceries and allow Lyle to get a little bit of work done.

"How will we get into town?"

"We'll walk, Bess," said Meg.

Bess hadn't walked anywhere in ages. She was mad at herself for allowing this to be known. But where was there to walk, and what point was there to walking, where she was from? The streets were ugly and adversarial and there were days when she could not bring herself to contemplate moving around on them.

She felt her jeans were too tight to walk in, so she went into Lyle's room with her knapsack to put on shorts. There were clothes heaped on Lyle's bed and the curtains had not been opened, so the room was dark and smelled of sleep and sweat and stale breath. When she emerged, Lyle and Meg were standing close together, Meg with her hands on her hips and with her head down.

"Sorry the room was such a fucking mess," Meg spat when they were out in the open air.

Bess was marvelling at the size of the trees. "God, no problem." The truth was Lyle's slovenly houseboat put Bess far more at ease than Meg's assiduously scrubbed apartment in the city the night before.

"It's really inconsiderate," said Meg.

"No, no."

"It makes me sick," said Meg.

Bess remembered Meg's parents' house, Bess's Uncle Alistair's, where Meg had lived right up until she was twenty-two with four of her seven brothers. It was a house of men, there could be little doubt. It was painted a greenish black colour and there was a shaving mirror above the sink in the kitchen. One time Bess dropped by to find a pile of freshly caught fish on the coffee table in the living room, and young Alistair with his boots propped up alongside of it, watching "The Price Is Right" and flicking cigarette ash into a bowl of tomato soup. Meg used to shriek at her brothers all the time and they would laugh at her. Findlay had once gone into her room and taken her birth control pills in order to give to his girlfriend, who couldn't afford them. At Meg's small, bright apartment the night before, she had done impressions of her brothers for Bess, who was punchy from her all-night flight and laughed until her ribs ached. Meg stuck out her front teeth and crossed her eyes and pulled her jeans down so that her stomach would hang over the waistband and the crack of her ass could be seen, and then she walked around bow-legged.

Meg was cosmopolitan now. She got them both iced cappuccinos and biscotti at the coffee shop, and Bess drank the cappuccino down like a milk shake and wanted another one. The jet lag lifted immediately and she looked around herself with renewed disbelief at the painful, vivid sky with the clouds hugging up against the mountains. Meg had purchased wild rice, salmon, and rapini, among other exotic items at the market, because Lyle was going to cook for them that night.

"You live here," Bess kept repeating.

"You could live here," said Meg. "Why don't you look for work?"

"Oh, Jesus Murphy," said Bess. It was inconceivable. "Dylan."

"Dylan would love it!"

"Of course he would love it," said Bess, not optimistically. That he would love it was not the point.

"You're thinking how hard it would be," intuited Meg. "Listen — it's not hard. I'm here. It seems so hard and then you get out here and wonder how in the name of God you were able to tolerate that hellhole you were in for so many years. It changes everything."

Bess was offended. What had been hard was getting out of her parents' house and into the little apartment with Dylan in the city. Meg had no idea what a triumph this dingy one-bedroom on a grey, violent street represented to Bess. Meg had never been there, and therefore had no way of knowing whether or not it was a hell-hole.

"I'm not saying you live in a hell-hole," amended Meg the moment Bess was thinking it. "I'm just remembering my own situation. You think you're stuck and you think you can do no better. Then you come out here, and the whole world opens up."

Meg spread her arms. Bess looked around.

On the weekend, Lyle's friend was supposed to take them out on his sailboat. He was called Wills, instead of Will, because he was from England, and Bess was obsessed with the idea that they were going to try and set her up with him. As pleased as she was about the sailboat, she could not bear the notion of being paired up with a stranger, and thought she might plead sick. The idea of sex had been a horror to Bess ever since the trauma giving birth to Dylan. She'd had a couple of passive relationships since then, but as soon as anyone tried to touch her, even made any careful suggestions, her gorge would rise and once she had actually thrown up in the fellow's presence. The guy had abruptly said, "Shall we go to 'er?" and Bess ralphed. After that, she decided not to bother herself with such things any more. It was embarrassing. Just something else to make her stand out from the rest of the world.

She phoned her parents' house that night and they told her that Dylan had refused to get out of bed the first day and ever since had been dragging himself around the house like a ghoul. Her father had taken him to buy a couple of new hens and that had cheered him up somewhat, but for the most part he was like "a little lost soul," as Bess's mother put it.

Bess winced at hearing what she had known was an inevitability, considering his behaviour before she left. As Bess was a freak, so was her son a freak. It was not healthy for two people to be so bound up with each other.

"When are you coming home?" was the first thing he said to her.

"It's really nice out here!" she said brightly. "Maybe we'll both come out here some time."

"Why didn't we both go out there this time?"

"Because I'm not a gazillionaire, I told you," she said.

"Kids *don't* cost twice as much to fly," Dylan stated for the hundredth time since Bess had announced her travel plans. He had taken it upon himself to find out about this at school, after Bess had tried to convince him otherwise.

"It's still more than I have right now, Dylan."

"Me and Pop bought some chickens, and I named one of them Ted. Do you want to talk to him?"

"No, I don't want to talk to the Jesus chicken."

"I'm going to go get him."

"I will kill you if you go and get the chicken."

"Talk to Nan." He was gone.

"He's running outside to get the chicken now," Bess's mother tittered on the other end of the line.

"For Christ's sake, Mother, don't let him bring that thing inside!"

"Oh, he just loves that bird."

Bess could hear the screen door slamming shut a second time.

"Here's Ted," said Dylan. "I'll hold him up to the phone."

"Do you know how much this is costing?" No answer. She was screaming at Ted. After a few moments, Dylan came back on the line.

"Did you talk to him?"

"I phoned to talk to you," Bess said sweetly, having used her time with the bird to take a couple of breaths.

"You can talk to me all you want when you come home," he reasoned.

"Sometimes moms need vacations."

"Sometimes kids need vacations too," her son rejoined.

Bess thought, *You little fucker,* blowing kisses into the phone.

She imagined Meg's life, tanned and healthy, independent with her own nice, woman's apartment full of brightly coloured woman things, partaking of grown-up, normal sex with her boyfriend on a houseboat. On an island on a houseboat. Without even a hint of nausea, Bess could only assume. Meg had wrenched herself from the family of boys, flown across the continent, and opened herself up like a flower, somehow. That was how. Merely by going away. Bess and Meg had used to go to the dances and the tavern together back home, resenting one another because they didn't have anyone else. Meg would pay Bess grim visits in the afternoons to break up the monotony of their endless, aimless days in their respective parent's homes. Whenever one of them was working, she would treat the other to booze and vice versa. It never occurred to them to do anything with their money except drink, there was so little of it. Bess was itching to interrogate her cousin as to the hows and the whys of her giving up drinking. It would have been inconceivable to Bess a couple of days ago, but as the clean, wet air and looming monster-trees and sun and clouds and water worked on her being, she could almost imagine forgetting she needed a drink some evening.

"But there's sun and water and trees back home," Meg observed as they struggled their way up a hill to see the view.

"But where?" panted Bess.

"All around!" said Meg.

"But where?"

If Bess ever forgot about drinking, Lyle was always there to remind her. He was an aficionado of all sorts of fine and tasty booze. He had a liquor cabinet right there on the houseboat just like somebody's dad, and every night brought out a different bottle for them to sample, saying what a pleasure it was to have another drinker on board to keep him company. They drank Jamaican rum and thirty-year-old scotch and Benedictine. Bess always drank too much of everything and felt embarrassed the next day, thinking if she had wanted to get drunk, there was always plenty of beer in the fridge — she should not have guzzled Lyle's good stuff. But Lyle was gracious and told her not to be ridiculous whenever she balked. Meg would sit nearby smiling at Lyle's stories and drinking Italian sodas to stay awake.

It turned out the friend with the sailboat, Wills, was gay, although Bess would never have figured it out for herself, and had to be told. He was a member of Lyle's book club, and a doctor who merely sailed from one coastal town to another doing locums at the various hospitals, occasionally docking his boat and flying inland for brief stints. (*What in Christ's name kind of doctor is that*, the father who owned Bess's conscience demanded.) Wills was one of the best-looking men she had ever seen, and Bess felt dowdy alongside of him. Meg and Bess sat up in front (bow? stern?) tanning themselves while Lyle and Wills stayed at the helm. Bess felt like she was rich, and felt guilty. The father inside her head wanted to know who she thought she was. All I ever do, Bess explained to the father, is go to work and eat food and talk to Dylan and go to bed at night. Goddamn lucky to have a job, grunted the father, especially in this economy. I am not saying that I'm not grateful to have a job, explained Bess. When you have responsibilities, interrupted the father, when you've got a small boy depending on you, sometimes your own goddamn pleasures have to take a back seat. Always, they do, Bess argued, helplessly getting angry. Well, who held a gun to your head and told you to have a baby all those years ago? Nobody did. Well? It's not just that my goddamn pleasures are supposed to take a back seat. It's that there are no pleasures. There aren't even supposed to be any.

"Isn't this beautiful?" said Meg.

Bess opened her eyes. The sea was the mountains and sky in reverse. A heron launched itself from a nearby crag of an island. She wanted to scream and pull at her own hair.

"Horrible," she grunted.

Meg glanced at her, not particularly surprised.

Meg hugged her knees. "Lyle's so hungover."

"Really?" Bess glanced back to see Lyle at the wheel, gazing steadily at the horizon as Wills leaned back, talking and gesturing with a beer can.

"Oh, come on, he looks like shit," said Meg, but the truth was he looked no different than since Bess had arrived. "He always drinks too much when there's other people around."

Guilt again for Bess. "I'm sorry."

"Jesus, it's not your fault!"

Bess felt like apologizing again, simply on instinct because Meg had yelled at her, but stopped herself.

"It reminds me of my father," said Meg. "Just sitting and drinking and sitting and drinking. Finding himself more and more fascinating the more he drinks. Assuming there's nothing on earth you would enjoy more than to sit there and listen to him explaining himself to you, endlessly, on and on, over and over again."

235

"Huh," said Bess.

"It made me crazy," said Meg. "He'd make you sit there and he wouldn't let you get up. 'Listen to me, I've got somethin' important to say to ya,' but it was always the same thing over and over again, and it didn't have anything to do with me. I might as well have been a doll, or a mirror."

Bess didn't know what to say, as she had never liked Meg's father to begin with.

"Lyle is nice," she offered.

"I know," said Meg. "He's a great guy. He is a wonderful, caring man." She leaned back and closed her eyes again.

They ate dinner on the sailboat, Wills making pasta for everyone, but once the red wine was gone, they headed over to Lyle's place to "unearth" another bottle of Jamaican rum. Wills told them hilarious stories about trying to teach Lyle how to sail when they first met, and thinking that Lyle was gay and trying to put the moves on him and Lyle being too drunk and obtuse the whole time to know what was going on. Almost all of Wills stories were about Lyle doing something foolish.

"He's just a tiny little boy," Wills told them, "underneath that *übermensch* exterior of his. Just a wee naive little boy at heart." Lyle was smiling and swirling the ice cubes around in his drink. Bess was relaxed when the men started asking about her own little boy, which, she understood, was perhaps the only thing about herself that made her interesting to them.

"He's a big bastard," she reflected sloppily. "Likes hockey and trucks. He'll probably be the kind of kid who spends entire afternoons lighting farts with his friends in the backyard."

Lyle looked alarmed. "You must do something."

"He sounds perfect," corrected Wills.

In the middle of all the hilarity, Meg had gone into the bedroom for some unstated reason and, after a few moments, called for Lyle to join her. Wills looked at Bess and clenched his teeth.

"So it begins," he said.

Bess leaned forward. "What?"

"You might want to sleep over at my place tonight."

"Why?"

Wills inclined his head towards the bedroom and Bess listened. Meg was crying. Lyle was speaking very low and Meg was shouting in whispers, and then she would cry again.

"What the hell's going on?" Bess hissed.

Wills rose. Bess couldn't believe the party was to end so abruptly. "I'm out of here. You should come. They'll be at it all night."

"No, no," Bess laughed. "They'll stop."

"They won't stop," said Wills.

They stopped at five in the morning, an hour and a half of silence went by, and then they started again, but only for fifteen minutes or so. Lyle came out of the bedroom and went into the bathroom and then he came out of the bathroom and walked out the front door. Bess finally went to sleep after that, and five hours later she sat up and saw Meg at the kitchen table with a cup of coffee and the newspaper in front of her.

"Today we should swim."

"How long have you been up?"

"I didn't sleep," said Meg.

"Jesus, go to sleep, Meg."

"No," said Meg. "There's no point now. I can't sleep in the day."

They were going to rent mopeds in order to drive up to the lake, but it turned out they needed a credit card number to give, and neither of them had a credit card, and Meg could not remember Lyle's number. They turned around and walked back towards the bike shop, to rent bikes. They hadn't wanted to do this at first because the ride was all uphill and neither of them were feeling particularly athletic.

"We are slaves to our credit rating," said Meg. "We are the outcasts of society."

Bess thought it was strange Meg wouldn't have a credit card, being gainfully employed, but it turned out she had screwed up in the past with an Irving Big Stop card in her early twenties. Bess had done the same with a Zellers card during quite a bleak time in her life. Feeding Dylan Zellers macaroni every day, Zellers chips, dressing him in Zellers jeans and Zellers shoes, taking him for sundaes at the Zellers restaurant. She told the story to Meg to cheer her up. Meg laughed and laughed and related a time when the only way she could get a drink was to order a complete meal along with the two or three beer she actually wanted at the Big Stop.

"Sitting there shaking with the DTs," she gasped. "Food growing legs, crawling around on my plate."

The lake was a blessing when they reached it, the two of them soaked in sweat, Jamaican rum seeming to ooze out of Bess's every pore. There was hardly anyone else around, and they waded in easily, as into a cool bath. Water got into Bess's mouth, and she gulped it in, it tasted so fresh. They floated on their backs and saw three eagles fighting over a fish.

At the houseboat, Lyle was still not there, and Meg made more coffee to drink and started looking around for food to cook for dinner.

"Lyle, Lyle, Lyle," she said as she paced around the kitchen. "Lyle is probably using his credit card to purchase something big and fancy right now."

"For you, maybe," said Bess. Meg made a barking noise at this. "Maybe he's with Wills," she suggested.

"Maybe he's getting his cock sucked," said Meg, "Now that the workers are on strike."

Bess had no idea what to say.

"That is terrible," Meg scolded herself. "What a terrible thing for me to say about Lyle."

Just as Bess and her cousin had finished a meal of cheese and grapes and apples and bread, Lyle and Wills came in with two bottles of wine and an armful of take-out food from the nicest restaurant on the island. They were in high spirits after spending the day sailing — "at sea," as Lyle put it.

"Alas, we were merely *at lake*," joked Meg. Lyle complained how could they have gone up to the lake without him, and Meg told him he hadn't been there to ask. Lyle said that he had been there at around noon to see if they wanted to go sailing, but the two of them were gone, and Meg said that they had left at 12:30, so he couldn't have been there at noon at all.

"So I'm just lying," said Lyle.

"I don't know," replied Meg, bland.

Wills gathered Bess into his arms, retrieving one of the bags of take-out at the same time, and waltzed her out the door. "Plenty of booze on the boat," he told her outside.

For the next few hours they sat drinking on his sailboat, Wills very decently pretending to flirt with Bess and find her attractive. He was the consummate host.

"I'd be happy to have sex with you," he was saying. "I mean, I'm a flamer, I do *flame*, as it were, but I'm not always averse to sleeping with women."

Bess doubled over at this and said that she didn't think she wanted the first person she'd slept with in years to be someone who claimed he "wasn't averse" to it. Then she put her head in her hands and reflected how pathetic this must sound. There was no nausea because the subject was so clearly academic. Wills was interested in the fact that she'd been celibate for years and tried to get her to confide in him, but Bess felt resentful all of a sudden and wouldn't do it. She was thinking about Lyle and Meg and wondering if it was not somehow all her fault. In the middle of the night, she had distinctly heard Lyle muttering something about his booze, and Meg's hiss had pierced through the wall: "Then why do you keep offering it?" At the same time, she was afraid they would leave her for Wills to look after the rest of the week, and she was unequal to the idea of becoming a favour someone was doing for his friends. Especially a man so lovely and legitimate as Wills the sailing doctor, to whom she also felt unequal, kind as he was.

Meg came wandering out of the dark a few hours later. "Came to get you," she said. "You guys didn't have to leave."

"How's everything?" Wills inquired.

"Fine, fine. He's gone to the mainland on business."

"He's gone to the mainland on business," said Wills. "You can't fly out at night."

"I know," said Meg. "But that's where he said he was going, and who am I to question?"

"There's late ferries," remembered Bess.

"Of course," agreed Meg. "There's late ferries. Why wait until morning when you can sit alone on a ferry for seven hours?"

Meg kept staggering on the way back to the houseboat, unable to find her footing on the dark path, where enormous tree roots snaked and crossed each other above the earth, forming natural human booby traps. "Look at me, I'm drunk," she kept saying. "Drunk on love." Clear-headed and brave, Bess found it in herself to ask if Lyle was mad at her for drinking all his booze.

"Number One," said Meg. "If somebody doesn't want you to drink all his booze, the sane and normal thing to do is to stop insisting they have more of your booze all the time. Clearly we all haven't been so meticulously brought up as to comprehend the gentle art of lying. Some of us have not had the privilege of such training, and can't be expected to understand the game, let alone win."

Bess waited for Number Two, but Meg was apparently finished. "Tell him I'm sorry," Bess said.

"I always tell him, over and over again," answered Meg.

At the houseboat, Meg got out the Jamaican rum and tried to make Bess have some more, but Bess only wanted to sleep. "This is what happens to those who love to offer, but hate to give," said Meg. "Their rum gets all drunk. It's a metaphor."

"No, I don't want to drink any more of his rum," Bess protested. "I'll buy him another bottle and I'll drink beer the rest of the time I'm here."

"It's the only way he'll learn!" Meg declared, shoving the bottle towards her. Bess crawled away from her, onto the couch, and pulled the blanket up.

Her stomach was shaky the next day. She had been dreaming about living in her parents' house again. She dreamt about her parents' house the way most people dream about high school and writing exams. Someone was supposed to pick her up and drive her to the airport for an important meeting, and Bess spent the whole dream getting ready for it — selecting the right clothes, putting on make-up, trying to find her shoes — and once everything was ready, her ride still hadn't come. In the dream, Dylan was a baby again and her grandparents were going to look after him for her, but she was vaguely worried about that because she knew her grandparents could die any moment, they were so old. In real life, they were both dead. Her parents' house had actually been their house, and she didn't know who in the family had lived in it before them.

It was a boring, useless anxiety dream and she woke up earlier than she wanted to, with a headache. Meg was sitting against the fridge with her eyes closed, and Bess almost booted her when she went to get cream for her coffee.

Meg opened her eyes and to Bess she looked as if she had spent the night smoking and drinking. She had deep and hungry lines around her mouth as though having used it to consume a multitude of poisons over the years. She looked like she had looked back home, only worse.

"What are you doing?"

"Meditating," said Meg. "When you haven't slept, meditation is like an acid trip. All these characters come and talk to you."

"You still haven't slept?"

"No, I can't sleep. Today we have to do lots and lots of fun things."

"I feel like shit."

"I know, but the only way to get through the day is to keep busy."

Bess didn't agree. She thought it might be nice to spend at least one day lounging around the houseboat, maybe strolling into town to drink more cappuccino and buy one of those enormous women's magazines that allow hours to pass effortlessly as page after page of unreality moves through your mind, catching on nothing. It might be nice to sit on the deck of the houseboat doing that, Bess thought. Meanwhile Meg was combing the phone book trying to find out about kayaking and whale watching. It was all expensive so they agreed to pack a picnic lunch and instead take the bicycles out to some sort of strange park that Meg had found a brochure for, the Castleman Family Farm, it was called.

It took an hour to bike to the Castleman Family Farm, and they were disappointed. Suddenly the road opened up into a great expanse of field, backdropped with woods, and tiny, empty buildings grew up from the tall, yellow grass. A plaque in front of one of the buildings stated that this, indeed, was the Castleman Family Farm. The Castlemans were one of the island's founding families, and had worked the farm for over a hundred years. They kept dairy cows. They were gone, now, though, the Castlemans and the cows. Bess and Meg moved from one empty building to the other, and peered in through the cloudy windows. In the cowshed there sat archaic milking equipment. In the building that was identified as having been the family homestead, there was nothing.

Both of them were thinking that it was exactly like back home, but nobody had made home into a park for people to come and wonder at. Nobody had ever biked out to their parents' hundred-year-old houses for curiosity's sake and peered in the windows. And the reason was that there were people still living in them, which didn't make things as quaint as when they were long abandoned. Anyone who might have lived there in the past was a safe and distant figure, about whom anything might be surmised. Meg stomped from one building to the next, pissed off, pronouncing the Castleman Family Farm to be the most depressing place she'd ever seen. A bunch of tourists drove up in a sport utility vehicle and let their children run around, snapping one picture after another of the crumbling cowsheds. One little boy tore through the grass, screaming, "I'm a farmer! I'm a farmer!" over and over again.

"I'm never having kids," gloomed Meg. Only five days ago, Meg had been outlining her plans to have no less than six kids, and she claimed she was going to give them names like Sunshine and Waterfall, and their nicknames would be Shiny and Fally. She had bombarded Bess with questions about Dylan her first night there until Bess thought she would scream, so hungover with guilt was she.

The flesh on one side of Bess's body began to tingle. She absently rubbed at it, and then it began to sting. "Something strange is happening to my body," she stated to Meg, who gaped at her.

"Are you turning into the Incredible Hulk?" asked Meg.

"Look," said Bess, holding out her arm, now red. "Ow."

"Ooh," said Meg. "Poison ivy? Is it itchy?"

"No, it fucking hurts," said Bess. She examined her leg, also burning, and saw it was covered with the infinitesimal red pinpricks as well.

The boy who had been screaming about being a farmer, now merely screamed and ran headlong at one of the sport utility vehicle women, jumping up and down before her and waving his arms. He was one of those ugly, orange-haired children with blotchy freckles whose faces turn violently red when they get angry or cry.

"It's nettles," said Meg, having examined Bess's skin. "It's nettles!" she called to the horrified grown-ups, gathering around their screaming boy.

"Nettles?" repeated Bess.

"Yeah, you know, nettles. We have them back home, I think."

"We do?"

"Yeah ... somewhere."

"I've never seen them before."

"Well ..." Meg murmured, doubtful. "They're around somewhere."

The tourists from the sport utility vehicle were looking at Meg, seeing her as an authority of some kind, hoping she would come over and explain what was happening. Apparently they had never experienced nettles either. Meg just stood watching the red-haired boy throw his continued fits of agony.

"Be honest with me. It can't possibly hurt as much as that little bastard is pretending."

"No," said Bess. "It just kind of ... surprises you by how it feels."

"Little snot-nose attention-seeking self-centred little rich *brat*," spat Meg with quick hate. Bess wanted something all of a sudden, but couldn't pin it down. It irritated her, combined with the pain in her skin. She wanted to get out of the sun. Have a cool drink somewhere and wait for her flesh to become her own again. She wanted to be somewhere else besides the dead Castleman Family Farm, surrounded by the ghosts of cows. She wanted to get off the island and go to Meg's small, bright apartment in the city and imagine it was actually hers. Wanted to be Meg as she was in the city. She did not want to be Meg as she was on the island. She was starting to realize, in fact, that she did not want to be *with* Meg as she was on the island. Then she thought of Dylan, and knew she wanted to be there instead, in their apartment on the grey street, sitting on the second-hand couch with the enormous faded afghan on it, knitted seventy-odd years ago by Bess's father's mother. Dylan on her lap, the two of them watching "Star Trek" repeats after supper, smell of toast and macaroni all around.

Meg broke down after dinner, having checked the answering machine as soon as they returned, getting only business messages for Lyle, nothing from Lyle himself. She went to the phone and dialled his cell, and then his pager, and then she made a salad and grilled some chicken for their dinner and did not eat it, crying instead. After dinner she phoned her own answering machine in the city to see if any messages were left on it, and after that was when she began to pace and talk and rage in such a way as to make Bess despair of their getting any sleep again that night. In the middle of her rage, she stopped and dialled Wills and asked him to come over, and Bess wanted to know what in the name of God she did that for.

"He explains things to me and he helps," said Meg. "He likes to talk about Lyle."

"Have they been friends for a long time?"

A pall dropped over Meg's face. "The only reason Lyle is friends with Wills is that Wills is in love with him," she brooded. "Lyle needs to be around as many people who are in love with him as possible."

Bess decided that she hated Lyle and a few hours later she had decided that she hated Meg and hated Wills as well. The two of them sat all night, speculating endlessly upon the secret thoughts and motivations of Lyle. Wills indulged her, feeding her obsession. Meg had been right: Wills liked to talk about Lyle. Neither of them wanted the drama to wind itself down.

Meg was reduced to clichés. "He thinks he's the centre of the universe!"

"Yes," said Wills.

"But he's not!"

"No," said Wills. "But he thinks he is."

"Forget about Lyle!" Bess shouted in exasperation, and Meg glared as if the words had been in cruel, bad taste.

"My God, Bess, this is my relationship we're talking about. This is my long-term partner we're talking about."

Bess felt guilty, like she didn't understand such things and had spoken presumptuously. Meg turned back to Wills.

"No man is perfect," she said.

"No."

"You have to accept your partner for who he is. I have to show him that I do that."

"Yes."

"But I can't do that if he's not here!"

"I know, love."

"Goddamnit!" Meg went to the bathroom and threw up.

"She hasn't slept for two nights," Bess told Wills.

"That's nothing. The record is a week and a half."

"Well, we should do something."

"Lyle is the only one who can do anything," Wills sighed. "It is for the rest of us to await his whim — to sit and suffer in communion." He poured himself some more wine and settled into the couch. Meg came out of the bathroom, red-faced and teary-eyed, and curled herself up in the crook of Wills's arm. He cooed at her uselessly. The two of them looked comfortable together and nearly content. Tomorrow was Friday, Bess thought, and the day after that was therefore Saturday, and then it would be Sunday, the day before which Bess could fly home. Three long days of the vigil remained. She had planned for herself a lengthy vacation, knowing there might never come another chance for such ease, and escape.

About the Author

Raised in Cape Breton, Nova Scotia, Vancouver resident Lynn Coady was nominated for the 1998 Governor General's Award for Fiction and the Thomas Raddall Atlantic Fiction Award for her first novel *Strange Heaven*. She received the Canadian Author's Association/ Air Canada Award for the best writer under thirty and the Dartmouth Book and Writing Award for fiction. Coady has published a number of short stories. Her articles and reviews have appeared in several publications including *Saturday Night*, *This Magazine*, and *Chatelaine*. She has also written award-winning plays and a screenplay.

Acknowledgements

God bless Charles for always being interested enough to peek at the stories before they were finished, and Christy Ann Conlin for her ongoing and supportive nebulous kinship.